A PROMISE TO THE DEAD

VICTORIA JENKINS

Published by Bookouture in 2019

An imprint of StoryFire Ltd.

Carmelite House
50 Victoria Embankment
London EC4Y 0DZ

www.bookouture.com

ISBN: 978-1-78681-687-0
eBook ISBN: 978-1-78681-686-3

1981

Afterwards, they sat in silence at the edge of the bed, side by side, their hands resting on the mattress, their fingers not quite touching. His clothes lay on the carpet near the bedroom door, abandoned in haste and a flood of desire; neglected in the insistency of their mutual intent. The heat that had rushed like fire through his body not long before was already cooled; in its place, he felt an emptiness that chilled his skin. He glanced at his bare hand resting on the sheet; pale and smooth, untouched by time.

It was the worst silence he had ever known, though in the hours and years that followed, he would become accustomed to far worse.

Trying to distract himself from the photograph that sat on the bedside table, he turned his head to look around the room, taking in details that until now had gone unnoticed: the pictures that lined the far wall, the clothes that had been slung over the back of a chair in the corner; the stubbed-out cigarette butt in a glass ashtray on the dressing table. He wondered what had gone on in this room, in this bed, and the thought made him nauseous with a violence he had never experienced before.

Earlier, not long ago, this had seemed like a good idea, something he had needed to do. He thought it would prove something, if only to himself. Yet now, trapped in the silence of the place and bound by a thousand thoughts he didn't want his memory to linger on, he felt strangled by an air he couldn't breathe.

A hand met his, fingers interlocking with his own. He looked down, sickened by the shiver the touch sent racing through him.

This wasn't how it was supposed to be. He had thought he would feel elated, euphoric – triumphant, perhaps, in some perverse kind of way – but instead he felt enclosed, trapped by an emotion for which he wasn't ready and for which he didn't have a name.

'I love you.'

He stood hurriedly, suddenly and awkwardly aware of his own nakedness, of how inferior and out of place he felt. He picked his jeans up from the floor and searched the pockets for his keys, trying to escape the gaze he felt resting upon him.

'Don't say that.'

A hand on his bare shoulder kept him back. He turned, allowing the trousers to fall to the floor. When soft lips met his own, he reciprocated, hating himself for it but wanting it at the same time, feeling the kiss breathe air back into him. His hands moved up, his fingers tracing bare arms, shoulders, throat. They moved towards one another, tightening as they closed their grip.

And when the face before him altered – the expression contorted, eyes wide with a fear he recognised – they kept tightening and didn't stop.

ONE

Matthew Lewis pushed his foot flatter to the accelerator, watching as the speedometer raced past fifty.

'Slow down, will you?'

His girlfriend, Stacey, was sitting in the passenger seat beside him, her bare feet pressed up against the dashboard; her toenails painted a lurid pink that managed to glow in the darkness. He glanced with contempt at the high-heeled shoes that lay kicked off in the footwell beneath her. Everything she was wearing that day had been chosen with the intention of pissing him off, and she had got exactly what she'd been after.

'You're not going up the A470, are you?'

He didn't respond. He was too angry to speak to her. After what he'd seen of her that day – after what half the city had seen of her that day – he didn't know whether he ever wanted to speak to her again. He knew she was doing it to try to make him jealous. Well, congratulations to her, he thought: it was working.

'There's police everywhere tonight,' she said, picking idly at a fingernail, the noise grating on the last of his nerves. 'They'll be looking for drink-drivers.'

Matthew's hands closed around the steering wheel. It was her fault they'd had to leave town in the first place; her fault that they now needed to avoid attracting any possible attention from passing police. If she hadn't been acting the way she had, they would have still been out enjoying themselves; or trying to, at least. He hadn't even drunk that much. He hadn't been able to relax, not while she was flaunting herself in front of him, although the few pints he'd had now felt like so many more.

He loosened the scarf that was wrapped around his neck. He had bought it from a pop-up stall on St Mary's Street when they were on their way to the stadium. Countless of these stalls erupted throughout the city's main streets on every match day, selling cheaply made merchandise for overinflated prices to parents relenting to nagging children, and adults who had enjoyed too many pints to know any better. There was something about match-day atmosphere that swept people along in its glorious optimism, even when the odds of a win were stacked against the home team. On this occasion, Wales had lost to Italy 13–12. It had been a poor game, non-eventful from the start, but it wasn't the loss that had dampened his spirits.

Who turned up to watch a rugby match wearing a short dress and heels?

He glanced at Stacey's legs, her pale flesh pinched pink by the cold, her bare knees pimpled in a smattering of goose bumps. With her face concealed beneath a mask of heavy make-up, and the push-up bra she had denied she was wearing doing its best to assist her breasts in a breakout bid, he barely recognised her as the person he had met nearly eighteen months earlier.

'Go over the mountain.'

'What?'

'The mountain,' she repeated, slowing her voice as though speaking to a child. 'You're less likely to be stopped by anyone up there.' When he didn't reply, ignoring her as though silence was in some way a form of victory, she rolled her eyes and turned to the darkened window. 'Do what you want,' she drawled, leaning against the headrest. 'Get pulled over for all I care … it's not my problem.'

Following her instructions but not prepared to admit she might have a point, he took the next right turn. It led them off the main road that headed north from Cardiff, through a small village lined with imposing detached houses that were a million miles away from the estate on which he lived. He took a good look at each in turn as they passed; in one, the curtains were pulled back behind a floor-to-ceiling window, exposing the comfort and luxury of the room and its inhabitants for the outside world to see. He felt a pang of envy for a wealth his family had never known. Maybe one day, he thought, when he did well for himself, he would be able to buy his parents a house like that.

At his side, behind the handbrake where he had propped it, his mobile phone began to ring. Grabbing it before his girlfriend could get her hands on it, he looked down at the lit screen.

Antony.

Matthew had texted his cousin before they'd left town, making an excuse about not feeling well. He didn't want to have to explain the real reason why they wouldn't be staying at his house that evening as had been the plan. No one wanted to admit that their girlfriend was an embarrassment.

He shoved the phone into the pocket of the driver's door, leaving it to ring through to answerphone.

'I don't see why we couldn't have stayed over.'

'Really?'

'Yes, really.'

'I can trust you with him then, can I?'

'With Antony? Are you taking the piss?'

Matthew's head snapped to the side, anger flashing from his eyes in the darkness of the car. He could feel his rage like a separate part of himself, a part that he hadn't known belonged to him. He didn't recognise it. No one had ever made him feel like this before.

'I think you're the one doing that, don't you? Turning up half naked, flirting with anyone who'll look at you.'

A smirk stretched across her face, lopsided and sarcastic. It managed to make her ugly. 'Awww ... are you jealous? Now you know how it feels.'

He gripped the steering wheel more tightly as he took a curve in the mountain road. They had left the lights of the village and been thrown into darkness by the high, overgrown hedges that ran either side of the lane. The sky lay blue-black and heavy over them, oppressive in its closeness and its expanse.

She was never going to let him forget it. One kiss, that was all it was. He had told her about it not long after it had happened – even though she would probably never have found out if he'd kept his mouth shut – and ever since his admission she had been making him pay for it, throwing out snide comments at every opportunity and treating him as though she couldn't let him out of her sight. He had always been taught that honesty was the best policy, but he realised now that he would have been better off saying nothing.

'This is pathetic.'

'No. You're pathetic.' She turned to the window, making it clear the conversation was over. He glared at the back of her blonde head, resentment festering inside him. He couldn't live like this any more, with everything on her terms. Tomorrow, once the nag of alcohol that was gripping his brain had released him, he was going to tell her it was over.

'What's that?'

The car was shuddering, making a chugging noise, as though its exhaust was being dragged along the road. The hedges had become trees now, their thick necks reaching skywards and their long arms stretching across the night to shroud everything that passed beneath them, swallowing the car within the tunnel they formed.

He looked at the dash. 'Fuck.'

He had planned on filling up the tank the following day after leaving Antony's house. They hadn't had time earlier that day; they had been running late and the traffic was notoriously bad on match days. He had forgotten the car was almost empty.

'Fuck!'

He pulled to the side of the narrow lane and slammed the palm of his hand against the window as the car ground to a stuttering halt.

'You're joking.'

'Yeah, I'm joking,' he snapped, unclipping his seat belt. 'Hilarious, isn't it?'

'Have you got any spare fuel in the boot?'

He looked at her, incredulous. 'Oh yeah, I always carry a can of petrol around with me, just in case.'

Her painted mouth, smeared pink at the corners, twisted into a sneer at his response before it snapped back to a frown. 'Can you phone someone?'

He took his mobile from the door and tapped in the passcode to unlock it. Its screen shot out a weak beam of light. 'No signal. Perfect. You?'

Scrabbling through her handbag, Stacey seemed to take an age to retrieve her mobile. The longer she took to find it, the greater Matthew's impatience grew.

'No.'

'Brilliant.'

'It's not my fault I've got no signal.'

'No,' he said, opening the car door, 'but it is your fault we're stuck up here.'

She folded her arms across her chest, trying to stave off the bite of cold night air that had swept through the car when he'd opened the door. She glared at him through narrowed eyes. 'If you hadn't been stupid enough to let the car run out of petrol, we wouldn't be here.'

'And if you hadn't acted like such a little slapper today, we wouldn't have had to leave town, would we?'

He got out and slammed the door behind him, its thud echoing between the trees that surrounded them. Beneath his rugby shirt, his heart hammered with adrenalin and frustration. He knew he shouldn't have invited her, but it was too late for that now. He already regretted what he'd just said, but it was too late to change that as well.

Glancing along the darkened strip of road that bent to the right ahead of him, he tried to estimate how long it might take him to find help. He had driven these lanes before, but he didn't really know them that well. He thought there might be a house within a mile or so, somewhere set back from the road. It wouldn't take him too long to reach it, not with the cold and the alcohol powering him.

'Where are you going?'

Behind him, Stacey had got out of the car. Her feet were bare and she had her arms wrapped around her skinny frame, unsuccessfully trying to keep the cold out. When she spoke, her voice was thrown to the breeze, barely reaching him though he was only metres away.

'Get back inside,' he called. 'It's freezing. I won't be long.'

He waited for her to get back into the car, knowing she would do so with little argument. If nothing else, running out of petrol was giving him the opportunity to take some time away from her, and anyway, she would only slow him down. Among other things, she was lazy. If something involved walking further than the end of the street, she would find an excuse to get out of doing it. The more he thought about it, the more he wondered what he was doing with her.

Fuelled by frustration and by the chill that bit through his jacket, he quickened his pace along the mountain lane, the path ahead lit by a full moon. He'd been walking a while before he realised he'd left his mobile phone in the door of the car, though he was unlikely to have got any signal anyway. With his hands shoved into his jacket pockets, he pushed on, surer now that there must be a house somewhere further along this road. He heard a screech overhead, a bird of some kind flitting between the trees above him, and the weight of drink that had tugged at his temples not long earlier lifted, sobriety bringing with it a disconcerting sense of unease.

He stopped at a hedgerow to tie his shoelace. Crouched to the ground, he felt himself enveloped by the darkness that surrounded him. An earlier sense of bravado had been replaced by an unsettling feeling of anxiety, and when he stood, he glanced around nervously, aware now of every shift in the leaves above him and every movement in the hedgerow at his side.

There was a gap in the hedge ahead. As he neared it, he saw a metal gate pushed open; the kind of metal gate that usually led to farmland, to keep cattle or horses shut into the field beyond. He squinted, trying to focus on what lay on the other side of the gate.

As he stood there, something in the distance caught his eye. He stepped towards the gate, his shoes sinking into the soft ground below his feet. His eyes narrowed, and for a moment he thought he had imagined it. Waiting there, he eventually saw it again: a distant flash of brightness that momentarily illuminated a corner of the field. He felt a wave of relief pass through him. A light meant signs of life, and signs of life meant help. He didn't need a lift far – the nearest twenty-four-hour petrol station was within a few miles – and if he couldn't get a lift back then he would just have to use a phone there to call a taxi. He didn't care any more how much it cost him; he just wanted to get home.

He stopped at the edge of the wide field that lay before him and scanned the blackness, his eyes still struggling to become accustomed to the dark. Then he saw it again – the glow of a torch or the flash of headlights – and this time he was sure that his eyes hadn't deceived him. Being closer to someone was enough to fill him with a comforting reassurance, and he began to move towards the light.

His eyes narrowed as he crossed the field, focusing on the near distance and the shapes that stood ahead of him: a van with its back doors flung open, and a man to the side of it, stooped low as though reaching to the ground for something. He hurried his pace. He was cold and he wanted to get back to Stacey. Though he was angry at her, he didn't want her to start thinking he had abandoned her up here.

He stopped as a sudden and unsettling uncertainty swept through him. There was something not right about this, not at this time of night.

If he turned back now, would he be able to find help elsewhere?

He stepped tentatively closer. He was going to speak, but as he neared the van, he saw something that kept the words held down, choking every syllable in the back of his throat. The blur of shapes began to sharpen, forming a clear picture that stood out against the darkened background. For a moment he couldn't move, stuck fast to the ground, his fear rendering him immobile. He needed to get away from this place. He needed help.

He turned to run.

Through the feeling of terror that swelled in his chest like the onset of a heart attack, his legs pushed hard, his feet pounding the ground as he raced back to the lane. A rush of blood filled his head, so that all he could hear was his own pulse throbbing in his ears. Reaching the gate, he turned back on to the lane, fighting to hear the sound of footsteps following him once he hit tarmac. There was nothing.

He sprinted as fast as he could, trying to work out how far away the car was. Then he remembered. There was no petrol. Panic gripped him, pushing frightened tears behind his eyes. Sprinting so hard for so long was making him feel sick, but he knew he couldn't stop. He started to recognise shapes in the darkness, the silhouettes of hedgerows he had passed on his way up. Not far now, he told himself. Don't slow down.

Straining his eyes against the flood of night that swallowed the lane ahead, he waited for the sight of his car to emerge. And then he heard it: a low rumble of engine noise in the distance that was soon behind him, stalking him. He was thrown into the glare of the van's headlights as they lit the road ahead of him. He spotted his car, so near now yet still too far away. The rev of an engine. The screech of brakes.

Then his body was thrown into the air as though he was weightless.

TWO

Detective Inspector Alex King and Detective Constable Chloe Lane stood at the side of the car and watched the white-suited scene-of-crime officer who was dusting the passenger-side door for fingerprints. The glare of the spotlights projected on to the man and his surroundings illuminated them like a studio set, as though the scene was set up with props and the people who moved within it were merely actors. The mountain road had been cordoned off for half a mile in each direction, though it was not much in use at that hour anyway. It was past 2.30 in the morning and the area was disconcertingly quiet despite the flurry of activity that had ensued upon the arrival of the emergency services. A team of officers was performing zone searches in the woodland surrounding them, their torch beams igniting life in the darkness.

'So much for a night off,' Alex said, giving Chloe a sympathetic smile. The younger woman had spent that afternoon planning her evening: an Indian takeaway for one and a film on the sofa. Having exhausted the subject of the limited vegetarian options available at Chloe's local Indian restaurant, conversation at the station had drifted to debate about whether a box set on Netflix was preferable to a film; the disagreement interrupting the monotony of a relatively quiet day. Both detectives realised they should have basked in the rare air of calm while it lasted.

'Remind me not to take meal recommendations from Dan again.'

'Not good?'

Chloe pulled a face and shoved her hands into her pockets. The air was bitingly cold and they stood with their coats zipped to their chins and arms folded across their chests. When the call had come in, Alex had been asleep, and she had pulled on yesterday's clothes, left abandoned on the chest of drawers in the corner. Somehow, even at this hour of the morning, Chloe managed to look pristine, her newly darkened hair swept back into a neat bun at the back of her head. The 999 call had come in at around 1.30, after a passing motorist had noticed the damage to the windscreen of the car, which was seemingly abandoned at the roadside. Unprepared to face the cold, the darkness or whatever else might have been lurking beyond the safety of his own vehicle, the driver had stayed in his car at the junction with the main road a further mile down the lane, where he had been able to get a signal to make the call. He'd had the right idea, Alex thought; instead, it had been left to the first attending officer to confront the scene that awaited them.

Alex looked through the window at the girl inside the car, who lay slumped face down between the front seats, her blonde hair matted with her own dark blood. She was wearing a dress that wouldn't have looked out of place on the kind of reality television programme Alex could never understand the popularity of, and which seemed inappropriate for an early-March night – short, strappy and a size too small. Despite her heavy make-up, her skin managed to look almost translucent in death. A single bullet wound to the back of the head had ended her life. It had been fired through the front windscreen.

The first attending officer had given Alex the handbag that had been retrieved from the floor of the car: a small silver clutch with a long metal chain handle. Inside, there was a candyfloss-pink lipstick, a tube of mascara, a mobile phone, a set of house keys, two ten-pound notes and a small collection of coins. Zipped into an inside pocket at the back of the bag was a bank card and a driver's licence. The photograph was unmistakably that of the girl slumped between the seats of the car. Stacey Cooper. Twenty years old.

A barrage of questions presented themselves, jostling for priority. What had the girl been doing on the mountain road at this time of night? Where had she been going? Had she been alone? And if not, why was no one with her now?

Chloe leaned towards the car and took a closer look through the driver's-side window. She had her own set of questions. 'If she was trying to escape from someone, why didn't she just drive away? Unless she was trying to escape from someone she was with.'

Alex didn't reply, for the moment lost in her own thoughts. Despite nearly two decades spent in the police force, she knew she would never get used to sights such as this. She didn't want to become desensitised to it, as she'd seen happen to other detectives. Recent thoughts of her imminent departure from the force returned to the forefront of her mind. More so than ever, she knew she was doing the right thing. She had hoped to leave at a quiet time, though she realised those times were few and far between. Now, she thought, as she looked at the poor girl whose life had been brought to an end so violently, she wouldn't be going anywhere.

She pulled a pair of disposable latex gloves from her pocket and slipped them on before opening the driver's door. The key to the 2004 silver Citroën C4 was still in the ignition. She turned it, expecting to hear the sound of the engine kicking into life. Instead, a low, dull spluttering sound emerged. She glanced at the dashboard. Empty.

'She'd run out of petrol.'

Scanning the inside of the car, she spotted a pair of high-heeled shoes lying in the passenger footwell. The angle of the girl's body – her right knee twisted awkwardly against the handbrake and her left leg stretched out towards the pedals – suggested she had tried to get into the back seat from the passenger side of the vehicle rather than the driver's side.

'Actually,' she amended, 'someone else had run out of petrol. I don't think anyone would attempt to drive in those shoes, do you?' She reached into the pocket of the driver-side door and retrieved a mobile phone. When she pressed a button at the side of the handset, the screen came to life with a photograph of a young man smiling for the camera, gripping what looked like a sports trophy. He was handsome in a way Alex imagined young women might find attractive, with a fashionable haircut and eyes that seemed to look beyond what they saw.

'Boyfriend?' suggested Chloe, taking the phone from her.

'Looks like. The car's probably his then.' Alex studied the windscreen from the inside. They would need ballistics to analyse the hole that had been made in the glass, but the size of it and the damage that had been incurred as a result suggested that the weapon used had been fired close to the vehicle. An expert would be able to tell them more; hopefully they'd also be able to identify the make and model of weapon used.

Placing a gloved hand on the back of the driver's seat and leaning over the girl's body, Alex stretched to study the sole of the victim's left foot.

'What are you thinking?' Chloe asked, watching her.

'I'm thinking she'd been outside the car at some point. Look.' Alex got out and Chloe took her place on the driver's seat. She leaned over and dipped her head to look at the girl's bare feet. The pale soles were speckled with gravel and dirt, a few tiny stones still embedded in her skin.

'Why would she get out of the car?'

'To help with something, possibly.' Alex stepped aside as the SOCO who had been scrutinising the other side of the car moved towards them. His brush worked the length of the window frame, his wrist deft in his task. 'But what?' she added, thinking aloud.

'They run out of petrol,' Chloe said slowly, backing out of the vehicle, 'and he gets out of the car.'

'The boyfriend?'

Chloe nodded. 'She then gets out too, following him perhaps, and they argue. Maybe she was annoyed with him for forgetting to fill up. Things get out of hand, he turns on her, she tries to escape and then …'

'Why does he get out of the car?' Alex challenged. 'If he can see from the dash that they've run out of petrol, he doesn't need to get out and look at anything. I don't know,' she said, her top lip curling. 'Shooting someone over an argument about an empty petrol tank seems a bit extreme to me.'

There were so many questions they needed to find answers to before they could draw any conclusions about the chain of events that had led to the young woman's death. Where had the couple been? Where were they heading? Did the man own a firearm, and if so, why had he been carrying it?

'He doesn't look the type to carry a gun.'

Chloe gave voice to the same thought Alex had been harbouring. Although she knew that killers came in every shape and size, and that assumptions based on appearance could prove dangerously misleading, the young man who had smiled at her from the lit screen of the mobile phone looked an unlikely suspect for a gun owner.

'DI King.'

Turning, Alex saw a uniformed officer approaching.

'There are tyre marks just up the lane. Can't tell if they're old ones or not.'

'I'll be there in a second.' She turned back to the car, studying the hole the bullet had made in the windscreen. If the gun hadn't belonged to Stacey's boyfriend, then that meant someone else had been there with them, either someone known to the couple or someone who was a stranger. For the moment, they had to assume that this girl and her boyfriend were the only people who knew what had happened up there.

In which case, one question seemed more pressing than any other.

Where was the boyfriend now?

THREE

Kieran Robinson had been missing for sixty-three hours. His sister knew this because the last CCTV sighting of him had been recorded at 23.36 three nights earlier, and as no one had seen him since that time, to her mind that was the moment he had officially become a missing person. As the minute hand on the clock above her parents' sink clicked forward, its sound echoing around the otherwise silent kitchen, she added to the time accordingly.

Hannah Robinson was familiar with the expression of being able to hear a pin drop, but in this instance it didn't seem at all suitable. The silence in the room was noisy and ugly and there was a tinny sound reverberating in her ears that she knew would grow as the day went on, as it had during those previous few days. Later, in bed, the noise would build to a crescendo and a pounding headache would keep her awake until the small hours. She would sleep a little, and then the pattern would repeat itself upon waking. They would do the same thing tomorrow: sit there, wait, achieve nothing.

Hannah knew how all this worked. She'd watched enough television shows and heard enough similar stories to know that time meant everything and that their lives would now be structured around it, dictated by the passing minutes. Every hour that passed in which Kieran wasn't found would inevitably chip away another piece of the hope that he would turn up alive.

'Would either of you like a cup of tea?'

Hannah glared at the family liaison officer, who seemed to have done nothing but boil the kettle since she'd arrived. She kept giving them empty reassurances that she would let them know as soon as there were any updates, yet all she had been able to offer them so far were regular top-ups of sugar and caffeine, which Hannah now felt sure were contributing to the migraines that were plaguing her.

The truth of it was, her own guilt was as much to blame as the FLO's ineptitude. She should be out there, she thought, doing something constructive; contributing something that might help put right what had gone wrong. She just didn't know where she should start.

She watched her mother, who was standing at the sink with her back to the room. She had recently had her blonde hair cut: a short, feathered chop that made her already prominent features look even sharper. It hadn't been appreciated when Hannah had pointed out as much. Her mother had reacted with a comment about Hannah's own purple hair – some smart-ass remark about the girl from that kids' book who got blown up like a blueberry. An argument had followed, as could have been predicted by anyone in the house. It was typical of her mother to go that one step further, to make it even more personal.

The sink at which Linda Robinson was standing was filled with dirty dishes and soapy water that had been left to go flat and cold; she wasn't there with the intention of doing anything, only with the aim of staring out at the garden so that she didn't have to look anyone in the eye. For countless hours during the past few days, Hannah had had to sit in the living room and listen to the sound of her mother wailing in the bedroom, unable to force herself up the stairs to offer any sort of comfort. They didn't have that sort of relationship; they never had. She was there, wasn't she? Under the circumstances, that was the best anyone could expect of her.

It was her father's job to be there supporting her mother, but yet again he had chosen to make himself scarce. He had a habit of hiding from his problems, though Hannah would never have anticipated that even he would hide away at a time like this. She wondered what her mother had done or said to keep him away. Regardless of his own failings, Linda had to be responsible for his absence at some level.

'When is anyone going to do anything useful?' Scraping the stool back across the tiled floor, Hannah stood and retrieved her mobile phone from the top of the microwave, her burgundy Doc Marten boots clomping across the kitchen tiles. She opened Facebook and scanned the posts relating to Kieran, but there was nothing new other than the wave of false pity that was currently swamping her newsfeed.

OMG, I only saw him last week.

Hope you're okay hun xx

Thoughts are with the family – let me know if there's anything I can do xx

All so meaningless, Hannah thought. She especially loathed the offers of help, as if anything these people could do would in any way improve the situation. She resented the gesture, knowing it was never meant anyway. People only ever said it when they knew full well there was sod all they could do and the offer would go unaccepted.

The FLO moved to Hannah's side, apparently immune to her hostility. She wasn't much older than Hannah, though the buttoned-up cardigan and the 1990s bob hairstyle made her look as though she could easily be two decades older.

'I promise you everything we can do is being done.'

'Waiting for his body to resurface, you mean?' Hannah stared the woman out, waiting for her to deny the accusation. She wasn't able to: it had already been said too many times. Kieran's mobile phone signal had been traced to the water around Cardiff Bay, where he had been on a night out that Thursday. Drunk was the assumption everyone had made. He'd had too much to drink, fallen into the water and drowned. Simple.

Only Hannah didn't believe it. They could keep saying it, but she would never accept it as a possibility. Something just didn't ring true. His body would have been found, for one.

And there was something else that didn't sit right with her. She could count on one hand, with a couple of fingers to spare, the number of times she had seen her brother drunk. The first had been on his fifteenth birthday, when he'd had three pints of snakebite and vomited all over the carpet in their mother's hallway. The second, not long after that, had been at a barbecue at a neighbour's house, where Hannah was certain Kieran had got drunk just to wind up their parents, who had spent the day arguing over something so insignificant she wasn't now able to recall it. The third and last time, over five years ago, had involved a litre of vodka and a game of spin the bottle, which Kieran had apparently repeatedly lost. In a drunken stupor and smelling of kebab meat and garlic sauce, he had turned up at Hannah's student flat in tears, confessing that he had kissed one of his male friends. The following morning he had made her promise that she would never tell anyone, and that they would never speak of it again. They never had.

Although she had seen him drunk, on none of those occasions would Hannah have said her brother was out of control; not so out of control that he might have injured himself or not been able to get help had it been needed. His experiences were no different to any of those of most other teenagers, and the years of sobriety and healthy living that followed suggested he had learned from his mistakes; something others took decades to do and some never achieved at all. He wasn't drunk on Thursday, Hannah was convinced of that if nothing else. He might have consumed alcohol, but to her mind there was simply no possibility that he had been drunk enough to fall into the water at Cardiff Bay and drown.

The silence in the kitchen was punctuated by a knock at the front door.

'I'll go.' The FLO left the room, leaving Hannah and Linda in an uncomfortable silence.

'Do you want to go for a drive?' Hannah asked, knowing her mother wouldn't leave the house while there was even the slightest chance Kieran might happen to just walk back in. Linda had closed in on herself since his disappearance, immersing herself in old photograph albums and home videos, poring over his images as though she might be able to recreate him somehow and place him back in the house with them. Though Hannah imagined her mother would vehemently deny the accusation, it was obvious to anyone that Linda had always favoured Kieran. He didn't annoy her in the way Hannah so often did, and Hannah supposed that had been enough to push him to the number one spot.

Linda shook her head. Hannah was relieved; she had offered to take her out in the hope that her mother would reject the suggestion, but at least no one could accuse her of not making the effort. When she turned to her daughter, Linda couldn't hide the impatience on her face. Without speaking, she managed to make Hannah feel that she was somehow responsible for her brother's disappearance. 'Are you staying for dinner?'

Slamming her mobile phone down on the breakfast bar, Hannah fought to hold back a wave of fury. What was the matter with everyone? Tea ... food ... as if everything could be cured through sustenance. She pulled her purple hair from her face and tied it back in a ponytail before heading for the back door, feeling her lungs tighten in their desperation for some fresh air, but her departure from the room was stalled by the FLO's return. She was followed by a young man wearing a grey shirt beneath an open navy-blue duffel coat. He was holding a police ID badge in his hand.

'This is Detective Constable Jake Sullivan,' the FLO introduced him.

'Has something happened?'

'We've still no leads on your son's whereabouts, I'm afraid,' DC Sullivan said, cutting short Linda's already severed optimism. 'Mrs Robinson, is your husband at home?'

'Darren's working away. He's not due back for a couple of days. I told the other detective that on Friday.'

The family had until today been seen mostly by a female detective: a woman not much younger than Linda who had burn marks to the side of her face that she did nothing to try to conceal. Hannah wondered what had happened to her. She had tried not to stare at the burns for too long, but the more she tried to avert her focus, the more she found herself unable to drag her attention away. It occurred to her that had she been afflicted with the same scars, she might have made an attempt to cover them with make-up. Maybe the other woman hadn't felt the need to hide. Perhaps that was something Hannah needed to try out for size.

'DI King,' DC Sullivan reminded her. 'You told her that your husband has been in Devon since last weekend?'

Linda nodded. 'Why, what's the matter?' Her attention shifted from the detective to her daughter, returning to DC Sullivan when he produced his phone from his pocket and searched it for something before passing it to her.

'Do you recognise this number plate?'

Hannah watched as Linda looked at the image on the phone. When she moved behind her mother to take a look, she could see the photograph was taken from CCTV footage. 'It's Darren's,' her mother said. 'You obviously know that already or you wouldn't be here asking me about it. Could you just please get to the point?'

'This recording was made on Thursday evening, near the Millennium Centre in Cardiff Bay.'

A silence followed. Hannah stepped back and moved away, but her mother continued to study the photograph as though staring at it for long enough might somehow alter what was shown there, removing any implication that put her husband under suspicion. Hannah knew more than her parent possibly realised. She knew that when he had been spoken to, her father had lied to the police about where he'd been on Thursday evening, telling them that he had been in Devon. If her mother's response to the image was anything to go by, Hannah suspected she had also been lied to by him.

'What are you saying?' she eventually asked.

'We need to speak with your husband, Mrs Robinson.'

'You've spoken to him already.'

'He needs to come back to South Wales,' DC Sullivan clarified. 'We'd like to talk to him face to face. I suggest you speak to him, and advise him that it's necessary for him to come home.'

In the silence that followed, Hannah tried to push back the doubt that was creeping closer to the front of her mind.. She knew that Kieran's disappearance alone should have been enough to bring their father back to the country. The fact that it hadn't made him appear increasingly suspicious, as well as inexplicably insensitive.

'You think he was involved in Kieran's disappearance?' her mother eventually said, her tone still clipped and defensive. 'This is ridiculous.' She thrust the mobile phone back at DC Sullivan. 'First you're saying there was an accident, and now what? Now you think Darren's hiding something?'

'He's lied to everyone about where he was on Thursday. Unless you already knew he wasn't in Devon as he said he was?' DC Sullivan raised an eyebrow that questioned her mother's honesty. Hannah anticipated that the look was only likely to be met with resentment.

She watched her mother's mouth fall open, apparently unable to articulate her outrage at the suggestion that she might have helped cover for her husband in some way. Instead, she looked to the FLO, exasperated. If she was searching for help, though, it was quickly evident she was looking in the wrong place. The woman really was as useless as Hannah had suspected.

DC Sullivan turned to Hannah and offered her a faint smile. She didn't return it, but he seemed undeterred by this. 'I know you've been asked this already, but how had your brother been in the days and weeks leading up to Thursday? Any unusual behaviour, or signs that there was something wrong?'

'Why are you asking Hannah?' her mother intervened, obviously still smarting from the detective's previous comment. 'I know my son better than anyone – I'd have known if there'd been something wrong. He was fine. If you're suggesting he's killed himself, then this is getting even more ridiculous.'

'I'm not suggesting anything, Mrs Robinson,' DC Sullivan said quickly. 'I'm just saying that sometimes we don't know people as well as we think we do.'

The FLO shifted uncomfortably in the corner of the kitchen, eyeing the kettle as though another cup of tea might help to resolve the tension that had gripped the room. Hannah noticed her mother suck in her top lip as her jaw tautened.

'You don't seem to have any updates on my brother,' Hannah said coldly, seeking an end to what seemed a pointless visit, 'so unless there's something else, I suggest you get on with the job of finding him. If you want to talk to my father, perhaps you should go and find him yourself.'

DC Sullivan hesitated. His pale face had speckled with red blotches, embarrassment settling upon his cheeks. 'I do understand your concerns for your son, Mrs Robinson.' He attempted to force eye contact with her, but his efforts were in vain. His comment had hit hard and there was no going back from it now. Linda's eyes were fixed to the floor, the fingers of her right hand gripping the kitchen worktop so tightly that her knuckles had whitened.

Hannah's eyes widened as though questioning why DC Sullivan was still there when they had made it obvious he was no longer welcome. 'Ask DI King to come next time, will you?' she said.

She followed him to the front door and slammed it shut with force once he was outside. Heading quickly into the front room, she pushed aside the closed curtain and watched the detective as he lingered on the pavement. Then she turned back to the room. The photographs of her and Kieran as children that had once lined the walls had all been taken down from where they had hung, replaced in recent years by a fresh coat of plaster and a lick of paint. Her mother could say what she wanted, but nothing was going to hide the truth: she didn't want Hannah's face looking down at her while she watched TV in the evenings. Removing only the photographs of her daughter would have made it too obvious, so she'd had no choice but to take them all down, Kieran included.

Hannah gritted her teeth and pushed her fists into the pockets of her skirt as she fought back angry tears. Where was Kieran? And where was her bloody father? She needed to speak to him, now more than ever.

Why had he been in Cardiff Bay on Thursday night?

And just what had he been arguing with Kieran about on Wednesday?

FOUR

DC Chloe Lane knocked at the door of the student property, noting with disgust the small mountain of bin bags left inside the front wall of the narrow strip of concrete at the front of the house, their contents – weeks old, if the stomach-churning stench of rotting waste was anything to go by – spilling out across the ground. The central panel of glass in the front bay window of the house had been smashed; behind it, a makeshift attempt had been made to protect those inside from the elements, the effort stretching as far as a flattened cardboard box and an intricate web of masking tape.

Her own student days were not a time she looked back on with particular fondness – her estrangement from her family had led to a dark period of isolation and choices she would have preferred never to have had to make – but one thing Chloe prided herself on was that she had always been hard-working and determined, and she couldn't remember ever having lived in a state anywhere near this, regardless of how tight money had been. She was no obsessive cleaner: having lived with Alex for six months the previous year, she imagined her superior would vouch for the fact. This, though, she thought as she held her breath at the front door, was beyond any reasonable excuses.

The door was answered by a young woman wearing a pair of long-sleeved cotton pyjamas and the previous day's make-up. She had been crying, her reddened eyes only partially hidden behind a pair of thick-rimmed glasses. Chloe presumed this was Gemma, who she had spoken to over the phone earlier that day. The girl's number had been stored on Matthew Lewis's mobile, and texts between the two arranging where and when to meet the previous day had been found when his phone activity had been accessed.

'Gemma?'

The girl nodded and stepped aside, allowing Chloe into the house. Inside, the smell didn't improve. Gemma, seemingly oblivious to the odour apparently embedded into the walls and carpet of the hallway, reached her hands behind her head and pulled her hair up into a messy bun, knotting it with an elastic band she had around her wrist.

'I'm sorry about the mess,' she said quietly, waving a hand aimlessly to her side. 'I keep reminding them I'm not their mother.'

Chloe followed her into the living room and picked her way through the debris to the sofa. A games console had been left on the floor, and the dirty carpet was littered with empty cider cans and the remnants of last night's takeaway: plastic containers housing leftover korma and tikka, a paper bag of prawn crackers, and a tub of curry sauce that had tipped over and been left to ooze on to the rug.

'How many of you are living here?' Chloe asked, wrinkling her nose.

'Five. I'm the only girl. You can probably tell that by the state of the place.'

She wondered how Gemma put up with living in this chaos on a daily basis, but she guessed the mess in the house was the last thing on the girl's mind at the moment. 'Where are the others?'

'In bed, probably,' she said with a shrug. 'Is there any news on Matthew yet?'

Chloe shook her head. She had given Gemma the few details they were in possession of when they had spoken earlier. She needed to know as much about the previous day as possible if they were to have any chance of forming a picture of what had happened to

Matthew and Stacey while they were up on the mountain road. Finding Matthew was their first priority, but with no leads and nothing so much as hinting at his whereabouts, the team was already feeling the pressure of time against them.

'His parents ...' Gemma bit her bottom lip. 'Have you seen them?'

'Not personally. They're beside themselves, obviously.'

Alex had been to the Lewises' house in the early hours of that morning, after leaving the scene of Stacey's murder on Caerphilly Mountain. Chloe, meanwhile, had undertaken the unenviable task of informing Stacey's parents of her death. Both couples had reacted as anyone might have expected, their initial shock morphing into grief and anxiety that quickly overwhelmed them.

'Tell me about yesterday.'

'We met up outside the train station and went for lunch on St Mary's Street, a couple of hours before the match started.'

'Where did you go?'

'The Italian on the corner, the one opposite McDonald's. I can't remember what it's called now. You know ... that chain place.'

Chloe nodded, knowing the restaurant Gemma was referring to. 'When you say "we" ...'

'There was me, Matthew, Stacey and two other friends from school.'

'That's how you know Matthew? From school?'

Gemma nodded and rubbed her left eye, leaving a smear of mascara across the bridge of her nose. 'We were in primary and comp together. I've known him all my life, really.' She looked away as though embarrassed for some reason. 'I've always got on better with boys. The girls at school used to hate me for it. They used to call me a slag, that sort of thing. It was never like that. I just find boys less complicated.'

Chloe wondered where that kind of boy had been when she herself was younger: the ones who were less complicated. She was being unfair, she thought, quickly chiding herself for her momentary cynicism. In her experience, people were complicated in equal measure.

When Gemma looked back at her, her eyes were glassy with imminent tears. 'Where the bloody hell is he?'

'We don't know. That's why it's so important you tell me everything you can. Even if it might seem insignificant to you, the more we know about Matthew and what happened yesterday, the greater our chances of finding him.'

'That's the thing, though ... I don't know anything really. I wish I did, I might be able to help then. We hardly see each other any more – we're both so busy with final-year exams. Yesterday was the first time we'd seen each other in at least a month.'

'Had you met Stacey before?'

'Once. At a party a few months back. Matthew didn't seem that keen on her at the time. Then they split up for a while – maybe a month or so. I was surprised to see her yesterday, to be honest.'

'You weren't expecting her to be there?'

'He just hadn't said anything about her coming.'

'It was Matthew who booked the tickets for the game, then?'

Gemma nodded. 'He always books the tickets. We try to go every year, for the Six Nations. It's kind of a tradition now, even when we haven't seen each other for a while. It gives us a chance to catch up.'

'You said Matthew and Stacey split up for a while. Do you know why that was?'

The girl nodded, but looked away again, avoiding Chloe's eye. She sighed before she spoke. 'We kissed, Matthew and I. I don't know why, it was bloody stupid. I've known him all my life and we've never done it before – I've never wanted to either. He's more like a brother than anything else. It sounds really weird now I've said that, doesn't it, but we were both drunk and it just happened.

Anyway, he told Stacey about it. I knew he would. Matthew's a good guy. He's honest.' She looked at Chloe now, her eyes almost pleading with her. 'Whatever happened up on that mountain, Matthew didn't hurt Stacey. I know it. He just wouldn't. He's never hurt anyone.'

'If you two kissed and Stacey knew about it, why would Matthew bring her to the game with you yesterday?'

'I don't know. I didn't get to ask him. I wanted to, but she didn't let him out of her sight all day.' Gemma picked at a loose thread on the seam of her pyjama trousers. 'If anything, I think maybe she came with him to prove a point. In front of me, you know, but also to him as well. She spent the day flirting with the other boys, all to get at Matthew, I think. It seemed to be working. He was on edge all day, and that's not like him. It was like she was trying to make him see what he'd be missing if they split up, or trying to prove the point that she could get someone else if she wanted to. The atmosphere was awful – it was really uncomfortable.'

Stacey's unusual choice of outfit for a rugby match was now starting to make sense. If there had been tension between the couple – visible enough for other people to have noticed them – then perhaps the theory that they had both got out of the car following an argument wasn't far from the mark. They just hadn't been arguing over the empty fuel tank, as previously presumed.

Gemma's face dropped as she realised the possible implications of everything she had said about Stacey's behaviour, as well as Matthew's reaction to it. 'He didn't kill her,' she said, shaking her head as though reading Chloe's thoughts. 'Matthew couldn't hurt anyone.'

The girl didn't need to persuade her, Chloe thought; it seemed as unlikely to her as it did to Alex, though with Matthew nowhere to be found, it was obvious that his guilt was the conclusion everyone was likely to jump to.

Just where was he now? If he hadn't hurt his girlfriend, there seemed no reason for him to hide. And if he wasn't hiding, it suggested he had been taken somewhere against his will.

But by who? Chloe wondered. And why?

FIVE

Darren Robinson took a drag of his cigarette and surveyed the expanse of open ground that lay in front of him. The building site had been prepped for work to start there the following week, and the project would be one of the biggest in a long while. He could have done with taking a break after the recent housing development he had worked on back in Cardiff, but taking breaks never made anyone rich, and besides, he needed to make himself scarce from South Wales for the time being.

In his pocket, his mobile started to ring. He took it out and looked down at the lit screen. Linda's name flashed up at him, the glare of its light as accusatory as her voice, berating him with its usual nagging tone. Returning the phone to his pocket, Darren waited for the call to end. She was bound to leave another voicemail; an addition to the four she had already left him that day, her tone increasingly frantic and less forgiving with each. Excuses usually came easily to him, but finding one for his absence over the past few days was proving a little trickier than usual. He needed to prepare his story before he headed home, but he hadn't yet finalised it in his own head. The longer he left his return, the guiltier he would inevitably appear. He didn't need to draw that kind of attention to himself, especially not now, with everything else that was now going on.

When his phone started to ring again, he gave a loud sigh and grabbed it from his pocket. He was just about to swipe left to cut the call dead when he saw that it was his daughter, Hannah. He wondered if she was with her mother, if Linda had persuaded her to try to get in touch after her own calls kept being ignored. Deciding he didn't want to take the chance, he let the ringing continue until Hannah was directed to the answer machine. Moments later, a voicemail notification pinged through. Darren unlocked the phone and put it to his ear.

'Dad … I need to speak to you. Where are you? Call me when you get this. It's important.'

There was a long pause, during which Darren could hear the faint exhalations of his daughter's laboured breathing. She was putting on too much weight, letting herself go, but it wasn't really for him to tell her that. He could imagine the response he'd receive if he advised her to step away from the fridge for a while, or not-so-surreptitiously left a leaflet for a local fitness class lying around. Sometimes you needed to be cruel to be kind, and as Hannah had never been the type to respond too well to kindness, Darren didn't think either idea was that unreasonable. Her mother should have been the one to give her a shove in the right direction where things like diet and health were concerned, but Linda had always been too wrapped up in Kieran to pay too much attention to their daughter.

Which was why it was a wonder she didn't know where he was. People didn't just disappear, no matter how much they might want to.

'Please,' Hannah finished. 'Just call me, okay.'

He deleted the message and finished his cigarette before stubbing it out on the dry ground beneath his boot. Devon had seen considerably less rain than South Wales during these past few weeks, and the forecast for the month ahead was so far looking good. The project would be able to progress quickly, providing that everyone else was prepared to put in the hours and the graft needed to get things moving. Relying on other people was the problem. Other people invariably let you down. In Darren's experience, the only person he had ever really been able to rely on was himself, and that truth had recently made itself even more evident to him.

He realised he had probably made a mistake listening to the message when he had. If Hannah had tried calling him straight back and found the phone engaged, she would know that he had his phone with him and had chosen to ignore her call. It would be yet another thing he would have to find an excuse for in preparation for his return home.

With a sigh, he scanned the empty ground again as he redirected his thoughts away from his family and back to his work. The area was substantial, with high fencing cordoning it off from the buildings that lay beyond: a small estate of 1990s homes, clustered together like Lego houses, with a primary school in the near distance, its metal railings painted a bottle green that stood out against the backdrop of brown and grey that characterised the estate. He couldn't imagine that the people already living there would be too happy with the number of new buildings that were to be constructed, but that was life: you had to accept what it gave you, whether you liked it or not.

It occurred to Darren that both his children – both kids in their own ways, despite their years – still had quite a way to go before they learned this.

Averting the flow of his thoughts, he contemplated the labour involved in constructing the one hundred and twelve properties that would form the development. Financially he would do all right from it – nothing he would be able to retire off the back of, but not exactly a profit to be sniffed at either – but the labour was beginning to do its worst. His back was in constant pain and his knees were starting to fail him. Years of hard physical graft had taken their toll, and though he was only fifty-one, Darren often felt like a man twenty years older.

Glancing at the signage that stood near the site entrance, he experienced a familiar tug of envy and resentment. Newton Homes. They were the real winners. The developers sat in their fancy cars, talking business into their latest smartphones, while the contractors were left doing the donkey work for a fraction of the financial reward. It seemed to Darren that money attracted money, and to get rich you needed to have started off with something: something more than he had ever had. It was a realisation that was making him increasingly bitter, though oddly the feeling also comforted him. Where he was now wasn't his fault.

He looked down at his phone and accessed the internet search engine. A tap of his finger on the bar threw up a list of his latest requests. At the top, typed in that morning while he had been in his hotel room, was the name of his son, Kieran Robinson. Though he had already read it once that day, Darren opened the article at the top of the search result list and absorbed its contents once again.

Police are growing increasingly concerned about the whereabouts of Kieran Robinson, who was last seen in Cardiff Bay on Thursday 8 March following a night out with workmates. The twenty-three-year-old, an apprentice bricklayer from St Melon's, left Haha's Comedy Club at 9.10 p.m. during the mid-set break. The last-known sighting of him was on CCTV footage taken near the St David's Hotel, where he was picked up on a recording at 11.36 p.m. His mobile phone was traced to the area, but a search of the waters around the Bay, carried out by a team of specialist police divers, yielded no trace of the young man. Police are particularly keen to learn where Kieran went and who he was with between the hours of 9.10 and 11.36. Anyone with any information that might help in the search is asked to contact South Wales Police.

Darren looked up and breathed in a lungful of cold air. He contemplated another cigarette, but he had already smoked too many of them that day, following one with another, replacing oxygen with nicotine as though it was the only thing keeping him functioning. He closed the internet page and deleted the entry from his search history. Finding the number he wanted, his finger hovered over the keypad. His previous messages could be seen on the screen; there were a string of them, with no replies to any having been received.

He could try to ignore him all he wanted, Darren thought. Some things were more than worth waiting for and he wasn't going anywhere.

He uploaded a photograph that was stored on his mobile and added a caption. *You have two days*, he wrote, *and then I'm going to tell Michael everything.*

He pressed send.

SIX

The small room on the ground floor of the police station was filled with people: reporters, film crew, police officers. Alex sat beside Matthew Lewis's parents at tables that had been moved to the head of the room, placing the couple beneath the glare of the cameras, where they were unable to avoid the looks of sympathy and doubt being passed their way with equal frequency. It was evident that the room was divided into two distinct halves: those who believed the couple's son had killed his girlfriend and those who questioned where he now was, believing his absence suggested there was a possibility he might be in some sort of danger. Either way, the mystery surrounding the events of Saturday night had garnered plenty of tabloid and social media interest.

Behind the tables at which they were sitting, a photograph of Matthew – the same picture that was pinned to the evidence board in the incident room – was projected on to a screen in the hope that someone who saw the appeal might recall having seen the young man at some point during the past sixteen hours. The photo had been taken the previous summer: a head shot of a smiling Matthew posing on a football field with a ball gripped beneath his arm. Alex had glimpsed the boy's mother eyeing the picture when she had entered the room with her husband, immediately moved to tears by the image of her missing son. Watching her reaction might have been enough to move Alex to tears too, had it not been for the gathered audience, who expected her to maintain a neutral outlook. She couldn't imagine the nightmare Matthew's parents were experiencing; she could only resolve to find out what had happened as quickly as possible. Guilty or not, they needed him back home.

Her thoughts strayed to the adoption application she was waiting for a response to. Becoming a parent was the most intimidating role she had ever signed herself up for, but things worth having rarely came without hard work and a little heartbreak along the way. If someone had told her ten years earlier that she'd be doing this alone, she might have thought them crazy, but a lot had changed during that decade, and she had learned that the only person she could ever really rely on was herself. She could do this. She'd be fine.

She looked at Matthew Lewis's mother, her pale face racked with worry, and the confidence she felt in her own abilities wavered. Before she could contemplate being a parent, she needed to finish her job as a detective.

News of what had happened on the mountain road the previous night had travelled with the typical velocity of grim tidings, with a number of different versions of events already doing the rounds of social media. As was so often the case, Alex was disheartened by the people's insensitivity. Inane, thoughtless remarks and so-called jokes across Twitter and Facebook only added to the suffering of those awaiting news of a person they loved and feared for, yet these comments were made so carelessly – in some cases callously – that Alex couldn't help but wonder what had happened to humanity. These people were so driven by a need for 'likes' that they were prepared to reduce themselves to cruelty to gain them. In the case of Matthew Lewis, there was little thought for the couple who now sat beside her, looking down at their hands in their laps, reluctant to face the onslaught of an equally insensitive press.

Matthew's mother glanced to her side and met Alex's eye. There was a dull emptiness within her gaze, something hollow and removed; so different from the eyes of the boy who had looked out from the screen of the mobile phone retrieved from the car the previous night. How easily the brightness could be dimmed, the light shut out. Alex attempted a reassuring smile, but she knew there was little she could offer in the way of comfort.

By all accounts, Matthew was a popular and grounded young man who was doing well at university and had no enemies. He had never been in any trouble with the police, and the suggestion that he might have owned or had access to a firearm was met with incredulity. The subject was so unexpected that the mention of it had been initially met by the boy's father with an awkward laugh, as though he believed himself caught momentarily in some parallel universe from which he would be just as quickly returned to his own life in which his boy was still upstairs getting ready for a night out with his friends.

The general public could come to its own conclusions, Alex thought, as it always seemed to, regardless of fact or common sense. Her own mind would not be shaken from the notion that Matthew was somewhere he shouldn't be, with God only knew who, and it was her responsibility to find him before he came to any harm.

The chatter that rippled throughout the room fell into a hush as the appeal began. DCI Thompson, dressed for the occasion in full uniform, addressed the waiting press with a general introduction before passing the focus over to Alex. She swallowed and cleared her throat, trying to forget that the cameras were trained upon her.

'Last night, sometime between the hours of 10.30 p.m. and 1.30 a.m., there was an incident on the mountain road that links Caerphilly with Rhiwbina. Unfortunately, this incident resulted in the death of a young woman.' She paused. Stacey's name had already been shared all over social media that morning, despite the best attempts of the police to keep her identity from the public eye for the time being. Regardless, Alex had been told not to state it at the appeal. With the details of the incident unknown, they needed to tread carefully. Though she believed Matthew himself to be in danger, she had been told he was to be still considered a possible suspect at this point. If there was any chance he might see the appeal, she mustn't do or say anything that might scare him away or deter him from coming forward.

'We are keen to speak to Matthew Lewis,' she continued, turning slightly to gesture to the photograph behind her. 'If anyone has seen Matthew or knows where he is, we ask that you get in touch on the number shown below.' She looked across to the boy's parents. 'I will now read a brief statement from the family. "We are devastated by what has happened and are fearful for the safety of our much-loved son. Matthew, if you are watching this, we ask that you come home or make contact with the police. We love you very much and just want you home safely."'

She folded the statement and returned it to the desk in front of her. 'We are keen to speak to anyone who used the mountain road between the hours of 10 p.m. and 2 a.m. last night. Thank you. That's all for now.'

Immediately the questions came thick and fast, just as she had known they would.

'What about Stacey's parents?' one reporter called out. 'Where are they?'

Alex's lip curled and she shot the man a glare. There had obviously been a reason for her withholding Stacey's name from her statement, yet he had chosen to ignore without a second thought the procedure the police were clearly trying to follow. In Alex's experience, the press were experts in disregarding the wishes of others, even when those others were in positions of authority. It was typical of a journalist to believe he was above the law.

'The victim's family are receiving specialist support from the police,' she said flatly. 'They are naturally distraught and we ask that their privacy is respected at this difficult time.'

'Do you think Matthew killed his girlfriend?' another reporter asked.

At her side, Alex saw Mrs Lewis's grip tighten around the glass of water that rested on the table in front of her, the surface of the drink trembling as it shook between her fingers. She clutched the glass as though it was the only thing keeping her from fleeing the room and the glare of attention focused upon them. Next to her, her husband sat motionless and distant, his eyes fixed sightlessly on the far wall, trying to blank out the audience that their misfortune had attracted.

'Finding Matthew is a priority.' She glanced across at DCI Thompson, briefly meeting his ever-critical eye. In the briefing before the appeal began, he had been explicit in his wishes that they remain vague about the details. It seemed to her now that being vague was helping to indirectly brand Matthew a potential criminal, and that doing so could jeopardise their chances of finding him alive, but she was under instructions and there was nothing she could do about it.

'What about Kieran Robinson?' someone else asked. 'Any updates?'

'Our inquiries are ongoing,' Alex responded through pursed lips. 'Needless to say, Kieran also remains a priority.'

She responded to a string of further questions, all with the same vague, non-committal answers. When the appeal ended, Matthew's parents stood hurriedly, his father brushing past her without a word. The snub felt personal. Though she hadn't directly accused Matthew, she hadn't expressed a belief in his innocence either.

Matthew's mother stopped in front of her and met her eye. Her jawline was set in a grimace and dark shadows of sleeplessness rested upon her sharp cheekbones. 'They all think he's guilty.'

'I can assure you, Mrs Lewis, we are doing everything we can to find out what happened to Stacey and where your son is.'

'Are you?' she challenged. 'What about those tyre marks that were found?'

Alex ushered the woman to one side, not wanting prying ears to overhear the details of the investigation.

'We don't have any reason to believe the marks are connected to what happened to Stacey.'

'And that's it? You're not even going to look into it?'

'We're currently in the process of trying to identify the vehicle through the tyre tread, but as I said—'

'But as you said,' Mrs Lewis repeated, cutting Alex short, 'you don't think it's relevant. I'm sure if it was your child missing you'd consider every possibility.'

She walked away, following her husband through the door into the corridor. The couple felt let down – by Alex, by the police – and at that moment she couldn't blame them. She knew that the only way in which she would be able to restore their faith would be to find their son alive.

SEVEN

The young woman in the station reception area was leaning on her elbows at the front desk, her angry face pushed towards the Perspex screen that separated her from the officer on the other side. Her purple hair was pulled back from her face in a ponytail that trailed the length of her back, and she was wearing a pair of Doc Martens that made her feet look far bigger than they probably were.

'Ginger,' she spat, pushing one foot behind her and pressing on to her toes, arching her back as though it was causing her discomfort. 'Skinny.'

The desk sergeant didn't have to think too hard about who she was describing; it was a brief yet accurate description that could only refer to one person working at the station. 'DC Sullivan?'

'That's him. Is he here then, or what?'

The desk sergeant glanced at his colleague in the office behind him. 'Saw him earlier,' the man said with a shrug, answering the look before returning to the paperwork he had been studying.

'If you'd like to leave a message, I'll make sure DC Sullivan gets it.'

The young woman gritted her teeth and threw her head back, casting her attention to the ceiling for a moment before returning it to the officer. 'No, I don't want to leave him a message. I want to speak to his superior ... now.'

'I'm sorry, but in that case you will need to tell me what it's about.'

She fumbled in the pocket of her jeans for her mobile phone before jabbing at its screen with a stubby finger. 'Kieran Robinson,' she said, putting the phone down on the desk and pointing at the photograph of her brother. It was the same photograph that had been used across the internet since his disappearance four days earlier: a grinning Kieran at a Christmas party, a length of tinsel draped around his neck and his arm slung around the shoulder of a faceless person who had been cut from the image. 'Recognise him?'

The desk sergeant's unchanging expression only enraged her further. 'Just another face to you, I suppose,' she said, throwing her arms in the air. 'What does it matter?' She slid the phone back towards her and returned it to her pocket.

*

'Everything okay?' DC Chloe Lane had entered the building through the main doors. She was looking windswept, her brunette hair unusually untidy as she hurriedly pushed it behind her ears. She slipped her jacket from her shoulders and hooked it over an arm.

'No,' the young woman snapped, turning to her. 'Everything is not okay.' She pulled her phone out of her pocket before jabbing in her passcode. 'Kieran Robinson. I'm his sister.'

'It's all right,' Chloe said, raising a hand and signalling for the woman to follow her. 'I know who you are. Come on through.'

Hannah Robinson shot the desk sergeant a look as she followed Chloe through a set of double doors and into the main corridor that ran the length of the station. Chloe ushered her into one of the family rooms and waited for her to take a seat.

'Everyone just forgotten about him then? Didn't take long, did it?'

'I can promise you that's not the case,' Chloe tried to assure her. Kieran Robinson had now been missing for almost four days. The last sighting of him had been well publicised in the hope that someone might come forward with information, but so far they were drawing blanks on all lines of inquiry. Where he had gone and what had happened to him after the last known footage of him was filmed remained a mystery, although the most popular theory was that he had fallen into the water and drowned.

His family couldn't accept that not finding Kieran's body didn't mean it hadn't happened.

'Why isn't there any progress, then?'

Chloe sympathised with the woman. It was frustrating when an investigation seemed to draw to a halt before it had really begun, but a lack of leads meant this was the case more often than the police liked to admit. The sad fact was that 48 per cent of cases that involved people who went missing after going on a night out remained unexplained. But no one wanted someone they loved to be the main character in one of those mysteries.

'It's Hannah, isn't it?' Chloe said. She remembered Kieran's sister from a news report broadcast over the weekend. 'We've looked at everything we possibly can with the information we currently have – Kieran's movements on Thursday evening, who he was with, where they went. You know his mobile phone hasn't been accounted for, but his laptop has been reviewed and there is really nothing at the moment to suggest that his disappearance is in any way suspicious.'

'Not suspicious? He's gone bloody missing, how much more suspicious do you need?'

'What I mean,' Chloe said, 'is that there's no evidence at this point to suggest that he has come to any harm.'

'Your most popular theory seems to be that he got pissed and drowned. That sounds like harm to me.'

'I'm sorry, Hannah. I wish we had more to tell you, but at the moment you know as much as we do. We're still making inquiries as to where he may have been during those missing hours between him leaving the comedy club and being out on the waterfront. I really am sorry. I know how difficult this must be for you.'

'No, you don't,' Hannah said flatly. 'You haven't got a clue.'

Chloe bit her tongue. She knew only too well how losing a brother felt – how being haunted by a mystery could consume a life, throwing everything else into doubt – but saying so wasn't going to ease Hannah's frustrations or offer her any form of comfort. Grief couldn't be compared or measured.

'He's just another statistic, isn't he?' Hannah challenged, leaning forward in her seat.

'Not at all,' Chloe said, feeling the heat of the woman's hostility burn her like a flame. 'I promise you we're doing all we can. We'll keep running the television and social media appeals and hopefully something will come in that can help move the investigation forward.'

'And that's it? That's the best you can do, is it?'

Chloe knew nothing she could say would help make the family's situation any easier. 'You've been assigned a family liaison officer?' she asked, wondering why Hannah had come to the station. Any queries or issues should have been directed to the FLO: that was what they were there for.

Hannah rolled her eyes to the ceiling. 'That woman who comes over to make the tea, you mean? Not sure how she justifies her salary. Anyway, I came here for a reason. DC Sullivan. He here?'

'As far as I'm aware. Do you need him for anything in particular?'

'Need him? The only thing I need is for him to stay the hell away from my family.'

The heat of Hannah's hostility intensified, and Chloe felt herself inwardly wince in anticipation of the revelation that might be about to follow. Whatever Jake had said or done, if it was enough to anger Kieran Robinson's sister in this way, then it would be sure to annoy Alex, something Jake seemed to have excelled at during the past few months.

'What are you referring to?'

'He more or less told my mum that perhaps Kieran *wanted* to go missing.'

Chloe gave an involuntary exhalation of despair. She didn't want to believe this might have been the case, but she knew Jake well enough to know it was more than likely. He was prone to opening his mouth before he engaged his brain; something that had landed him in deep water on several occasions. 'What do you mean, more or less? What exactly did he say?'

Hannah sighed. 'He said, "Sometimes we don't know people as well as we think we do."' She sat back and folded her arms, her mouth twisting into a grimace as she waited for Chloe to respond.

Chloe tried to keep her reaction neutral, but it was almost as though Hannah Robinson was taking some sort of solace from her discomfort. She didn't entirely blame her. If the family already believed the police weren't treating Kieran's disappearance seriously, then Jake's remark had only served to aggravate their dissatisfaction.

'In what context was it said?' The comment was crass, but Chloe struggled to believe that even Jake could be so insensitive as to say something like that. She could only think – and for his sake, hope – that it had been poorly timed and misinterpreted in some way. Yet knowing him as she did, there was a part of Chloe that doubted it.

'Context? There's an appropriate context for that sort of comment, is there?' Hannah shook her head, exasperated. 'My mum's in bits about Kieran. She's climbing the walls not knowing what's going on. That was the last thing she needed to hear.'

'I'll have to speak to DC Sullivan about this,' Chloe told her, knowing that any attempt to defend him to this woman would be pointless. Where Hannah was concerned, it seemed, the damage was already done, but Jake needed the chance to relate his version of events. There was always another side to everything, though he was going to need to come up with something pretty inventive to keep Alex off his back on this one.

'You do that,' Hannah said, sitting back and letting it be known she was going nowhere. 'In the meantime, I'd like to make this complaint formal.'

EIGHT

The last thing Alex wanted to be greeted with on her return to the station was the news of Hannah Robinson's complaint against DC Jake Sullivan. Frustration powering her pace, she sought out the young constable, finding him midway through a telephone conversation at his desk in the incident room. Waiting for him to end the call, Alex tried to swallow her anger until they were away from the prying eyes and ears of the rest of the team. Gossip was never anything but detrimental, and until she had heard both sides of the story, she didn't want news of the complaint to reach the rest of the team. She tried not to pass judgement before knowing all the facts, but where Jake was concerned, it had become too easy to assume the worst was correct.

'My office,' she mouthed.

He slouched into the room five minutes later, his shoulders hunched. This constant air of just-woken-up was one of the things Alex most disliked about Jake. She wanted to shake some life and energy into him. There were different approaches to the job they did, each with its own merits, but sometimes Alex felt Jake tried too hard to carve out his particular style of detective work, appearing so blasé that anyone might have been forgiven for thinking he didn't care for the cases he worked on.

His manner now suggested he realised exactly what he was guilty of, but if he was aware of the inappropriateness of what he had said to Kieran Robinson's mother, Alex couldn't help but wonder what on earth had made him go ahead and say it in the first place.

'We've had Hannah Robinson in. Kieran Robinson's sister. She said you made an inappropriate comment about the nature of her brother's disappearance.'

Jake's failure to deliver any kind of response to the claim suggested he knew what Alex was referring to. A red flush was already starting to creep up his neck, spreading across his checks like a mottled rash. For someone who so often came across as arrogant, this characteristic seemed oddly out of place.

'What exactly did you say?' she asked, closing the door to her office. 'Hannah claims you suggested Kieran might have wanted to go missing. Is that correct?'

'That's not what I meant. It came out wrong.'

Alex sighed. 'You think?'

She sat at her desk and studied Jake's face with an attention that was visibly uncomfortable for him. 'Making inane comments within the four walls of this station is one thing. This is something else entirely. So come on then … if it came out wrong, how was it meant, exactly?'

Jake shifted from one foot to the other and shoved his hands into his trouser pockets. It made him look like a schoolboy summoned to the head teacher's office, heightening Alex's irritation still further. She wished he had a little more about him: some spark of wit that went beyond the standard bantering office humour that was his usual forte. She even suspected she'd have a greater respect for him if he was to argue with her on something rather than attempting to simply skirt around the subject.

'I was trying to offer them some comfort.'

'By implying that Kieran might have made a conscious decision to leave his family with this worry hanging over them? That he could have killed himself, even? How in any way might that act as a source of comfort?'

Jake's thin lips remained tightly clamped together, his jaw tensed as though forcing back a reaction he knew wasn't likely to be well received. 'They think something bad has happened to him. I was just saying maybe it hasn't, that's all.'

'Because suicide would be somehow easier to cope with?' Alex didn't bother to keep the exasperation from her tone.

'I never said the word suicide.'

'I don't think you needed to. The insinuation was there.'

Jake shifted on the spot, avoiding Alex's eye.

'So what do *you* think might have happened then?' she pressed him. 'Because the rest of us are working with the evidence … it's what we're supposed to do. You did show up for your training, didn't you?'

Jake looked past her, his tongue pushed into his cheek and his focus fixed to a point on the far wall. It was clearly taking everything he had to hold back what he really wanted to say. 'I don't know,' he admitted eventually, his words clipped. 'The comment was misjudged. I'm sorry.' His tone suggested there was no remorse within him at all.

Alex sat back. She didn't want bad feeling among the team, particularly during a case of this scale. As irritating as DC Sullivan could be on occasion, she didn't believe he had intended any malice. Stupidity wasn't a crime, though at times it could prove to have just as many consequences.

'I don't want you to have any further dealings with the family for now.' She sighed. 'DCI Thompson's going to get hold of this, and it'll be for me to defend you. Again.'

Jake nodded, still not meeting her eye. Alex was no longer sure his body language was a result of embarrassment. There was an arrogant detachment to Jake that she had always disliked, though since it apparently went unnoticed by everyone else, she had sometimes wondered if she was imagining it.

'I don't expect you to.'

'You're a part of this team. Start proving you deserve your place here, please.'

He left the office and returned to the incident room, where shortly afterwards Alex joined him and the rest of the team. She needed to update everyone with what they now knew about Matthew Lewis and Stacey Cooper.

'Right,' she said, bringing the chatter around her to a close. 'Here's what we know so far. Stacey was twenty and employed as a receptionist at a health spa in Blackwood. Matthew is twenty-one, studying football coaching at the University of South Wales.'

'You can get a degree in football?' DC Dan Mason said, raising an eyebrow. He had been a member of the team for as long as Alex could remember, and over the years had proved to be a solid and reliable detective. Events of recent months had shaken him, reaching too close to home, but hadn't stopped him from being as steadfast as ever. They had, however, made him more cynical than he'd been before.

'You can get a degree in just about anything nowadays,' Chloe responded.

'Both live at home with their parents,' Alex continued. 'We know that on Saturday they'd been to Cardiff to have lunch with friends before going to the stadium to watch the game against Italy. After the match ended, they went to the Prince of Wales on St Mary's Street, still with the same group of friends. Both Matthew and Stacey were drinking, and we know that the plan had been for them to stay with Matthew's cousin Antony, who lives in Roath. I've spoken to Antony. He received a text from Matthew at just gone half ten to say he and Stacey wouldn't be going over. No explanation. He tried calling Matthew but there was no answer. Matthew's phone records confirm this.'

'Argument?'

'Between Stacey and Matthew? After speaking to the friends they were with in town, it seems likely. Apparently there was a bit of tension between them. It seems Matthew wasn't happy with the way Stacey was behaving.'

'What does that mean?' Dan asked.

'Flirting with his friends, mostly. Matthew had kissed another girl a while back, one of his friends – he told Stacey about it, and by all accounts she seemed to be doing her best on Saturday to get her own back.'

'Is that enough of a motive for him to have killed her?'

Alex shook her head, her scepticism obvious. 'It doesn't make sense. As far as anyone knows, Matthew didn't have access to a gun, and even if he had, why would he have been carrying it in the car with him on Saturday? I don't buy it at all. This is South Wales, not Compton. We should hopefully know more once we get the details of the weapon back. Someone else was involved at some level, whether it was someone who was in the car with them that night, or someone they met along the way.'

'Hitchhiker?' Jake suggested.

'They were young, but I don't think either of them was stupid. Who in their right mind would stop to pick up a stranger at that time of night?'

'People do stupid things all the time,' Jake said, defending his suggestion. 'We'd all be out of a job if they didn't.'

He didn't meet her eye, but Alex caught the implication. What she had said to him in her office had hurt, and he was still smarting from it. She had to admit he had a point. Alex herself wasn't exactly free from a history of poor decision-making. Her divorce had been followed by a string of liaisons with her ex-husband; too many to be plausibly referred to as misdemeanours. More recently, an encounter with Dan had brought her poor decision-making into the workplace. Regardless of what happened next, she still felt she had some making-up to do. The next chapter in her life was where she felt certain she could begin to right the wrongs she was guilty of.

'He was driving under the influence of alcohol,' Chloe said. 'That's pretty stupid for a start.'

'Which leads us, perhaps,' Alex said, shaking herself back to the present, 'to what they were doing up on the mountain road. He lives in Blackwood, she lives in Nelson. The quickest way from Cardiff back to either of their homes would've been straight up the A470, particularly at that time of night, with the roads quiet. So why take the mountain route? Had he planned to meet someone there, the person who was responsible for killing Stacey?'

She knew she had to cover all possibilities, but even as she asked the questions Alex felt in her gut that nothing this premeditated had led to the couple being up on the mountain road that evening. The silent response that came from the rest of the team seemed to suggest the same.

'If that was the case,' Dan said eventually, 'then where's Matthew now? Say he had organised for someone else to be there. Wouldn't he have waited for us to arrive, made out they'd been attacked at random and then claimed he was a victim too?'

'Exactly,' Alex said with a shake of her head. 'You're right. It's too implausible.'

Reaching for the laptop on the desk in front of her, she clicked on the opened file. A close-up of the gunshot wound inflicted on Stacey Cooper was projected on to the screen behind her. 'We've got the post-mortem report back, but unfortunately it doesn't tell us anything we don't already know. For now, we're just going to have to work with what we've got. These images have been sent to ballistics. They're also analysing the damage to the windscreen. Hopefully, once the wound and the bullet itself have been analysed, they'll be able to identify the type of weapon used.'

She paused and turned away from the image. 'Look … this is unfamiliar territory for the majority of us. Shootings are thankfully still rare in South Wales. Our priority for now is to find Matthew Lewis. He remains innocent until proven guilty, let's remember that, please. Keep pressing his friends for information – perhaps they know more than they're letting on. With regard to who else might have been up on that mountain ...' Alex sighed, surrendering to the limited details in their possession. 'There's no CCTV for miles in any direction, so we've no chance of tracking any other vehicles that way. The woodland has been searched around the area where the car was left, and so far we've found nothing. Both Stacey and Matthew appear to have been popular, so social media might prove useful on this one. Let's keep the appeals for information regular, please.'

She stretched out an arm, diverting the team's attention to another face that looked down from the evidence board. 'Kieran Robinson. There's been an update on the CCTV reviews that you should all be aware of by now. Darren Robinson's van was picked up near the Millennium Centre on the night Kieran went missing. We know Kieran had been working recently with his father as an apprentice builder. On Thursday night, he'd been to a comedy club with a group of subcontractors who'd all been involved in the construction of a housing development in Whitchurch. The evening had been paid for by the development's owners, Lawrence and Wyatt Properties – an end-of-project bonus, apparently. Darren Robinson didn't attend – he told everyone, including his wife, that he was in Devon, working on another job. So what was his van doing in Cardiff Bay on the night Kieran went missing? We've yet to get hold of him since the CCTV footage has been picked up, but it'll be interesting to see what he has to say for himself when we do.'

As Alex brought the meeting to an end and the rest of the team began to return to their desks, she noticed DCI Thompson lingering at the side of the room, waiting to speak to her. Despite the general belief that he would remain in place for a brief time until a permanent replacement was appointed, he was still based at the station in Pontypridd. He had been transferred following the retirement of Superintendent Blake, who had been Alex's superior for much of her career. With the post having remained unfilled,

DCI Thompson had been given little other option than to stay in Pontypridd, which hadn't at first been met with much enthusiasm. His initial frustration at being removed from his position in Bridgend had been gradually shadowed by a reluctant acceptance that he might be with them for an indefinite period of time, and although the majority of the team continued to find him aloof and a little bit strange, Alex was growing increasingly used to his ways. To claim she either understood or liked the man would have been an exaggeration, but she was at the very least finding him more tolerable to work for than she had just a few months earlier.

'DC Jake Sullivan,' he said.

'It's been dealt with.'

Thompson's eyes widened. 'Meaning?'

'Meaning I've spoken with him and I'm satisfied that the comment he made to Linda Robinson was simply poorly timed and misjudged. I'll make sure he apologises to the family in person.'

'How long are you expecting to wait before we hear from ballistics?'

'Could be days.'

'You still think Matthew Lewis could be in danger? If he killed Stacey, he could be lying low somewhere.'

Alex raised an eyebrow. 'Where?' She shook her head. 'I don't think he's responsible for Stacey's death, but he's the only person who knows what happened up on that mountain. The sooner we find him, the better.' She realised she hadn't answered the question directly, exactly what she hated anyone else doing. 'Yes,' she added. 'I do think he could be in danger.'

'But nothing's come in yet?'

'Nothing useful, no.'

They were interrupted by one of the DCs, as though he had been waiting around the corner just to prove her wrong. 'Boss. We've had a call in. Someone's found a body.'

NINE

Dear Elise,

I have something I need to tell you. I am writing this so that when I next see you I won't need to go through it again. When the time comes, I would prefer to focus on us, if that's possible – if you can find it in your heart to forgive me. By the time I've finished writing, I hope you'll understand why I've done the things I have. There is so much suffering in this world, but you of all people don't need me to tell you this. I try to help alleviate the pain, though I know they won't see it in this way – not in the way you will. Yours is the kindest heart I have ever known – your soul is the most forgiving. You see the good intentions where others only see intent, and your outlook on life is something I have tried to learn from, though I'd be lying if I claimed it has been easy.

I think about you every day. I want you to know that those others mean nothing to me, not in the way you do, but it is hard to undo something that has been done for so long. It is hard to fix something that has always been broken.

I took a life. There ... I've said it. Those four short words look so simple when they're written down like this, as though they weigh nothing, and I suppose it's true that the load does become lighter over time. There are things I wish I could change, yet regardless of everything that has happened, I wouldn't change the course of events that led my life to yours. I would do it all again in a heartbeat, all to get to you.

I'm beginning to ramble, and for this, too, I apologise. There is so much I need to say to you, but finding the right words seems an impossible task, one I need to get right, as much for myself as for you. I am not a bad man. If all that comes from writing to you is your acceptance of this, then I will consider it worth every uncomfortable second, because believe me when I tell you that this isn't easy for me to do. Despite everything you may be tempted to believe, I need you to believe that I am not a bad man. You've had plenty of time to form your own opinion on this and I know there have been occasions when I've let you down. Trust me when I say I never meant to.

Life is complicated, sweetheart – you know this as well as I. Please don't be too quick to judge me. Give me time and I'll explain everything as best I possibly can. There were things I couldn't guarantee you, promises I was forced to break, but this is something I can do for you now with a pledge that everything I say will be the truth, all of it, with nothing left hidden.

I miss you. I need to be with you again.

Benny x

TEN

At the motorway service station where they had arranged to meet, Chloe found Darren Robinson sitting in McDonald's drinking coffee from a cardboard cup. In his early fifties, he was dressed in his work gear: black cargo-style trousers, black boots grey with dust, and a short-sleeved T-shirt despite the cold bite of the March weather. Chloe flashed her ID as she took a seat opposite him.

'Will this take long?'

She didn't answer the question. The man's behaviour was odd to say the least: his son had gone missing and his wife was distraught as a result, yet he hadn't returned home to be with her since learning of Kieran's disappearance, and he had lied to the police about where he had been that night. Though he had agreed without argument to meet up with Chloe, he was acting as though a conversation with the police was something his busy life simply couldn't accommodate. Just why was this man being so cagey?

'Your son's still missing, Mr Robinson.'

He sat back and glanced around the room, folding his arms across his chest before returning them to his sides. He looked tired, his eyes bloodshot from lack of sleep, and Chloe wondered whether the thought of Kieran's possible whereabouts was keeping him awake at night or whether there was something else preying on his mind; something he was desperate to keep hidden from them.

'I'm aware of that.'

'I need you to explain why you lied to us about where you were on Thursday night. You said you were in Devon on a job, but your van was picked up on CCTV near the Millennium Centre in Cardiff Bay.' Chloe put her phone on the table between them, pointing at the photograph shown on the screen. 'You can't be in two places at once.'

Darren looked briefly at the photo before looking back up at her. His eyes darted to the left as though something had caught his eye, but it seemed to Chloe that the delay was nothing more than an attempt to give himself time in which to formulate his response. With a sigh, he placed his hands on the table, open-palmed, as though this conscious gesture of apparent honesty would be enough to make her change her mind about him. 'I was going to go to the comedy club, meet the rest of them there, but I decided last minute not to go.'

'So why not just tell us that on Friday?'

Darren reached for his coffee, changed his mind and returned his hands to his lap. Chloe noticed he didn't wear a wedding ring, though this wasn't unusual. It was possible that he didn't want to lose it or damage it at work, or that he just never wore one. If it had been any other man than Darren, Chloe might have thought nothing of it, but everything about Darren Robinson was becoming a source of suspicion. 'I'd been drinking,' he said, scratching his left ear. 'I'd been out that afternoon. Finished work early and went to the pub. I'd had too much to drink. I shouldn't have been driving. I didn't want to tell you I'd been back to Cardiff – if I'd told you that, I would have had to tell you about the drink-driving.'

He was lying. Chloe watched him shift in his chair and run his hand across his head before returning to his coffee.

'Why did you change your mind?'

'What?'

'About going to the comedy club,' Chloe reminded him. 'You said you changed your mind.'

'Headache. I realised I'd had enough to drink already.'

'So where did you go instead?'

'Stayed at a mate's in Cardiff.'

'You live in Cardiff,' Chloe reminded him, unable to keep the sarcasm from the comment. 'St Melon's isn't that far a drive from the Bay, is it? Why not just go home?'

She waited, but Darren didn't answer. He'd already told so many lies; she wondered why just one more seemed such an issue for him.

'Your friend would be able to confirm you stayed there, would he?' Chloe persisted, noting the way Darren twitched and shifted every time he was asked a further question. It was like watching a trapped wasp struggle beneath an overturned glass: frantic at first, then increasingly weary as its energy failed and it accepted the fact that there was no escape.

'She,' he corrected her. He sat back in his chair and rolled his eyes to the ceiling before glancing over his shoulder as though he was making his confession to a mate down the pub and didn't want anyone he knew to overhear. 'Look,' he said, having gauged the reaction on Chloe's face, 'that's another reason I didn't want to say where I'd been. The friend I stayed with, I've known her for years and it's completely innocent, but Linda won't see it that way, will she?'

Chloe picked up her phone from the table and opened her notes app. 'I'll need this friend's name and contact details,' she told him, sarcasm once again escaping from her, this time at the word 'friend'. She waited as Darren retrieved his own phone and read out the woman's phone number. 'Why didn't you go home the following day?'

'I had to get back to Devon for the job.'

Chloe sat back, scepticism stamped across her raised eyebrow and the curl of her top lip. 'So you drove all the way to Cardiff from Devon for a night out you didn't even go on, and then drove all the way back again? '

Darren shrugged. 'I won't see a lot of the boys again,' he said casually. 'Had to make the effort, didn't I.'

His words hung in the silence between them for a moment. They both knew there was a chance he would never see his son again. Despite the cliché that people didn't just disappear, there were occasions on which exactly that did happen.

'Is that everything then?' he asked.

'How would you describe your relationship with Kieran?'

Darren studied her for a moment, wary of the question and its possible implications. He looked like a man who knew he was at risk of stumbling over his own lies and was consciously dodging the trip wires he'd strung out for himself. 'Fine,' he said tentatively, as though any answer he gave might in some way incriminate him. 'Good, actually. I mean, I gave him work, didn't I? I wouldn't have had him there with me day in, day out if we didn't get on well, would I?'

'How did that come about?' Chloe asked, ignoring his question. 'Kieran studied art at college, didn't he? Seems a bit of a jump for him to make – art college to labouring.'

'You're not much older than Kieran. Know anyone who studied art?'

Chloe shook her head.

'Exactly. That's 'cos there's no jobs at the end of it. He was twenty-three and bloody clueless … his qualifications weren't worth the paper they were printed on. No one else would give him work 'cos he had no experience. I tried to help him, that's all, like any father would.'

'*Was* twenty-three?' Chloe repeated, picking up on the man's use of the past tense.

Darren's face changed instantly, darkening as he held her eye. There was a challenge in his stare that she realised was intended to be intimidating. 'Is,' he corrected himself. 'Look,' he said, his voice sharpening, 'I know what you're trying to do. You think it's strange I've not been home, and maybe you're right, maybe I should be with my wife, but this is hard for me as well, you know. We've all got different ways of coping with things.'

He continued to hold her gaze, his face softening as though in an effort to make Chloe believe that his words were genuine. Darren Robinson might be no fool, she thought, but neither was she. She had seen enough men like him to know not to believe a thing he said.

He looked away as a young family passed them, a newborn in a baby carrier screaming with all the force of its tiny lungs, an older child competing for attention above the din, proudly letting anyone within a half-mile radius know that he needed to use the toilet.

'Are we done then?'

'You haven't drunk your coffee,' Chloe pointed out.

Darren stood. 'Gone off the idea.'

He pushed his chair back and made his way towards the exit, Chloe watching him as he left the building and returned to his van. She was certain of one thing: nothing Darren Robinson said was to be taken at face value.

She searched her phone for Alex's number, waiting just a few seconds before the call was answered.

'He's a liar,' she told her. 'He's not quite as skilled at it as he likes to think, though. I just can't work out what he's lying about.'

'Everything, perhaps?'

Chloe's mouth rose at the corner. 'Maybe. Where are you?' Their conversations tended to be punctuated with the background buzz of passing traffic; Alex was often in the car, where she complained she seemed to spend half her life, but the only sound now was her voice, hushed to little more than a whisper. While she'd been staying at Alex's house, Chloe had shared lifts to work with her. The journeys had given them time to talk, free from other distractions. Though her move to Pontypridd, a few streets away from the police station, had been just what she'd needed, Chloe missed those chats.

In truth, she missed Alex. For reasons she was remaining tight-lipped about, her colleague hadn't been herself recently.

'Thornhill. A body's been found in a garden.'

'Not Matthew Lewis?'

'I don't know anything yet. I'll keep you updated.'

ELEVEN

The semi-detached house was on an estate that dated back to the 1960s. Ongoing building work was evident, with piles of bricks and plastic sheeting filling a drive that was barely wide enough for a single car. Crime-scene tape had already been secured around the property, and the sight of the police car pulled up outside on the pavement had been enough to ensure that the obligatory throng of rubberneckers had congregated in the street, whispering among themselves and pointing questioning fingers at number 14. So far, the police had been able to withhold the fact that human remains had been found in the garden.

If shock had a face, it would have been that of the woman standing in the hallway as though she had stumbled by mistake into a stranger's home, a stranger's life. She was in her late thirties and was wearing a fitted grey skirt that hugged her hips and a pair of scuffed court shoes that added three inches to her height. She had been brought home from work by the call she had received from the builder over an hour earlier, and was yet to take off her coat, having lingered in the hallway with a uniformed officer, neither really knowing what to say to the other to fill the silence while they waited for the detective's arrival.

'Ignore them,' Alex said, closing the door on the sight of the neighbours cluttering the road. 'Is there somewhere we can go?'

Without a word, Natalie Bryant went into the front room, where the curtains were still pulled closed. The room was a mess: pieces of furniture were piled on top of one another, a TV unit was propped precariously on a sideboard, a bookcase was crammed so full with DVDs and board games that it looked as though it might topple over at any moment.

'Sorry,' she muttered, indicating the chaos that surrounded them. 'Everything from the other rooms has had to be stored in here.'

Alex waved a hand, dismissing the apology. The last thing Mrs Bryant needed to think about was the state of her house.

'How long have you lived here?'

'Five years. Just over five.' She pressed the fingertips of her right hand to her forehead as though pushing back a headache. 'We saved for so long to move here.' Her eyes glassed over, shocked to tears by the turn of events that had overtaken this seemingly normal Monday.

'I don't understand this,' she said, turning to Alex. 'I mean, there's got to be a mistake or something, hasn't there?'

There was a noise behind them and the women turned to see a uniformed officer in the doorway. Alex excused herself and followed the officer down the hallway to the back of the house. It seemed Mrs Bryant hadn't dared to venture out into the back garden since she had arrived home, not wanting to confront what was waiting there. Either that or she had been advised by one of the builders not to.

Alex found herself in the shell of what had previously been the kitchen, recognisable only by a few remaining units and a stopcock on the far wall. The room stood bare and cold, tiny shards of broken tiles cracking underfoot as she followed the man to the back door. Outside, the builders had been in the process of digging up the garden ready to lay foundations for an extension. Their machinery stood silent now, turned off at the macabre discovery beneath the patio slabs. Tools lay on the ground, abandoned beside flasks of tea.

'The pathologist has been held up in traffic,' the officer explained.

In the garden, two builders were standing with a second uniformed officer, the three of them grouped by the fence as though keeping a safe distance from the chilling sight that had been excavated just feet away from them. Alex stepped towards the hole in the ground, seeing first the length of fabric that the body had been wrapped in. It might once have been any colour, but the earth had turned it a muddy brown, and time and insects had worn it threadbare. Whichever builder had pulled back the material to see what was hidden within it had dropped it back over the remains, concealing it once again from sight. Perhaps he had done so in an effort to protect his colleagues, she thought, or maybe it had been for his own benefit, as though covering the body might erase the memory of the discovery from his consciousness.

Alex took a latex glove from her pocket and put it on before crouching beside the hole. The fabric was recognisable as a curtain by the row of plastic hooks that could be seen running along one edge, more than half the hooks now missing. She hadn't seen a pair of curtains with that kind of hook in a number of years. Her parents had once had a similar pair in their living room, and the memory dragged Alex back in time for a moment, a familiar tug of nostalgia clenching her gut as it had so often during that past year.

When she leaned forward to pull back the fabric, a human skull greeted her. The dark orbs in which a pair of eyes had once been now stared unseeing past her. The featureless bone was still connected to the torso of the skeleton, its arms crossed across its front. Alex didn't need a degree in forensic pathology to know the remains had been here for a number of years.

'Who found it?' She looked up at the builders. The younger of the two – a man no older than his early twenties who was wearing a beanie hat and an expression of panic that looked so ingrained it might as well have been tattooed on his face – raised his hand tentatively, as though he was still at school and confessing to something that would get him sent to the head teacher's office.

'How long have the two of you been working on the extension?'

'Just started last week,' the other man told her. He turned his head as he coughed. 'Found some unexpected things in my time, but this ...' he added, shaking his head as he dragged the back of his hand across his mouth.

'We'll need you both to give statements, if you've not already done so.'

Alex stood and went back into the house, where she found Natalie Bryant still in the front room, waiting for her. She had been crying, and at the sight of Alex, she quickly wiped her eyes.

'You said you've been here just over five years, Mrs Bryant. Do you know who lived here before that?'

'There was an elderly couple living here. They died. I don't know much more than that, I'm sorry. I don't really remember much about that time, if I'm honest – I'd not long given birth and I wasn't in a great place. It all seems such a long time ago now. This house was supposed to be our fresh start. We've been saving for the extension since we moved in. The thought of it being there all that time ...' She ran her palm over her face before pressing the heel of her hand against her right eye. 'Sorry ... I don't mean "it". I just ... You know what I mean.'

'You have a son?' Alex said, looking at a framed photograph that lay at the top of a box filled with books, stationery and sporting trophies.

Natalie nodded. 'Rhys. He'll be six in the summer. Thank God he's at school and hasn't had to see any of this. How would I explain it to him?' She sidestepped a pile of boxes as she moved to the window and pushed aside the curtain. 'You'd think we'd done something wrong,' she said, looking at the neighbours who were still lurking on the opposite pavement. 'So what happens now?'

'Is there somewhere you can stay tonight?' Alex asked.

'We can go to my in-laws – they're not far.'

'Your husband ...'

'I've called him. He's on his way home.'

When reports of the builder's call had made it to the incident room, the initial assumption had been that the body of Matthew Lewis or Kieran Robinson had been found, but it had soon become obvious that the remains at 14 Oak Tree Close were not those of anyone who had gone missing recently. Alex was unsure of her response to learning that the discovery didn't involve either of the young men the team were currently searching for. It meant there was a chance both Matthew and Kieran were still alive, but on the other hand it meant a whole new case would be competing for their attention and burdening their workload.

It never rains, she thought.

She left the room and opened the front door, grateful for the gust of fresh air that was blown into the hallway. Outside on the street, the gathering of neighbours had grown, the increased police presence attracting greater attention. Alex went across to them and raised a hand. 'If you could all move back, please, away from the tape.'

'What's going on?' a man asked.

'Just move back, please.'

She turned to a uniformed officer who was standing nearby and rolled her eyes. It never failed to surprise her how nosy people could be, as well as how inappropriate.

Her mobile began ringing in her coat pocket. It was one of the DCs back at the station.

'Boss. Got something for you on the Matthew Lewis case. How far are you from Caerphilly Mountain?'

Thornhill was only a few miles from Caerphilly, just over the border between the counties on the edge of Cardiff. The road on which Matthew Lewis's car had been found was a five-minute drive from Alex's current location.

'Close. Why, what's happened?' She almost added the word 'now'. They had wanted leads, but she could have done without everything turning up at once.

'Someone's found something in one of the fields. Ticket stub from the rugby match on Saturday.'

Alex's initial hope that something useful had been discovered there was quashed. 'The stadium's quite a big place,' she said, cynicism etched through her tone. Tens of thousands of people had attended the match in Cardiff that Saturday; it seemed unrealistic to expect the ticket stub to prove fruitful in any way.

'How many of them might have been in that field, though?' the officer reasoned.

Alex accepted the point. If nothing else, it offered a faint glimmer of hope in what had until now been a case halted by a series of dead ends.

TWELVE

Seeing the police car waiting further along the lane, Alex pulled into an area designed for passing other vehicles and cut the engine. She knew these lanes well: her own home was not far from here, just a few minutes' drive down the other side of the mountain towards the town centre.

The police car was parked in front of a metal gate. If her memory served her correctly, the gate was usually closed. A couple of horses had once roamed around in the field beyond it, often lingering where they would be visible to passing cars, their sad eyes gazing wistfully out. Alex couldn't remember having seen them for a number of years now, and she wondered what had happened to them.

She had called Chloe on her way there, arranging for them to meet on the mountain. Chloe had been on her way back to the station, nearly at the A470, and the lanes had involved only a brief detour. Chloe had parked near the spot where Matthew Lewis's car had been found and was now waiting with a uniformed officer and the man who had found the ticket stub earlier that day. He was in his late sixties and dressed as though he was about to embark on an Arctic expedition, a thick padded coat zipped up to his chin and a hat pulled down over his ears. A terrier tugged at the lead he was holding.

'Didn't think too much of it at first,' the man told them, 'but then I realised it was for the match on Saturday. Bit strange being up here, this far from town. Then I saw the news about that young couple. Strange business, that.'

Alex shot Chloe a look, both women sharing the same thought. The zone searches that had been carried out overnight on Saturday had stretched half a mile in each direction from the point at which Matthew Lewis's car had been found. This land was over a mile away. If the ticket stub belonged to Matthew Lewis, what had he been doing so far away from the car? Why had he been in this field?

She took the stub from the uniformed officer. It had a serial code along its edge: it would be easy enough to find out who had purchased it. 'Where exactly did you find it?'

The man stepped across the muddy ground at the entrance to the field. 'Just there,' he said, pointing to an area part way into the field. 'I had to chase the dog in here. Should have kept her on her lead.'

Alex looked back at the wet ground they had just crossed, silently cursing herself for not having extended the search this far. They had assumed Matthew had gone missing much closer to the spot at which his car had been found. The land was pitted with various indentations that had churned up the field's boundary, but the previous night's rain had ruined their hopes of finding anything that might prove useful. If the ticket stub had been discovered yesterday, they might have been able to identify a vehicle from the tread marks left in the mud.

Her disappointment obvious, she followed Chloe into the field, leaving the dog owner and the officer still standing near the gate.

'Reckon he's legit?' she asked, catching Chloe up.

'Him?' Chloe nodded back in the direction of the gate.

'Why's he dressed like that?'

Chloe smiled. 'You think he's hiding something under there?'

'Very funny. You never know.'

'Except when you do.'

'Why was he up here? Not him, I mean. Matthew.'

'No idea. But look.' They were nearing the middle of the field, where the land, having previously inclined, now reached its peak.

Alex followed Chloe's gaze. Ahead of them, almost hidden from sight of anyone passing along the lane, was an old farmhouse. Its chimney stack could be seen outlined against the woodland that stood behind it, with the upstairs windows – most of the glass smashed and the frames rotted – visible as they moved forward.

'Never knew that was here,' Alex said.

The building was small and in a state of disrepair. Part of the roof was missing and the downstairs windows had also been smashed. What had once been a garage stood to one side, its broken doors hanging loose, the inside of the building now victim to the effects of the inclement weather. Moss clung to the woodwork in thick clumps.

Alex followed Chloe as her colleague headed towards the farmhouse.

'What was he doing here?' Chloe asked, thinking aloud.

Alex said nothing. For the moment, they were only assuming that Matthew had been here. Even if the ticket stub turned out to have belonged to him, it didn't mean that he had ventured any further into the field. There was also the possibility that someone else had come into possession of the stub and it was he or she who had dropped it up here.

Yet Alex doubted the probability of such an event. The more she thought about it, the more it seemed unlikely that, despite the fact that so many other people had been to the match on Saturday, any of them had had reason to be in this field. Matthew had been here, she felt sure of that. Had he left the car and walked up here to find help getting petrol? If so, what was it that had drawn him into the field? It wasn't far from the spot where his car had been found, but in the pitch dark, and with no phone, walking over a mile seemed an almost reckless decision to have made. Maybe he had had no other option.

They stopped outside the garage. Inside, ancient shelving units housed rusted paint tins and tools that were probably of no use for anything any more. There were no signs of life around the building and no vehicles to be seen either inside the garage or out.

'Why would he have come here looking for petrol?' Alex said. 'Or help in getting any, at least. You can see this place hasn't been lived in for years.'

'Perhaps he couldn't tell that in the darkness.'

'It's the only thing that makes sense – the only possible reason we have for him to have been this far away from the car. I don't believe anyone else was with them, at least not when they stopped. Someone else came on the scene later, after Matthew had left the car.'

'So you think Matthew wasn't even there when Stacey was shot? Could he be hiding somewhere, scared of taking the blame for her murder?'

'If he wasn't there, he might not even know she's dead.' Alex turned to scan their surroundings. 'There are no other houses between here and the spot where the car was found, are there? This would have been the first place he would have reached.'

'Why not just call someone?'

'There's no signal up on the mountain road,' Alex told her, knowing this from personal experience. She had always found that there was an area of at least a mile and a half in which all mobile signal was lost. In fact, the thought that it would be an unfortunate place to break down had more than once crossed her mind as she had driven through.

A wave of sadness swept over her. Just a little further along the mountain road, her signal was usually resumed. If Matthew had walked half a mile or so further he would have been able to call for help – if he had taken his mobile with him. Would that extra half a mile have undone whatever had happened up here? Would it have saved Stacey Cooper's life?

Chloe turned and looked back across the field towards the gate, where the dog walker and the police officer were still standing, both gazing in the direction in which Alex and Chloe had headed. 'We've just said how remote this place is, though. We could barely see it from the road, and that was in daylight.'

Alex put her hands on her hips and scanned the land around her. 'Maybe he knew it was here somehow.'

'Alex.' Chloe gestured ahead, her attention drawn to a patch of earth that looked different to the rest. She moved forward and crouched down, running a hand across the uneven surface, lifting a handful of soil and letting it fall through her fingers. 'This has been disturbed. Look.'

Alex followed an L-shaped track mark that had been scoured into the ground. The lines were straight, carefully outlined, the indentations methodically etched. The soil between them had been turned over, as though it had been half dug before being filled in again.

'Christ,' she muttered.

A picture was beginning to form: something far more sinister than she might have imagined. Was Matthew Lewis here, buried just feet beneath where they stood?

THIRTEEN

Dan was sitting at his desk in the incident room. On the computer screen in front of him was a list of names and dates: the records relating to the ownership of number 14 Oak Tree Close, Thornhill. The house was a 1960s red-brick build, with a stone porch above the doorway and protruding upstairs windows to the front. It seemed as innocuous as any other semi-detached property on any other housing estate. No one could have guessed at the dark secrets its patio was concealing, and news of the discovery at the property had caused shock waves throughout the local community. Unearthing the secret had been one thing, but getting to the truths that had been buried with the body was likely to prove a much more complex task.

Until recently, Dan had kept an open mind about most things. Though the job had at times been more challenging than he could ever have anticipated as a young man signing up to his chosen career, he had managed to stay positive about most aspects of life. People were good in the main, and that goodness prevailed over evil in the majority of cases. Only it didn't seem that way any more.

He returned his focus to the screen, shaking himself free of his dark thoughts. Number 14 had been purchased five years earlier by Natalie and Jonathan Bryant, having previously belonged to a woman named Carol Smith. Before her, the house was owned by a couple called Stan and Peggy Smith, who had lived there for almost forty years. It wasn't an uncommon surname, but Dan wondered whether Carol Smith was the couple's daughter, and whether she had inherited the house from her parents.

He was in the process of trying to find the whereabouts of Carol Smith when Jake came over from the other side of the incident room. He was carrying a mug of tea, though the dark bags that lay heavy beneath his eyes made him look as though he had stayed up late the previous night enjoying something far stronger.

'You heard about Matthew Lewis?'

'What?'

'The burial site up on the farmland. Nothing there.'

Dan turned in his seat and pushed a hand through his greying hair. 'So what are we working with?'

Jake shrugged. 'Boss reckons now that Matthew might have interrupted an intended burial. Someone else's.'

'Jesus. Talk about bad timing.'

'Just had a call in about him, as well.'

'About Matthew?'

'Someone thinks they've seen him.'

'Where?'

'Cardiff. Queen's Street.'

Dan rolled his eyes. 'Right. Them and how many others, I wonder? You'd better check it out, though.'

Although they so often relied on the help of the public, more often than not, sightings of people who had been reported missing or wanted by the police turned out to be false leads. However, the rare occasions on which a member of the public did come forward with something useful meant that they couldn't afford for any call to go ignored. No one wanted to be responsible for dismissing a genuine lead as yet another time-waster or glory-hunter.

*

Jake sipped his tea and returned to his desk to contact the shops near the supposed sighting of Matthew Lewis. If he had been where the caller suggested, he would have been picked up somewhere on CCTV. He checked the details, noting the names of the shops and their contact numbers. Clicking on another tab, he returned his focus to the Facebook page he had been looking at earlier. He had been scrutinising Matthew Lewis's timeline for signs of anything that seemed amiss, but so far his search had offered him nothing. Everything he had seen suggested that Matthew was a regular twenty-one-year-old, with his page consisting of the usual shared memes, banter between friends and updates on his progress at university. There was certainly nothing to suggest he was the type of man who might be harbouring a firearm and a desire to kill his girlfriend.

An email notification flashed up at the top of the screen.

Jake glanced around the room. Dan was engrossed in his task of tracking down Carol Smith. The rest of the incident room team were similarly engaged in their work, all trying to identify any leads that might help them find Matthew Lewis. With Kieran Robinson's whereabouts also a priority, it felt like each of them was tackling the workload of three people.

Returning his attention to the screen, Jake moved the mouse to the search engine at the top of the page and typed in Kieran Robinson's name. He found him within a brief scroll of the results: a thick mop of dark hair, brooding eyes and almost Mediterranean skin; a handsome young man whose smile didn't quite stretch to his eyes. His profile picture had been taken the previous summer, showing Kieran sitting on a park bench, shaded from the sun by the overhanging branches of the trees that stood behind him.

Jake moved from the page and opened the email that had just been received. Earlier that day he had made a request to Facebook for access to Kieran Robinson's inbox messages: on missing persons investigations the data was usually forthcoming. As requested, copies of Kieran's recent messages, both sent and received, had been included within the email. Jake reached for the bottle of water that lay in the top drawer of his desk and took a long drink. Screwing the plastic cap back on, he began to read the conversations between Kieran and the people he had been in contact with during the weeks leading up to his disappearance.

His most recent interaction had been with a girl named Georgia Harris. *I miss your face*, she had written two weeks earlier. Kieran had replied with a heart emoji. *I miss the free lifts home*, he had responded. The conversation continued in the same light-hearted vein, the two exchanging friendly banter in which each mocked the other's shortcomings, and it quickly became apparent that Georgia and Kieran had studied on the same art course. There was talk of plans to meet up, though the manner in which the exchange of messages drifted to its end suggested that these plans might never have come to fruition.

Jake finished his tea and glanced over his shoulder again before turning his attention to the next strand of messages. In this case, the conversation was one-sided. *Is everything OK?* someone called Elliot West had asked almost a month earlier. Kieran hadn't responded. *You can't just ignore me*, Elliot had persisted. The following week, when there had still been no reply from Kieran, Elliot had sent another message: *Okay, it's like that then. Nice. Thanks for nothing.* The next day, he had written: *This how you treat everyone you have sex with?* Kieran had then blocked Elliot from sending him any further messages.

Jake returned to Facebook and typed Elliot West's name into the search bar. There were a number of results thrown up, an array of faces greeting him from the screen like a game of Guess Who?. He scanned them in turn, wondering which might belong to the sender of the messages to which Kieran hadn't wanted to reply. Stopping at one face, he guessed there was a chance this might be him. He looked the right age, early twenties like Kieran, but Jake would need confirmation before he chased him up. He would contact Facebook to find out if this Elliot West and the sender of the messages was one and the same person.

It was obvious what the messages referred to, but Jake wondered whether Elliot had been upset enough by Kieran to wish him harm. The tone of the messages was one of disgruntlement, and Kieran's refusal to acknowledge Elliot's attempts at a dialogue had clearly not been met with appreciation. With another glance in Dan's direction, Jake closed the window on the screen.

He wondered where DI King was. He hadn't seen her in a while, which for the time being suited him fine. She had made her mind up about him long before now, and Jake had always been aware of her ambivalence towards him. Following the complaint from Hannah Robinson, he felt the need to prove himself to her more than ever. If there was a link between Elliot West and Kieran's disappearance, he wanted to be the one DI King had to thank for it.

FOURTEEN

Alex arrived at the station early on Tuesday morning knowing that she and the rest of the team were likely to have a long day ahead of them. She got herself a coffee from the machine in the corridor and took it to her office, sipping it at the window as she watched the world begin to wake below her: service buses pulling away from the bus station across the road, traffic waiting at the set of lights that stood just beyond the station car park, the dark grey of an early-spring sky paling into a hazy blue as the light of morning drew nearer.

She thought about the letter that was still in her bag; a letter she had read more than ten times, carefully unfolding and folding it, consuming each and every word as though she was able to taste it. There was something almost archaic about receiving a letter; this type of letter, at least. Paper still came through her door in the form of council tax statements and television licence reminders, but what was rare now were the types of letters that provoked an emotional response; the kind that could change a person's day, lift their spirits with just a few lines.

Alex was reminded of the letters she had found among her mother's things after she had passed away the previous year: long, handwritten missives exchanged between her mother and father before their marriage. In them, both had declared feelings Alex could never remember having seen displayed when she was growing up, although she knew from bitter experience that the optimistic, joyous early days of a relationship were short-lived, and that the reality of marriage – the reality of life, once the sheen of the honeymoon period had worn off – allowed little time or space for the affection her parents had evidently felt for one another at some stage in their past.

Dear Ms King, the letter began, *we are happy to inform you that your application for adoption has now been reviewed …*

Putting her coffee cup on the windowsill, Alex went to her desk and retrieved her bag from the floor. The letter was tucked into an inside pocket, still in its envelope. She opened it once again and scanned it, checking it carefully, as though her previous readings of it had been wishful thinking; as though her own eyes had been somehow capable of deceiving her. She had missed nothing, she thought, lingering over each sentence, devouring each word as though they were fuelling her body. This was real. It was happening, finally.

Her thoughts were broken by the ringing of her phone. When she answered, she was greeted by the serious monotone voice of the forensic anthropologist who had attended number 14 Oak Tree Close the previous day. She had thus far encountered him on only one occasion. Her initial impression was that someone as downcast and sombre as he seemed to be was probably ill suited to a job in which death and violence formed the basis of each day. She'd bet he was a riot at parties.

His call was earlier than expected. He was efficient if nothing else, she thought. Hopefully his efficiency that morning would be catching. They were desperately in need of something that would power the positivity of the team.

'I can tell you that the body is that of a male aged early twenties at the most,' he told her. 'There's evidence of a hyoid bone fracture, so the most likely cause of death is strangulation. The deterioration of the remains is obviously an issue, but there's no doubt in my mind that that's how he died. I've sent a sample of bone to the lab for DNA extraction – it is possible we might gain some further information that way, but it's a time-consuming process.'

'The remains aren't too old for that?'

'I don't want to raise your hopes,' he admitted. 'It's one of the worst examples of decomposition I've seen. But it's been done in cases where the remains are much older than this.'

'When do you think he died?'

The pathologist exhaled noisily. 'Ballpark estimate? Between thirty and forty years ago. Like I said, the condition of the corpse makes it very difficult to be any more specific. I'm sorry. There is one other thing, though. When we reassembled the remains, two bones were missing. The metacarpal and the phalange. Third finger of the left hand.'

'The ring finger?'

'Indeed. Been cut clean off at the knuckle.'

Alex paused, absorbing the information. Presumably, anyone who had gone missing would have been reported as such, though previous cases had proven things were not always that straightforward. She wondered whether the ring finger had been removed from the young man before or after death. What reason could there possibly have been for it to be taken?

'Anything else we can work with until any possible DNA results come back?'

'I'm sorry. It's frustrating, I know, but that's all we have for now.'

Alex thanked the man and ended the call. She wondered how he managed on occasions when he was forced to make a genuine apology, given that everything he said sounded like a recital of the phonetic alphabet.

It wasn't the conversation she'd hoped for, though she knew that to expect anything other would have been naïve. How many young men of that age group would have been reported missing during a ten-year time frame? And then there were the others – the truly lost, the ones who hadn't even been reported as such. An investigation on this scale was a massive undertaking, particularly with the disappearances of Kieran Robinson and Matthew Lewis also on their hands, and the murder of Stacey Cooper to solve.

The ring finger, Alex thought, pushing her hands through her hair. An accident prior to death, or something that had been done afterwards? The particular finger seemed so specific; symbolic, somehow. She looked at the case notes relating to Matthew Lewis and Stacey Cooper that were spread out on the desk in front of her, and sighed. Beside them waited Kieran Robinson's files, their contents offering nothing that had so far given them any help.

Pushing back her feelings of despondency, Alex left her office. In the incident room, the rest of the team were waiting for that morning's briefing. The atmosphere was depressingly flat, with the majority clearly dejected by the lack of progress since Saturday. They needed something to happen that day to reignite some motivation and drive.

'We now know that the stub found on farmland a little over a mile from where Stacey Cooper was killed does belong to a ticket purchased by Matthew Lewis,' Alex told them. 'For those of you who weren't here yesterday evening, I'm sure you'll have already heard that we've also found what looks like a half-dug shallow grave on that same farmland.'

There was a ripple of murmurs among the assembled team.

'Our theory is this,' Alex said, turning to the faces that looked down at them from the incident board. 'We know that Matthew ran out of petrol on the mountain. He probably had no mobile signal, so there was no other option than to get out of the car to find help. Stacey stayed in the car to wait for him. He walked as far as the farm. Now, he either knew that the building was there and headed for it in the hope of getting help, or he saw something else that drew him there.'

'Lights perhaps,' Chloe suggested.

'You're saying someone killed him and dug a grave up there for him?' Jake asked.

'No. If that was the case, why didn't we find Matthew's body in it?'

'You said the grave was half dug,' Dan chipped in. 'So what are you thinking … he interrupted whoever was in the process of digging it?'

'Seems more likely. Those lanes are pretty quiet at night and the field in which the ground was dug is secluded from the road. We think Matthew inadvertently interrupted someone – someone who then went on to kill Stacey to keep her quiet. The tyre marks on the lane have been analysed, and the report I received last night says they're recent and likely to have been made by some kind of transit van.'

'That narrows things down,' Dan said.

'There are a few theories to consider. One is that Matthew was hit by this van. It's also possible he was abducted by whoever was driving it. We've all made gut judgements about this young man, but we still need to consider the possibility he may have been involved in Stacey's murder.' Alex stepped to the evidence board and drew a finger across the map of the mountain that had been pinned there. 'Whichever theory we favour, it seems likely that at some point, he was here,' she said, jabbing a finger on the section of map that marked the field in front of the farmhouse. 'The tyre marks were here, a hundred metres or so from the car in which Stacey was killed.'

The image of Matthew pinned to the board caught her eye: a young man with bright eyes and dark hair, his whole life seemingly ahead of him. Instinct told her he was a victim here, and if the theory that he had also been injured or harmed in some way proved correct, they were dealing with the cruellest twist of fate. Had Matthew and Stacey stayed with his cousin as was originally the plan, neither of them would have been on that mountain on Saturday night.

'So you think Matthew managed to escape from the field, but whoever had been up there followed him in the van?'

Alex nodded. 'With what we've got, I think that seems most likely at the moment. Someone followed him, hit him, then shot Stacey to keep her quiet. There's every chance Matthew might still be alive, but whoever was driving that van may well have hit him with enough force to disable him.'

'Then put him in the van and took him somewhere,' Dan finished for her.

Alex nodded. 'All our focus needs to be on finding Matthew Lewis and Kieran Robinson,' she said, her voice resolute.

'Do you really think there's any chance Matthew's still alive, though?' The sceptical expression on Jake's face said he thought the possibility unlikely. 'If whoever we're talking about here killed Stacey, they'll have killed Matthew too, won't they?'

'We continue to think and act as though he is alive,' she replied firmly.

Her attention stayed on the photograph of Matthew Lewis for a moment. What exactly had he seen up in that field? And then there was the question of *who* he had seen. Who had that makeshift grave been intended for?

'Nothing from ballistics yet?'

Alex was brought back to the room by Dan, who roused her from her thoughts with his question. She shook her head. 'I'm hoping that by tomorrow we should have something. What have you got on 14 Oak Tree Close?'

'Before Natalie and Jonathan Bryant, the house belonged to a woman named Carol Smith. The former owners were Stan and Peggy Smith, so it looks as though the property was signed over to Carol by her parents. If that's the case, the house would have belonged to the family at the time of our victim's death.'

'Been in touch with Ms Smith yet?'

Dan shook his head. 'Just found her details now. She works for the council.'

'Right. Chloe, I'd like you to come with me, please. Dan, try to find out as much about the family as you can. The more we know about the house and who lived there, the quicker our chances of identifying our victim. We're waiting for DNA results, but that could take a while. In the meantime, we keep our focus on finding these missing young men. Let's look into the farmland, please … who owns it, why the house is standing there derelict. Any updates, as always, I want to know about them straight away. Any questions?'

When she was met with silence, Alex brought the meeting to a close. Chloe lingered, waiting for a moment alone with her.

'What if that grave was dug for Kieran? I know it might seem far-fetched, but two young men go missing within a few days of one another … it's not entirely impossible, is it?'

'I had the same thought last night. And if it wasn't intended for Kieran, then who was it for?'

Neither detective wanted to consider the possibility that another victim might be involved in the mystery surrounding Matthew Lewis's disappearance, but nor did they want to believe that the grave had been intended for Kieran Robinson. They had to believe that he might still be alive.

'Are you okay?' Chloe asked. 'You look tired.'

Alex smiled, playing the part she had grown accustomed to. Chloe was the only person she had come close to telling about the adoption application, yet she had chosen not to confide even in her. This was something she needed to do alone; besides, she hadn't wanted the past few months with Chloe to be tainted by the knowledge that they might be the last. 'In that case, you can treat me to a coffee on the way.'

She was keen to get away from the station and get the investigation moving at a quicker pace. Most of all, she was keen to meet with Carol Smith. It was impossible to conceal a body beneath a patio without someone living at the property being aware of it.

FIFTEEN

Chloe ran a finger beneath the collar of her shirt and rolled her eyes in Alex's direction. The council building was a shrine to glass, with the reception area consisting of floor-to-ceiling windows that arched to form a part of the building's roof. Though it was only March and the air outside was still wintry cold, the heat trapped inside the building gave the misleading impression that the external temperature was far greater. Around them, a vast area of open space was home to little more than two sofas and a plastic stand stacked with leaflets, and the place still had that new-carpet smell Alex associated with the first drive of a new car. In summary, the council offices' reception area was a shocking waste of space and money. No wonder so many people had complained at the extravagance of the building when it was constructed just a few years earlier.

They were greeted at reception by a woman who was optimistically dressed for a much warmer spring than the one that was struggling beyond the glass. She wore a short-sleeved pink blouse bedecked with an enormous white bow, and her hair was scraped back into a bun so tight it appeared to be giving her a DIY facelift. She acknowledged the two detectives as they approached the reception desk, offering a smile that stretched right across her face.

Alex showed the woman her identification and told her they were looking for a Carol Smith. Emerging from behind the desk, the receptionist displayed a pair of tights so heavily patterned they looked capable of bringing on a migraine if stared at for any great length of time. Alex wondered if the woman's clothing choices affected her mood. Maybe, she thought, that was where she had been going wrong all those years. Perhaps she needed to start wearing more pink.

'I'll show you to Miss Smith's office,' the receptionist said cheerily, bustling her way through an electronic turnstile before holding her key fob to the sensor so that Alex and Chloe could follow her through. 'She's up on the second floor.'

Alex thanked her, and the two detectives followed her into the lift. On the second floor, they walked the length of the corridor to find Carol Smith in her office, a tiny triangular room tucked away in a far corner of the building. She couldn't have looked more of a cliché had she tried. She wore a pale blue suit with a silver brooch pinned to the lapel, and a pair of glasses rested on the end of her nose. Her greying hair was pulled back into a bun. At the side of her desktop computer, waiting at arm's reach, was a coffee mug that looked as though it hadn't met with a washing-up bowl in quite some time.

'Detectives?' she repeated, after Alex had introduced herself and Chloe. She stood from her desk and nervously smoothed down the front of her skirt, looking from one woman to the other questioningly. 'What can I do for you? Sorry,' she added, raising her palms as she looked around the small office. 'I'd offer you a seat, but … I don't usually entertain guests.' She gave a nervous laugh.

'That's fine, Miss Smith,' Alex said. 'We can stand.'

Carol Smith didn't sit back down; instead, she stepped from behind her desk and shifted from one foot to the other, her unease palpable.

'We're here about a property you once owned,' Alex explained. 'Number 14 Oak Tree Close.'

Carol nodded. 'Okay,' she said, apparently unaware of the events that had played out at her former home just the previous afternoon. 'I sold it a number of years ago now, though.'

'There's building work going on at the property at the moment,' Alex explained. 'The owners are having an extension built.'

The woman nodded. 'Lovely. I mean, naturally it's a bit strange for me to think of any changes being made there. I grew up in that house, you see, so it'll always stay as it was in the seventies for me. But things have to move with the times, don't they?'

She cast a smile at the two detectives, looking disconcerted when it wasn't returned by either woman. The smile evaporated, replaced by her initial expression of unease. She looked from one woman to the other questioningly.

'Sorry. I'm not sure I understand why you're telling me about an extension.'

'Unfortunately,' Alex told her, 'the building work has been stalled by the discovery of remains buried beneath the patio.'

She watched Carol Smith's reaction carefully. If the woman knew anything about the body found in her family's former home, she was one of the best actors Alex had ever seen. She looked from one detective to the other once again, her mouth moving as though making an attempt to form words, but no sound escaping it.

'Remains?' she said eventually. 'As in, human remains?'

Alex nodded. Carol Smith raised a hand to her mouth.

'Was the house passed down to you by your parents?' Chloe asked.

Carol nodded. Moving her hand from her face, she ran it over her hair and then sat back down at her desk, turning her attention briefly to her computer but not appearing to take in any of the details that waited for her there. 'Sorry. This has come as a shock, obviously. My parents signed the house over to me years ago, before they died. That was over a decade ago. How old ... I mean, how long was it there? I'm sorry ... there must be some mistake, surely?'

The words were an echo of Natalie Bryant's, disbelief momentarily suggesting that an error could be made with a discovery as huge as this; that an initial assessment had been little more than a misjudgement and the remains weren't human after all.

'Between thirty and forty years,' Alex told her. She and Chloe watched the woman's reaction as she did the mental maths to work out the decade in which the body would have been buried. The realisation that it must have happened at some point during her own childhood drew itself across Carol Smith's face, dragging at the corners of her mouth in a painful grimace.

'That can't be right,' she mumbled, almost inaudibly.

'Why not?'

Carol looked up. 'I mean, I was just a kid then. I was still living at home. There must have been a mistake.'

'There's no mistake, I'm afraid. We are currently trying to make an identification of the remains. That's where we may need your help.'

'My help?' Carol turned to Chloe, though it had been Alex who had spoken. It wasn't the first time that someone had sought comfort from Chloe in response to Alex's words. Not for the first time, Alex considered the fact that her younger colleague was so much more approachable than she herself was. There had been a time when the fact had offended her, but she was beyond that now.

'I'm sorry,' Carol said, raising her palms in apology. 'I don't know how I can help you.'

'I know it was a long time ago, but whoever was responsible for concealing the body in the garden was likely to have been someone you came into contact with at some point, at the very least. We're going to need as many details as you can give us – friends, family members … anyone who had access to the property between the mid seventies and late eighties. I know,' Alex added, noting the reaction that flooded the woman's face, 'it's a big ask. Do you have any other immediate family?'

Carol exhaled loudly. 'Family around at that time, you mean? No. I was an only child. I mean, I've got aunties, cousins, that sort of thing, but no one close, no.'

'We'll need contact details for them,' Chloe said.

They left the office with a promise from Carol that she would get the contact details of relevant friends and family members sent over to them before the end of the afternoon. Alex hoped for all their sakes that the woman had a decent memory. She was in her early forties, so would have been in her early teens at most at the time of the burial. Alex knew what her own recall of details was sometimes like; expecting Carol to remember every person who might have had access to the house was asking a lot, though she already wondered whether the contact details would prove necessary.

'Just think,' she said, once the lift doors had closed and she and Chloe were away from any possible prying eyes, 'someone has access to your home and manages to dig your garden up, bury a body there and lay a patio over it without you noticing.'

'Seems unlikely.'

'Exactly.'

The lift stopped and the doors opened on to the reception area, where the two detectives put their conversation on pause until they were back in the car park.

'So it must have involved at least one of the parents?' Chloe said, finishing Alex's train of thought.

'Probably. Not unless whoever lay the patio was responsible for putting the body there, but he'd have had to be working alone and managed to get it past the people living there. I can't see how it can't involve at least one of the parents in some way.' Alex reached into her pocket for her keys before unlocking the car. 'I don't think Carol Smith knows anything about it, do you?'

Chloe shook her head and got into the passenger seat.

'We just need to find out who that body belongs to,' Alex said, starting the engine. 'Then we need to find out what he was doing there.'

SIXTEEN

Alex and Chloe returned to the station to find Dan on the phone at his desk. His focus was on the screen of his computer when they entered the incident room, but when he saw the two women, he ushered them over, thanking whoever was at the other end of the line before ending the call.

'That was the auctioneers the farmhouse on Caerphilly Mountain is currently listed with. It's been up for auction with them a total of eight times over the past five years, but there's only ever been one bidder. That was back in 2015 and the sale fell through. The place is in such a state that people are afraid to touch it, by the looks of things. Too pricey to put right.'

'And the current owner?' Alex asked.

'These guys.' Dan pointed at the website on his screen, a property development company called Carter and Morgan Homes. The main image showcased a grand detached building overlooking the sea, its glass-enclosed first-floor balcony scattered with sunloungers and tables decorated with half-filled wine glasses. It was the epitome of the kind of lifestyle popularised by reality television shows and design magazines, doubtless aspirational to many but to Alex's mind unrealistic for anyone whose life had even the slightest element of responsibility.

At the bottom right of the page, in a separate image, two men wearing expensive suits posed for the camera, their smiles flashing unnaturally white sets of teeth.

'I'm obviously in the wrong job.'

'They don't get to work with us, though,' Chloe said, perching herself on the corner of Dan's desk. 'Just think what they're missing out on.'

With a smile, Dan turned his chair to face both women. Alex felt a pang of something she had not yet felt – a nostalgic tug at her chest at the thought of leaving these people she had grown to think of as friends as well as colleagues. They had been through so much together and a part of her had taken for granted their being there, as though it was fact that they would always remain so. Losing her mother the previous year should have been enough to teach Alex that nothing and no one was permanent, but she had always been adept at ignoring any realities she didn't want to face.

The fragility of time was making itself known and had finalised that adoption application as though signing it for her. Alex was forty-five; she knew that if she didn't make the move now, she never would.

She looked back to the photo on the screen. 'Have you managed to get hold of either of them?'

'Not yet. Might not be too easy, either. One lives in Dubai, the other's currently on holiday in Bali. How the other half live, eh?'

Alex sighed. If that was true, then neither man would have been in the country at the weekend. It put her no closer to finding out who had been on that mountain road with Matthew Lewis and Stacey Cooper on Saturday night. Had someone else known that the property was deserted and that both its owners were out of the country for a while? It was unlikely that whoever had been digging that grave had done so on a whim. The time and place were most certainly premeditated, with whoever had been up there mistakenly confident that they would be uninterrupted.

'The farmhouse doesn't really seem their style,' Chloe said, scrolling through the gallery of properties featured on the website. 'Everything on here is glossy and modern. Why buy a derelict place like that?'

'I thought the same. I asked the woman from the auctioneers –
she said she's not sure of the details, but from what she understands,
Damien Morgan made the purchase years ago, when the property
came back on the market. She thinks it used to be in the family;
that he might have purchased it through nostalgia.'

'So why not do anything with it?' Chloe wondered. 'These two
hardly look strapped for cash.'

'Maybe it turned out to be more of a hassle than he realised,'
Alex suggested. 'Is Morgan the one living in Dubai?'

'Not sure. I'll get on to it.'

Alex's mobile phone began to ring. She retrieved it from her
pocket and glanced at the screen, not recognising the number.
'DI King.'

It was someone from the ballistics department calling with
the results of the bullet analysis. 'I've just emailed over the report
on the weapon used to kill Stacey Cooper,' the man told her.
'Take a look and get back to me if you want to go over any of
the details.'

Alex gestured to Dan, who moved from his seat so she could
take his place. She accessed her inbox on his computer, quickly
typing in her password. As promised, the email was there waiting for
her. She opened the attachment and read through the details, with
Chloe and Dan close enough to also absorb the contents of the file.

'A .22 air rifle,' she said.

'An air rifle was powerful enough to do that?' Dan queried,
his tone laced with disbelief. He glanced across the room to the
evidence board, where the graphic image of Stacey Cooper's head
wound was displayed.

It seemed sickening that a weapon capable of causing a fatality
could be legally kept by anyone in the name of so-called sport. Alex
was aware of a number of cases in which people – some of them
children – had been killed by a misfired air rifle. In the right hands,

they were as deadly as any other form of firearm, and this was no accident. Whoever had fired the gun that had killed Stacey Cooper was clearly an experienced shot. She wondered whether it was the first time the killer had used the weapon to murder someone.

'According to this,' she said, scanning the contents of the email, 'a rifle is lethal enough if aimed at close range and with accuracy. Or if it's been modified with the purpose of making it more deadly. Look.' She minimised the report and left her email account for a moment. A quick internet search demonstrated how frighteningly easy it was to purchase a modification kit that would make a rifle even more dangerous.

'What's the point of gun laws if it's all this easy?' Dan asked. Bitterness laced his tone, as it had tended to recently. His eyes met the burns that lined Alex's face, and she caught him looking away quickly, as he so often did. She knew he blamed himself.

She shrugged. 'Ridiculous, isn't it? Basically, anyone with access to the internet can get their hands on one of these if they happen to be that way inclined.'

'So where do we start in terms of trying to identify who owns this type of rifle?'

'Gun clubs, shooting ranges ... let's start with the obvious. The farmhouse ...' she said, directing their attention away from the weapon for a moment. 'It may have been standing empty for years, but someone knows it well enough to be aware of that. I wonder how many viewings it's had since it's been up for sale. Whoever was up there digging that grave is familiar enough with the place to know they were unlikely to be interrupted.'

'Someone linked to the auction company?' Dan suggested.

'Or a potential buyer,' Chloe added.

'Get back on to the auctioneers,' Alex said to Dan, 'and find out if we can get a list of people who've viewed the place. Let's get hold of Carter and Morgan as well,' she added.

She left Chloe and Dan at Dan's desk and went to the evidence board at the far side of the room. Stacey Cooper and Matthew Lewis looked out at her, their smiles hauntingly tragic. How different those faces would have looked if they had known what was waiting for them just around the corner. It was a blessing that most people lived in ignorance of their fate.

She lingered on the face of the young man, searching his eyes for answers. Had she built her first impressions of him on a misconception, assuming he was no more than a typical twenty-one-year-old? Her belief in his innocence had felt firm, but it wouldn't have been the first time she had made a mistake. Either way, the notion that too much time had passed and that she had already failed him – that she had already failed Stacey – felt all-consuming. It was a feeling she was too familiar with: one she wished she had never had to experience.

'Where are you?' she asked beneath her breath.

SEVENTEEN

It had been easy to find Elliot West. He worked in a department store in the centre of Cardiff, selling designer suits to people who had cash to burn and a desire to stay ahead of current trends in men's fashion. Having been directed to the right department by a young woman at the perfume counter, the first thing Jake noticed about Elliot was that he looked nothing like his social media profile pictures. This was no surprise – people rarely did – but in Elliot's case the difference was so stark that anyone meeting him for a date thinking they were to spend the evening with the man they had seen on Facebook would have been forgiven for bailing out early on the grounds of being drawn there under false pretences.

'Elliot West?' Jake said, flashing his police ID.

The young man turned from his colleague mid-laughter, amused by some exchange that had just taken place between them. His grey eyes met Jake's before they briefly scanned the length of his body. 'Yeah.'

'DC Sullivan.' He glanced at Elliot's colleague. 'Is there somewhere a bit quieter we could talk?'

'What's this about?'

Taking the hint, the other young man left Jake and Elliot alone, heading to the payment desk, where he kept an inquisitive eye on the conversation he had been forced to leave.

'Kieran Robinson,' Jake said, showing Elliot a photograph on his phone. 'Know him?'

Elliot glanced down at the screen, though it was already apparent he didn't need to take a look at the image awaiting him. At the mention of Kieran's name, he swallowed nervously, his Adam's apple rising and falling. 'Shall we go to the staff room?'

Jake followed him through the store, eyeing the displays along the way. He liked to think of himself as stylish, but with his rent as high as it was, police salaries were going to have to increase substantially if he was to ever afford the clothing for sale in this place.

'I've seen his picture on the internet,' Elliot told him as they passed a display of scented candles that were still overpriced despite the claim that there was now 50 per cent off the RRP. 'I know what happened to him. Well ... I suppose everyone knows by now, don't they?'

They stopped at a door marked *Staff Only*, and Elliot turned quickly, his face crestfallen as he realised the implication of his statement. 'I mean I know he went missing. Is missing. I don't mean I know what happened to him. I don't know anything.'

He waited a moment for Jake to respond, but when the detective said nothing, he pushed the door to the staff room open. He waited for Jake to enter before him, following him and closing the door behind them. The room was small, with a square table at its centre and a worktop and sink to the right. An array of tea- and coffee-making equipment was lined up on its surface, artfully arranged by someone who apparently had too much spare time.

'Tea?' he asked, waving a hand casually at the worktop.

'How did you know Kieran?' Jake asked, ignoring the offer.

Elliot sat on one of the chairs crammed in around the small table. 'I didn't. Not really. I only met him once.'

Jake already knew what had happened between Kieran and Elliot. It didn't take a detective to work it out, with the scorned tone of Elliot's Facebook messages making the situation abundantly clear. He wondered whether Elliot had been hurt enough to take revenge for the bitter sense of rejection he had clearly experienced at Kieran's refusal to reply to him.

'Did you have sex with him?'

Elliot folded his arms across his chest and looked up at Jake with indignation, a determined defiance stamped across his face. He obviously hadn't anticipated the question so soon in the conversation, nor had he expected the detective to be quite so forthright. Jake had predicted awkwardness – embarrassment, maybe – but Elliot displayed neither.

'Yeah. It was a couple of months ago now. Just the once, and then he ignored me.' Elliot shrugged, feigning nonchalance.

'We've seen the messages you sent Kieran via Facebook,' Jake told him. 'You seemed quite upset by his rejection.'

'Rejection?' Elliot pulled a face, his top lip twisting in an attempt at a sneer. It was a poor effort at making himself appear not to care. He looked Jake up and down as though hoping to unnerve him. It seemed to offer him a momentary confidence. 'Like I said, it was only once.' He shrugged again. 'Life goes on.'

'Where were you on Thursday night?'

'The night Kieran disappeared, you mean? Am I under suspicion now?'

Jake said nothing, letting him know he was still waiting for an answer.

Elliot sighed and shook his head. 'I was at a party, actually. A mate's twenty-first. I'll give you his number if you like.' He reached into his pocket for his mobile phone. Tapping in a passcode, he accessed his photo gallery and held the phone out across the table for Jake to see. The photograph showed Elliot sandwiched between two other people – a boy and a girl in fancy-dress outfits – all three pulling duck-face poses for the camera. 'There,' he said, his point proven. 'That's me at the party.'

Jake retrieved his own phone and copied in the name and number Elliot gave him. 'Do you know anything else about Kieran that might help us find him?

With another shake of the head, Elliot stood. 'Look,' he said, 'I'm sorry about what's happened, I really am. But if I'm honest, I'm not that surprised. That boy had issues.'

'What do you mean by that?'

'Back-of-the-closet job,' Elliot said casually, checking the clock that hung above the sink. 'He wanted it and then he didn't. I don't think he knew *what* he wanted, to be honest. Look … I'd better get back to work. I'm sorry I can't be more help. I hope you find him.'

Jake followed him back out on to the shop floor and watched him head back to his department. No one knew, he thought: no one else had mentioned Kieran's homosexuality, not even his family. His sister seemed to think she knew her brother better than anyone else, yet even she didn't appear to be aware of it. He wondered whether Kieran's disappearance was related to his secret, and how the two might be linked. If there was one thing Jake knew only too well, it was how dangerous a secret could be.

EIGHTEEN

Alex was heading out of the station when she spotted Hannah Robinson near the front reception area. The young woman was lingering by the doors, her phone clutched in her hand as she paced the steps that led down to the car park. When she caught sight of Alex, she stopped and thrust the phone into her pocket as though she had been caught doing something she shouldn't have been. Her purple hair and the scowl she wore like a permanent accessory made it impossible for her to appear inconspicuous.

'Hannah. Can I help you with anything?'

Hannah opened her mouth to say something, but closed it again without speaking. Telltale signs of tears were evident in the smudged mascara at the corners of her eyes. It was a side of the young woman Alex hadn't seen before, yet even in a moment of apparent vulnerability, Hannah still managed to radiate an anger that was tangible. When Alex had first met the Robinson family, Hannah had maintained an aloofness bordering on aggression. Alex had let it pass: the young woman's brother had been reported missing; of course she was angry. Now, though, knowing what she did of Hannah's reaction to Jake, she suspected that her anger was rooted in something deeper.

'Do you want to come inside?'

Wordlessly Hannah followed Alex into the station, her heavy boots thudding dully across the tiled floor. Alex led her through the waiting area and down a corridor to an unused office. She didn't think taking her to an interview room was appropriate under the circumstances; the setting would only add to her apparent reluctance to speak. Whatever Hannah was there for, her demeanour on the steps suggested she was only half sure about sharing it with the police. If the family really knew nothing about Kieran's disappearance, Alex thought, they were doing very little to help themselves appear innocent.

She gestured for Hannah to sit before taking a seat beside her.

'I need to tell you something,' Hannah said eventually, after a silence that seemed to run on for an uncomfortable length of time. She paused and glanced around, surveying her surroundings. The room looked as though time had forgotten it: empty mugs still waiting on the table, and piles of paperwork stacked on top of a filing cabinet in the corner; the blinds at the window left closed, shutting out any signs of daylight. The cash injection that had been administered to the first floor of the station, on which the incident room and Alex's own office were situated, hadn't stretched to the lower reaches of the building, which were in general home to suspects.

'Kieran,' she said, looking at the carpet between her boots. 'Last Wednesday, I heard him arguing with my dad.'

'Arguing over what?'

'I don't know. I popped in just to pick something up, and they were upstairs. My mother wasn't there – she goes to the gym most evenings. Waste of time, that is. Anyway, when I went in, I could hear Kieran shouting.'

'What was he saying?'

She paused and bit her bottom lip, casting her eyes to the ceiling. 'He was calling Dad a liar.'

Alex paused, studying the guilt making itself increasingly apparent on Hannah's face. 'Why didn't you tell us this before?'

'I didn't think it was relevant.'

'Your brother was reported missing a couple of days later,' Alex said, as though Hannah needed reminding. 'Everything is relevant. And you obviously know that, or you wouldn't be here telling me now.'

The young woman's face flushed, but she held Alex's eye, defiant. She was twenty-seven years old, yet there was something childish about Hannah Robinson; something petulant and headstrong, like a teenager who was too used to getting her own way and would throw a toddler's tantrum if anyone dared to challenge or question her.

'What else did you hear?' Alex asked, not bothering to hide the impatience in her voice. Darren Robinson's absence during the search for his son had thrown up immediate red flags; now it seemed his daughter had helped protect him from any further suspicion.

'I honestly wasn't there long. The truth is, I didn't want the hassle. I'd had a long day, I was tired. I couldn't be bothered with the drama.'

'Why do you say that? Do your father and Kieran argue a lot?'

'No, not them so much, but my parents argue like they're in training for some sort of world record.'

'I need to know exactly what you overheard, Hannah. All of it.'

She exhaled loudly, puffing out her cheeks. 'Kieran said something like "How could you do this?" Then he called Dad a liar. Dad told him he needed to calm down. I just left. I wish I hadn't now.'

'Why do you say that?'

'I would have known what they were arguing over then, wouldn't I? I'd know for sure whether Dad might be involved in Kieran's disappearance, because I know that's what you're all thinking, it's obvious to everyone.'

Alex was tempted to point out that her father's absence hadn't helped deflect suspicion, but the obvious didn't need to be spoken.

'My father isn't involved in this.'

'And yet you're here telling me about the argument.' Alex sighed and pushed back her chair. 'You should have told us this before, Hannah.'

The young woman looked down at her hands, a single tear escaping her right eye and tracking a line through the heavy make-up that had been applied in an attempt to conceal her tiredness. Her tears were the first sign she'd shown that day of anything other than defiance, but Alex wondered to what extent they were truly for her brother.

'I knew it would make my dad look guilty. I don't think he's done anything wrong, but ...'

'But ...?'

With a sigh, the young woman tilted her head back and looked up at the ceiling. 'He's been acting really weird, hasn't he? He should be here, at home, but he's stayed away as though nothing's happened.' She chewed on her bottom lip again and sat forward in her chair, her arms folded across her stomach. Alex noticed her pinching the skin on the backs of her arms, squeezing it between her thumb and forefinger. It must have hurt, yet Hannah didn't flinch. 'You do think he's involved, don't you?'

An argument between Kieran and Darren changed everything. If Kieran was as angry on Wednesday evening as Hannah was suggesting, it was likely he might still have been in a fragile state of mind when he'd gone out on Thursday evening. Perhaps he'd drunk more than his sister claimed he would have, regardless of his apparent years of sobriety.

Was there now a possibility that Kieran had actually chosen to leave?

But there would be a trace, Alex reminded herself, casting the idea aside once again. Wilful disappearance might once have been achievable, back when life was in many ways so much simpler, but twenty-first-century technology meant it was now far more difficult to vanish completely.

'You've wasted time by keeping things from us. If you're trying to protect your father from something, it needs to stop now. We can't help any of you while you're hiding things, least of all your brother. I need to know everything there is to know if we've got any chance of finding Kieran—'

Alex stopped abruptly. It was too late: the unspoken word had been caught somehow, breathed into the air without her having to lend it her voice.

'Alive,' Hannah said quietly, finishing the sentence. 'Any chance of finding him alive.' There was another moment of prolonged silence, made all the more uncomfortable by Hannah's laboured breathing, the heavy sound of it filling the small room. She reached into her bag and took out a bottle of water, draining what was left of it. She was crying now, moved to tears by something: guilt, or just frustration.

'I swear to you,' she said, returning the bottle to her bag, 'I don't know anything else. I wish I did.'

Alex stood and went to the door. 'So do I,' she said bluntly. She left the room and went out into the corridor, leaving Hannah alone with her thoughts for a moment. Perhaps it would give her time to realise the scale of the damage she had done by stalling the investigation into her brother's disappearance. They needed to speak with Darren Robinson again, and the sooner the better. Chloe was right: Darren was hiding something, whether relevant to his son or not.

'Boss.'

The desk sergeant approached her, holding out an A5-size padded envelope. *DI King* was handwritten on the front in capital letters. 'Just been handed in.'

'Thanks.'

Alex took the envelope and returned to Hannah to walk her back to reception and see her out before making her way up to the first floor to find Chloe. There was nothing more to be achieved by keeping the young woman at the station; though Hannah had withheld information from them, Alex was pretty sure it was another family member who held the secret to Kieran's disappearance.

NINETEEN

Damien Morgan was still in Bali and Dan hadn't been able to reach him at his hotel, being told each time he had contacted reception that Mr Morgan was unavailable. He had left a message on his home phone on the off chance that someone was staying there while Morgan was away, and when his mobile rang that afternoon, it was a woman returning his call.

'I'm Damien's wife,' she explained.

'Oh, right. Okay.' Dan had presumed that Morgan's wife would be on holiday in Bali with him. 'Is your husband on a business trip?'

'No. It's purely pleasure, I'd imagine.'

The woman's hostility burned through to Dan's ear and he wondered what had gone on between the couple.

'I'd like to speak to him about a property he owns – a farmhouse on Caerphilly Mountain.'

'This is about that girl and the missing boy, isn't it? I've read about them. It's terrible. Why do you want to talk about the farmhouse?'

'A ticket stub belonging to the missing boy was found near the property, and there's evidence of disturbed land that we'd like to speak to Mr Morgan about. Do you think you'd be able to get hold of him for me?'

'I'll try, but I doubt it. We're supposed to be having a break from each other, you see, so I don't know whether he'll return my calls. What do you mean by disturbed land?'

'I think it's probably best I speak to your husband first, Mrs Morgan.'

'I'm still his wife,' she said. 'I should know if there's anything going on.'

'There's really nothing for you to be concerned about,' Dan tried to reassure her. 'We're simply following through with our inquiries at the moment.'

'Fine,' she said, her annoyance obvious. 'I'll tell him to contact you if I get hold of him.'

Dan thanked her and ended the call, getting up from his desk to head to Chloe's on the other side of the incident room.

*

It hadn't taken Chloe long to compile a list of sellers who supplied the range of air rifles identified by ballistics in the shooting of Stacey Cooper. The details that had been provided were specific enough to narrow the weapon down to a particular model, one that was only available to order from online suppliers, though Chloe didn't see how that might help them identify their killer.

'This is never going to help us. Where the hell am I supposed to start with all this?'

She stared at the list shown on the screen of her computer. As was so often the case, time and resources seemed to be against them. The scale of the task ahead of her already felt near impossible.

'You don't need a licence to buy or own an air rifle of this kind,' she said, turning to Dan. 'We're relying on the sellers to have kept records of every sale. How many are likely to have done that?'

Dan raised a doubting eyebrow, silently agreeing with her scepticism. 'We can live in hope.' He moved to her side and perched on the edge of her desk. 'That sighting of Matthew Lewis,' he said, making inverted-comma signs with his fingers. 'Not him. There's a surprise.'

It was yet another endless lead, a case of mistaken identity on the part of the eager member of the public who had thought himself helpful. They were no closer to finding out where Matthew was, and with each day that passed, they were unable to avoid the fact that the likelihood of his still being alive was growing smaller by the hour.

'Great.' Chloe minimised the list of gun sellers and pulled up the internet page she had looked at last. It was a search of local shooting clubs.

'Looks like shooting's more popular than we realised,' Dan said, studying the screen. 'By the way, I've managed to get hold of Damien Morgan's wife.'

'They're back in the country?'

'She never left. He's still in Bali. Been there for the past fortnight, apparently. Sounds as though they've recently separated, or they're on a break at least.'

'Any idea why?'

'I've not managed to speak to him yet, but his wife seemed guarded about it. Judging from her tone, I'd say any blame lies with him, or at least she thinks so.'

'So if he's been in Bali for the past two weeks, he's out of the frame?'

'Looks like.' Dan sighed and gave her an optimistic smile. 'Unless we're looking for more than one person. Onwards and upwards, I suppose.'

Chloe felt her mobile phone vibrate in her pocket. She had a WhatsApp message from Scott: a photograph of a vegetable curry he had told her he was going to attempt. He had stayed at her house the previous night, with a day off work in prospect and no intention of moving any further than to the kitchen. She smiled when she noticed the edge of his face at the side of the photo, grinning over the curry while giving the camera a thumbs-up.

Looks amazing, she texted back when Dan had returned to his desk. *Shame I probably won't be back in time to enjoy it. X*

A moment later she received a reply. *Still no closer? Keep going. I'll put some in the fridge for you. X*

She returned her phone to her pocket and her attention to the computer screen, pushing to one side the momentary pang of resentment she felt at being kept away from the comforts of home. This was the life she had chosen, and she had chosen it with good reason. She couldn't allow her recently discovered happiness with Scott to get in the way of that. There was a way of making both lives work for her, and whatever approach was needed, she was determined to find it.

Shifting her thoughts back to the case, she continued her search. At the sound of her name, she turned to find Alex heading for her desk.

'We need to tighten our focus on Darren Robinson.'

Chloe raised an eyebrow. 'What's he done now?'

'His daughter's just been in. She heard him arguing with Kieran last Wednesday evening.'

Chloe pushed her chair back from her desk. 'And she didn't think to tell us this sooner?'

'Didn't think it was relevant, apparently. Didn't want to drop Darren in the shit, more like.'

Chloe glanced at the padded envelope Alex was holding. 'What's that?'

'No idea. Any joy?' she asked, gesturing to the computer screen.

With a shake of her head, Chloe scrolled through the list of search results as a demonstration of the scale of the task she had ahead of her. 'Like pissing in the wind, as you would say.'

Not for the first time, she found herself unable to keep her eyes from Alex's scars: the pale streaks that snaked up her colleague's neck and face. There was a part of Chloe that still blamed herself for what had happened. Even though Alex had reassured her that her injuries would have been far worse if not for Chloe's intervention, Chloe had relived those moments over and over, constantly seeking a different outcome, in which Alex's suffering was erased entirely and the scars ceased to exist.

Alex ripped the corner of the envelope and dragged her finger across the sealed edge. 'I guessed as much. Sorry. We have to try.'

Looking back to the screen, Chloe began to explain the complications they were facing. 'God knows how many of this particular range of gun have been sold. Shooting things is a lot more popular than I thought. Fancy finding that a source of enjoyment: going out and having a pop at things just for fun. I don't understand how—'

'Fuck!'

Chloe turned to Alex, the room falling abruptly silent. A couple of members of the team seemed to be holding back sniggers at the unexpected expletive: Alex rarely swore, and certainly didn't make a habit of doing so while at work.

But Alex wasn't laughing. She had jolted back from Chloe's desk as though she had been bitten, dropping something on the floor and staring at it as though waiting for it to attack again. Chloe followed her horrified gaze and felt a wave of bile rise in her throat.

At Alex's feet, resting on the hard carpet of the office floor, lay a finger.

TWENTY

Dear Elise,

I've just read over my previous letter and I'm sorry if nothing seems to make sense. By the time I've completed this, I hope things will be clearer. I need to make them clear as much for my own sake as for yours, if only to make peace with the decisions I've taken. When you return to me, I want us to start anew, put all this behind us, firmly in the past. I think it's possible. I have to believe that it is possible.

Not long before you left, you asked me a question I never answered. Do you remember what it was? I am able to recall it as though it was only yesterday. It was a Saturday morning, still before sunrise; you were sitting in the kitchen with my newspaper open on the table, your attention fixed on its contents as you sipped your first cup of tea of the day. If I close my eyes, I can imagine you now as vividly as I saw you that morning, as though you are still right here in front of me. You looked so beautiful in the dawn light as it came through the window.

You were reading an article about the divorce of a famous couple: two Hollywood actors who between them should have had the world. You said, 'Well that's it, then ... if they can't make it, we're all doomed.' There was a hint of a smile on your face, yet your words were soaked with such sadness. And then you asked me something I tried to ignore – something I perhaps should have just answered there and then.

'How many people have you loved before?'

I suppose it was the unexpectedness of the question that made me falter – it wasn't the sort of thing we asked one another – and I remember trying to find anything I could as a distraction. It was untrodden territory for us and I was scared to step upon it for fear of detonating a landmine that would explode between us and rip the two of us apart. I was a coward then, but I am braver now. You have made me stronger. If you were here, I would give you the answer to your face.

One.

Before I loved you, I had only loved one other.

Benny x

TWENTY-ONE

The house looked lifeless, with no sign of any lights on inside, but Darren knew that Linda was at home: her car was parked on the driveway and she rarely went anywhere without it. He pulled his van up alongside it and cut the engine, waiting a few moments before opening the door. Everything was going to come out sooner or later: secrets always did in the end. They had always known that, and yet they had kept theirs locked between them as though they were strong enough to hold it together by themselves. The police were too suspicious of him for it not to emerge eventually. His marriage was dead in the water; it had been for some time now. There was nothing left to lose by telling Linda the truth.

The sound of the front door closing behind him seemed too loud in the silence of the hallway. He pushed off his boots and kicked them to the side, padding to the kitchen in his socks. Her silhouette at the breakfast bar made him jump. He had thought that maybe she was upstairs in bed; instead, he found her sitting in the darkness, wearing her coat. He hadn't seen her since Saturday, and in that time she seemed to have changed so that he almost failed to recognise her. Linda Robinson, once so confident and headstrong – the things he had loved about her that had become the things he had grown to loathe – was now a broken woman, deflated by events of the past five days.

'Where have you been?' It seemed she was beyond anger; in its place, her voice was exhausted, defeated.

'Kieran knew,' he said, deciding that wasting time would only prolong the inevitable. She was going to hate him regardless of the order the words came out or how he attempted to soften the blow. She hated him already.

In the darkness, Linda's eyes homed in on him, her disbelief quickly replaced by panic. 'Knew? What do you mean, he knew? Knew what?'

Her husband's inability to look her in the eye and the wordless response that seemed to scream through the silence of the kitchen gave her the answer she needed. It had always been her greatest fear, ever since Kieran had been a little boy. She should have told him herself, but there had never seemed to be a right time. The longer it went on – the more weeks that had rolled into months and months that had grown into years – the easier it had become just to say nothing. It had seemed harmless, until now.

'Wednesday night. I came home and he was upstairs in our bedroom.'

Linda looked ghostly in the darkness, her face paling further with her husband's every word. 'What was he doing in our bedroom? He never goes in there.'

'He said he needed his birth certificate. For an application form or something.'

She was shaking her head, disbelieving. 'He would have asked me for it.' It couldn't be true; Kieran would have said something to her. One of them would have told her at the time.

But why would they? she thought. Darren was barely there any more, and when he was, they hardly spoke to one another. Kieran had become increasingly distant, shutting himself up in his room for days on end or simply disappearing out of the house, always secretive about where he had been and what he had been doing. It seemed she was the last person anyone in her family wanted to confide in.

'I don't know what he was doing in there. I only know that when I went upstairs, he was furious with me, calling me all sorts. When he left, I just thought he needed time alone to calm down.'

'You didn't think to go after him, after what he'd found out?'

'I just told you,' Darren said, his frustration rising, 'I thought it was best to give him some space.'

Linda stood and pushed the stool back, its legs scraping across the tiled floor. 'Why didn't you tell me this before?'

'I thought he'd just gone somewhere to cool down for a few days. I thought maybe when he came home he'd have come round … that you wouldn't have to know anything about it.'

Linda looked at him, incredulous, before turning to the fridge and taking a bottle of wine, already half finished, from its door. The yellow strip light cast a momentary glow across the room before she closed the fridge again, taking a glass from the cupboard and filling it. 'I bet you wish he'd disappeared years ago, don't you?'

Darren didn't respond. There was no right answer: whatever he said was only going to make her angrier. She knew how he felt, how he had always felt; he had never been anything but honest with her, in those early days at least. Going over it again now wasn't going to get either of them anywhere. It wasn't going to help bring Kieran home.

'You need to tell the police. It might help them find him.'

He couldn't speak to the police, but he couldn't explain that to Linda. 'That probably won't help,' he said, gesturing to the wine.

With a dexterity her husband hadn't realised she possessed, Linda swung around and threw the glass at him. He managed to dodge its path, darting to one side as it hit the wall behind him and smashed into pieces.

'You never loved him!' she screamed, her eyes flashing with a rage that was animalistic. 'You never even tried to!'

Darren stayed where he was, wine and broken shards of glass at his feet. He had never seen her like this. Any anger Linda had previously felt had manifested itself in bouts of silent isolation; when she was upset, she'd preferred to be alone with her misery, where she could let it fester and grow. He had never witnessed any violence from her, but he knew that didn't mean it didn't exist. People were capable of anything under the wrong circumstances.

'That's not fair. And you know it's not true.'

'Isn't it? I know it, Hannah knows it – Kieran especially knows it. No wonder he's the way he is.'

With a shake of his head, Darren stepped back and flicked the kitchen light switch. They were thrown into the harsh glare of the bulbs that hung between them, almost naked but for the copper mesh that encased them like metallic webs. He had always hated those light fittings. He hated a lot about the house, but it was easier to just let Linda have her own way. Now, too late, he realised that letting Linda have her own way was only easier in the short term.

'You keep blaming me, but the truth is, Kieran's the way he is because of you. You've babied him, mollycoddled him like some little mummy's boy, and now he's a grown man who doesn't have a clue about real life or how to stand on his own two feet. The same goes for Hannah. Why do you think she acts like she does, always angry at something, always looking to start an argument with anyone who looks at her the wrong way? You've smothered Kieran and done fuck all for Hannah, and that's why the pair of them are so fucked up. You want to blame someone for the state of those kids, Linda, then take a look a bit closer to home. You know, maybe Kieran's buggered off somewhere just to get some peace and bloody quiet, to escape your clutches. He's got the right idea—'

Suddenly Linda lunged to the draining board and grabbed a knife left propped in the cutlery tray. Darren barely had time to acknowledge her movement, let alone respond, until he felt a searing pain and looked down to see the knife embedded in his body.

He stared in horror at his stomach, his eyes widening at the small circle of blood seeping through his clothing, the shock of the sudden and unexpected pain rendering him almost incapable of speech.

'You crazy bitch,' he gasped, his fingers reaching for the handle, his palm soaked red with his own blood. 'What have you done?'

TWENTY-TWO

The team gathered early on Wednesday morning with the news that the mother of missing Kieran Robinson had stabbed his father the previous evening having spread faster than nits in a junior school. Alex had found out on her way to the family home: officers had attended a call about a domestic incident, and Darren had already been taken to hospital, where he had undergone emergency surgery. Linda Robinson was currently in custody facing a charge of attempted murder. It was a turn of events that no one had expected.

'Do we know the details of what happened?' asked Dan.

'Not yet,' Alex told him. 'I'm hoping Darren might be a bit more forthcoming than his wife. She's currently refusing to speak to anyone.'

Alex had been to the custody suite to see her earlier, but Linda Robinson was refusing to so much as make eye contact. Alex felt an underlying sympathy for the woman. Her son had been missing now for almost a week; during that time, her husband appeared to have done nothing to support her, and had indeed made himself a suspect. Perhaps Linda too thought he was involved in their son's disappearance in some way. Until she was able to speak with Darren, Alex doubted she was going to get any closer to the truth.

'Think she knows he's involved in their son's disappearance somehow?'

'It's a possibility, but why wouldn't she just tell us?'

'Is she protecting someone else?' Dan suggested. 'What if incriminating her husband means exposing her daughter? Hannah lied to us as well. Whole family's starting to look dodgy.'

Alex pressed her fingertips to her forehead. 'I thought the same. But I don't know. Hannah's angry, but I think that's just her default setting. I just can't see her being involved in any of this.' But it wouldn't be the first time you've been wrong, a voice in her head told her.

'What's Darren's current condition?' Jake asked.

'He had emergency surgery during the night, but he's currently stable. Chloe and I will be going to the hospital later to speak to him.'

'So we've no idea what happened between him and his wife?'

'Not yet, but Darren Robinson remains our focus at the moment. I'd like us to take a closer look at him – let's get access to his emails and phone history. There's something going on there, something I reckon Linda knows about.'

Alex paused and looked up at the most recent addition to the evidence board: a photo of the severed finger that she had received the previous afternoon. 'You all know about this,' she said, pointing at the image. 'The print has been taken, but no match has shown up on the system. Our victim at number 14 had a finger removed either prior to or following death. It's impossible that the finger I received yesterday belongs to the same victim – this one has only been recently removed from its owner. We need to consider the timing. Bit of a coincidence, isn't it – me receiving that finger just after a body with a finger removed is found?'

'What are you saying?' Dan asked. 'You think the two are connected in some way?'

'I'm not sure yet,' Alex admitted. 'I don't believe in coincidences though.'

'The finger couldn't have been frozen all this time?' Jake asked. 'Someone's kept it and sent it now they know the remains have been uncovered?'

Though Alex had considered this herself, it was impossible. The remains were decades old, but there was no doubting that the finger she had pulled from that envelope was recently removed.

So who the hell did it belong to, and why had someone chosen to send it to her?

She shook her head. 'Not for the amount of time we're looking at here. I've reviewed the CCTV footage from the front of the station.' She leaned forward and clicked on an image, projecting it on to the screen behind her. 'We need to find out who this young man is.'

The screenshot from the CCTV footage showed a boy aged between eleven and thirteen standing next to a bike. With one hand he gripped the handlebars as he propped the bike against the side of the station's front steps; in the other he was holding the envelope that Alex had received the previous afternoon.

'Let's get this image out to the public, please. Someone knows who this boy is. My guess is he didn't have a clue what was in that envelope. Right,' she said, shifting the focus of the meeting, 'we've had the DNA results back for the body under the patio.' She looked at Dan. 'Have you managed to run the results through the database?'

Dan had been the first member of the team Alex had seen that morning when she'd arrived at the station. They had been eagerly awaiting any possible results from the DNA testing, with both detectives intrigued by the potential history surrounding the mysterious and macabre discovery. It was likely that whoever the person beneath the patio was, he had been reported missing at some point. Someone had been missing him for all these years, grieving for a son, a brother, a boyfriend, the not-knowing making it impossible for them to ever find closure. Now, decades later, this person could be returned to their family for the ending they deserved.

Dan stood and joined Alex at the screen. She stepped aside to allow him access to the laptop, where he logged his ID number and passcode into the system. Murmurs spread among the team as he accessed his emails and opened the relevant attachment, sending an image to the screen behind him.

'We're looking at the 1980s,' Chloe said, studying the screen. 'Possibly even earlier. Even if the victim had committed a crime back then, there was no recording of DNA on the system at the time.'

'I know,' Dan said, 'but look.' He pointed to the image: two separate patterns that looked like interlocking coils. He felt for a moment like a science teacher in a secondary school. 'According to the experts at the lab, in genome sequencing half this pattern comes from a person's mother, the other half from their father. Look.' He ran a finger along the pattern of the genome sequence on the right-hand side of the screen, stopping part way down. Then he returned the team's focus to the pattern on the left, stopping again midway. 'This pattern belongs to the DNA of our body under the patio. The other one came up on the database.'

'It's a partial match?'

'Yup. Not enough of a match for a sibling, but there's no doubt we're looking at a family member, someone still fairly closely related.'

'So who have we got?' Alex asked.

Dan turned back to the laptop and accessed the PNC. A moment later, a man's face was gazing down at the team. He looked young – the stubble that lined his jawline seemed oddly out of place – and the wide-eyed expression of fear suggested this was his first encounter with the police. His record on the database showed he had been arrested almost five years earlier for a driving offence when he was aged just nineteen.

'Dean Williams. He's definitely related in some way?'

Dan nodded. 'Apparently you can't argue with the science.'

Alex gave him a grateful smile. 'Thank you, Dan.'

It felt as though they were getting somewhere with something, at least. She just wished that the progress had been in the case of Matthew Lewis. Whoever the poor man buried beneath the patio at number 14 turned out to be, they could do little to help him now other than to seek belated justice on his behalf. For Matthew, the passing days mattered much more.

She turned to study the face on the screen. Scanning the personal details stored in the file, she noted the young man's address, hoping that they'd find him still living there.

TWENTY-THREE

While Alex went in search of Dean Williams, Chloe was looking for a man named Gareth Lawrence. Feedback from the auctioneers who had listed the farmhouse on Caerphilly Mountain showed Lawrence had been the last person to view the place, just three weeks earlier. As she drove to the property company's offices in Cardiff, it seemed to Chloe that the team was juggling an impossible workload with the three cases they were currently investigating. The pressures of the last few days – the long hours that had led them down a series of frustratingly final dead ends – had been obvious in the tired faces gathered in the incident room that morning. They needed something positive: something that might offer some hope in the search for Matthew Lewis.

Yet in her heart, Chloe knew hope was futile. Matthew Lewis was dead. They just needed to find out why he had been killed and where his body was. They needed to find out who that burial ground had been prepared for.

Lawrence and Wyatt Properties was based in offices on Cathedral Road, a street characterised by imposing period properties that housed orthodontists' surgeries, solicitors' practices, hotels and recruitment agencies. There was a bustling energy about this particular route into Cardiff, with the wide expanse of playing fields that lay at its head making it a place where the city met the suburbs; where the busy pubs and coffee shops that sat between offices offered a twenty-four-hour metropolitan energy that made even Chloe, in her sleep-starved state, feel a little rejuvenated.

'Can I help you?' the woman behind the reception desk asked.

Chloe showed her ID. 'I'm looking for Gareth Lawrence.'

'He's not here today, I'm afraid. He's not due back in until next week.'

Chloe surveyed the small waiting room. There were display boards at the window, advertising available properties for sale and rent. The company's branding and its mission statement had been well considered, its marketing spiel, aimed squarely at young professionals, offering the promise of an affordable step on to the property ladder.

'I thought Lawrence and Wyatt were developers,' Chloe said, gesturing to the photographs.

'Part developers, part estate agents,' the woman explained. 'They've probably got goodness knows what else going on too. They're both incredibly ambitious and driven.'

Chloe wondered whether the woman was receiving bonuses for her sycophantic praise of the partners who paid her salary. 'Is Michael Wyatt available?'

'He's in a meeting at the moment, but I can let him know you're here?'

'If you could, please.'

Chloe took a seat and leafed through a property magazine on the coffee table beside her chair. She had always rented and had never seen the need to own her own home, although more recently she had started to understand why so many people felt comfortable with the idea of ownership, even when it resulted in an increase in outgoings. It offered a permanence that Chloe's life had never had; something she had never strived for or felt she was missing out on. Perhaps that was changing. Perhaps being happy had a lot to do with her sudden change of outlook.

'He'll be with you in a few minutes,' the receptionist said, emerging back into the room.

Chloe offered her an insincere smile. The woman's tone was indifferent at best; condescending at worst. She wondered if Gareth Lawrence and Michael Wyatt thought as much of themselves as this woman seemed to. Refusing the offer of coffee, she returned her focus to the magazine.

Five minutes later, Michael Wyatt arrived. He was in his mid to late fifties, with thinning grey hair and a pallor that screamed for an encounter with a heatwave. His shirtsleeves were rolled back, revealing an expensive watch. Dan was right, Chloe thought: property development seemed to be where the money was, although if the man's pale flesh was any indication of his tastes, it appeared that sun-bleached beach holidays weren't his cup of tea.

'DC Lane,' he said, offering Chloe his hand. 'Would you like to come through?'

Chloe followed him into a narrow corridor that led to his office: a small, sparsely furnished room painted an oppressive dark blue. A series of prints on canvas lined the wall above the desk, each showcasing a property that presumably belonged to the company.

'We're making inquiries about a farmhouse on Caerphilly Mountain,' she said, taking a seat opposite his. 'This place.' She took her mobile phone from her pocket and found the screenshot she had taken of the auctioneer's advertisement for the property.

Michael Wyatt leaned forward and looked at the image. 'I'm aware of the place. I've never been there, but I'm pretty sure Gareth visited for a viewing a few weeks ago. I know he'd mentioned the place to me.'

'The auction company told us he'd been there. Did he say much about his viewing?'

'Not much,' he said, with a shake of the head. 'Only that it wouldn't be right for what we do. It's got a certain charm about it in the photographs, but I don't think it lived up to the expectations. That one would be a labour of love, I think.'

'Wouldn't be right for what you do,' Chloe repeated. 'What do you mean by that?'

'We develop housing estates in the main, rather than individual properties. That's just the way the business has grown over the years. Most of the properties you'll have seen advertised out front are part of recent projects. A lot of them are affordable for first-time buyers.'

'You've done very well for yourselves,' Chloe stated, with genuine admiration. She respected anyone who worked hard for their success, having learned from experience that it was the only way you could ever be certain of claiming something as truly your own. 'Do you mind me asking how you got started?'

'Bought a flat, did it up, sold it on. It became quite addictive.'

'Why do you think Mr Lawrence would have been interested in the farmhouse? As you say, it doesn't seem to fit in with the kind of development you usually manage.'

'He's always fancied the idea of opening a hotel,' Wyatt told her with a roll of his eyes. 'Bit of a boyhood dream he's not yet let go of, I think. I'm not so keen on the idea myself – I prefer to sell up and move on. I think he liked the location.'

Chloe wondered what Alex would make of such a proposition. Her own home was just a couple of miles from the road on which Stacey Cooper had been killed, with the site of the derelict farmhouse even closer. From what Chloe had seen of it, the appeal of the place was its wildness, and she doubted men like Gareth Lawrence and Michael Wyatt cared much for nature or landscape, not unless it was within a half-mile radius of their own homes.

'The houses on offer in the window,' she said. 'Where are they situated?'

'Whitchurch.'

'You know Kieran Robinson, then?'

'Not personally, but I'm aware of him. I've seen his photo on the news, read about his disappearance. His poor family – they must be sick with worry.'

'Have you met his father, Darren Robinson?'

'A couple of times, briefly. We've only used him on more recent projects, but I had to take a back seat for the majority of the last one. Family issues.'

'Do you mind if I ask what those issues were?'

'My daughter.' He stopped for a moment and looked away, turning his gaze in the direction of the office door. When he spoke next, Chloe noticed the lump in his throat rising and falling. 'She passed away last year.'

'I'm sorry to hear that.' She shifted in her chair, uneasy at having made the man revisit his recent loss. 'Can I ask what happened?'

'She had a rare kidney condition. There was no suitable match for her.'

Chloe drew in her bottom lip, not knowing what to say. The subject of his daughter's death was evidently something Michael Wyatt had still not grown accustomed to talking about, and perhaps never would. Chloe had been told a long time ago that time was a great healer, but the bearers of this promise had proven misleading with their assurances. Time hadn't healed; if anything, it had merely embedded the pain a little deeper into her skin, etching it like a scar that was invisible to everyone else.

'So you've not been working as much as usual?'

Michael shook his head. 'Family first.'

'Absolutely. You weren't at the comedy club last Thursday night, then?'

Michael shook his head. 'Stand-up isn't really my cup of tea, particularly not now. The boys like that type of banter, though – Gareth thought it might be their kind of thing.'

'You paid for it all, did you?'

'Not me personally. The company paid.'

'A very generous bonus.'

'Is it? Doesn't say much for other companies then. Look, truth be told, I'd rather see them enjoy it than the taxman. It might not be the norm, but the boys did a great job in a short space of time. A few things held us up at the start, so the deadlines were tight. Keep the workers happy, I say.'

Tell that to DCI Thompson, Chloe thought. The man wouldn't have known a smile if it had jumped out from behind his desk and kissed him.

'Could you let me have Mr Lawrence's contact details, please?'

Michael Wyatt waited for Chloe to unlock her phone before reciting his business partner's number from memory. 'We've worked together for over two decades,' he explained, reacting to the impressed look she offered. Memorising phone numbers wasn't something she was familiar with; the only number Chloe was able to recall was her own.

'Can I help you with anything else?' he asked.

She shook her head. Her phone had started ringing as she held it in her hand. 'Sorry,' she said, swiping the call to answer. 'I'll see myself out.'

Pausing Jake mid sentence, Chloe waited until she was outside the building and on the street before prompting him to continue.

'Where are you?' he asked.

'Lawrence and Wyatt's offices in Cardiff.'

'Lawrence there?'

'No. Why?'

'I've got Darren Robinson's phone history here,' Jake told her. 'His messages make for interesting reading. Looks as though he's been trying to blackmail Gareth Lawrence.'

TWENTY-FOUR

The woman who answered the door was in her early to mid fifties. She had shoulder-length light-brown hair that curled at the sides of her neck and was flecked with only the slightest signs of grey, and she was smartly dressed in a pair of tailored trousers and a knee-length cardigan. With a bag slung over her arm and her car keys in her hand, it was evident that she had been about to go out.

Alex introduced herself and showed the woman her ID. 'I'm looking for Dean Williams,' she explained. 'Does he still live here?'

'No.' The woman's grip on her bag tightened at the mention of the name. 'Why, what's he done now?'

Alex wondered why the reception of the young man's name was so frosty. As far as his police record was concerned, his first misdemeanour had been his last.

'You know Dean then?'

'For my sins,' the woman said with a sigh. 'He's my son. He moved out about a year back. Why are you looking for him?'

'Your son has done nothing wrong, Mrs Williams,' Alex reassured her.

'That's a first. And it's Barrett now,' the woman corrected her. 'Nicola Barrett. I divorced Dean's dad years ago.'

'Do you think we could go inside to talk?'

The woman hesitated, her unease growing increasingly apparent. 'I'm sorry, I was just on my way out. I've got an appointment in town.'

'I won't keep you long.'

Alex followed Nicola Barrett into the house. The woman stopped in the hallway, waiting for Alex to close the front door behind her.

'Does the address 14 Oak Tree Close mean anything to you?'

Nicola shook her head. 'Should it?'

Alex reminded herself that she needed to tread sensitively. This woman's son was a relative of the person whose body had been buried beneath the patio, meaning that she too would be connected to the man, perhaps even more closely than her son was. It was likely that whatever arrangements Nicola Barrett had made for that day, the news that Alex was about to deliver might force her to postpone them.

'Ms Barrett, we're making inquiries into a possible missing person.'

'A possible missing person?' the woman repeated, noting Alex's specific choice of wording. 'What do you mean?'

'Is there anyone in your family who's been reported as missing?'

The woman's face changed, her eyes glazing over almost instantly. 'My brother. He went missing a long time ago now, though. 1981. I was just a kid at the time. Please tell me what's going on.'

Despite the decades that had passed, Nicola's reaction made it apparent that her brother's disappearance was as raw now as it had been all those years ago. Alex looked to her left, into a living room, gesturing for Nicola to lead the way through. She did so without question, sinking on to the end of a corner sofa and looking at Alex expectantly as the detective took a seat at the other end.

'I'm afraid a body has been found, and the DNA retrieved from the remains is a partial match with your son. It's very likely therefore that the body is that of your brother.'

Nicola nodded steadily as she stared at the carpet, absorbing the information with a quiet acceptance. 'Okay.'

Alex waited, but the woman offered nothing more. 'What was your brother's name?'

'Oliver. Oliver Barrett.' Nicola stood and went to a set of drawers at the far side of the living room. Crouching to the bottom drawer, she rummaged among its contents, removing a handful of photographs. 'I don't have many of these,' she said. 'We never used to take them like we do now, did we?'

Handing the photographs to Alex, she sat down again. Alex studied them: some of Oliver on his own, some of him with Nicola; one of the two children with their parents. There was an obvious similarity between the siblings and Alex wondered what Oliver would have looked like now, whether he would still bear such a close resemblance to his younger sister.

The photographs were mostly from the late 1960s and the 1970s, though in one, Oliver was an older teenager: a serious-looking boy with dark eyes, a pair of thick-rimmed glasses resting on his nose. The last photograph showed brother and sister posing together on a beachfront – Oliver in ill-fitting shorts and a striped T-shirt, Nicola in a summer dress – both pulling faces for the camera.

'I knew he was dead,' Nicola said, her eyes fixed on one of the photographs. 'After all this time, you give up hope of anything else.'

She paused and looked away, her lips thinning. 'You know, I've imagined this day so many times over the years. Each time different in some way. I thought I'd know how I would feel, how I would react, but … I don't know. I don't know what to feel.'

She stood and took the photographs back. 'This address,' she said, still maintaining her composure. 'Why did you ask me if I recognised it?'

Alex watched her as she moved from detachment to acknowledgement. Though she must have realised that her brother's disappearance might have involved something sinister, she was now forced to face up to the brutal fact that he had been murdered all those years ago. Her face fell as she fitted the pieces together, crushed beneath the weight of the truth.

Alex told her everything they had so far: the discovery of the body during the preparations for the extension, the DNA result on the bones recovered, the partial match with Oliver recorded on the police database. Nicola listened carefully, not speaking as she absorbed the truth of her brother's fate; a truth she had waited almost forty years to hear. All the unanswered questions, all the doubt and suspicion, the anger and the pain; everything seemed to have led up to this moment. And yet the answers she needed more than any others were the ones that were still left unrevealed.

'I knew he hadn't run away,' she said. 'It never made sense. It wasn't Oliver. We'd already been through so much.' She shuffled through the photographs, lingering on each in turn. 'I suppose you know our background … what happened to our parents?'

Alex nodded. She had looked at the case files concerning Oliver Barrett's disappearance: they'd revealed a family history steeped in tragedy. Both parents had died of cancer within a short time of one another, just a few years before Oliver had gone missing.

'We'd always been close,' Nicola said, still staring at the photographs, 'but losing them made us even closer. I knew he hadn't left me.'

She wiped away a tear that had slipped from her left eye and turned her head as though embarrassed. 'How did he die?' she asked, and yet her face said something different: that she didn't really want to know.

There was no way to soften the truth. 'All the evidence suggests your brother was strangled.'

Nicola's resolve crumbled and she leaned forward with her arms clutched around her stomach, her cry choked at first before it burst from her.

Alex swallowed uncomfortably, moved by the woman's agony. 'I am so, so sorry.'

Nicola's fingers tightened around the photographs, gripping them as though it was Oliver she clutched, desperately clinging to the last pieces of him.

'I'm sorry that I have to ask you this, but did Oliver ever have an accident involving his hand?'

Nicola's eyes narrowed. 'His hand?'

'Had he lost a finger?'

The woman studied her, her expression blank. There was a moment of silence before a guttural sob filled the room, the implication of Alex's question hitting Nicola with the force of a truck. She shook her head. 'No,' she managed.

She stared at the top photograph, a tear landing on the image. 'Someone killed him,' she said quietly, her voice slipping across the words. She took a deep breath and turned back to Alex. 'Look at him,' she said, holding out the photo: a young Oliver, leaning forward to the camera and grinning as he posed on a tricycle. 'Why would anyone have wanted to hurt him?'

'I don't know. But I promise you that we're going to do everything we can to find out.'

TWENTY-FIVE

Despite the emergency surgery he had undergone in the early hours of that morning, Darren Robinson was awake and chatting with one of the nurses, seemingly without a care in the world, when Alex and Chloe arrived. No one would suspect his son was still missing or that his wife had just hours earlier plunged a kitchen knife into his stomach.

His expression changed when he saw Chloe. 'I'm the victim here,' he said defensively.

'Mr Robinson,' Alex greeted him. 'We meet at last.' She smiled at the nurse, who glanced at her ID before leaving the room.

'Found my son yet?' His voice had assumed a weakened tone, as though feigned vulnerability might help him escape the onslaught of questions that was about to come. The performance was a little too late.

'We may be closer to finding out what might have happened to him, yes.' She pulled the visitor's chair over to the bedside and sat down, the closeness seeming to make Darren uncomfortable. He looked at Chloe, who was standing at the foot of the bed.

'Didn't really answer the question, did it?' he snapped, the weakness in his voice gone as quickly as it had appeared.

'I apologise,' Alex said, her words thick with sarcasm. 'Evading the truth is obviously something you would recognise, since you're an expert in it yourself.'

Darren grimaced and looked to the closed door, as though contemplating whether he might be able to make an escape, or if the nurse who had recently left the room might return to rescue him from his imminent interrogation.

Placing a handful of printed sheets on the bed beside him, Alex waited for him to pick them up and take a look. His face fell when he realised what they were, and he exhaled loudly, closing his eyes and tilting his face to the ceiling.

'Want to tell us what this is all about?'

When there was no reply, Alex picked up the transcript at the top of the pile. '"I want what's mine",' she read. She scanned down the sheet of text messages sent from Darren's number to that of Gareth Lawrence, co-owner of Lawrence and Wyatt Properties. '"I want my money. Pay up or I'll tell Michael everything."'

'Whatever you're thinking, this has got nothing to do with Kieran.'

'You're not denying an attempt at blackmail then?' Chloe said. She pointed to another of the sheets on the bed: an invoice for materials addressed to Michael Wyatt and signed off by Darren Robinson. 'We've checked with your suppliers and we know you only purchased half the materials listed here. Anything you want to explain to us?'

'Go and speak to Gareth Lawrence,' Darren snapped. 'See what he's got to say for himself. Oh no, sorry ... your lot don't do that, do you? You'd rather pick on the little guy – the ones who can't afford to buy themselves out of trouble.' He winced and shifted beneath the bedsheet. 'This is bullshit.'

'So what's he done then?' Alex challenged, riffling through the pages. 'Enlighten us, Darren. You sent a text message to Mr Lawrence on Sunday with a threat to tell Michael everything. You demanded your money. What money would that be?'

Darren said nothing.

'Your silence suggests guilt. I'm presuming the invoice has been altered to add materials that were never bought, am I correct? It looks as though you've been taking money for a lot of work that was never completed.'

Knowing he had been backed into a corner, Darren had little choice but to respond. 'Presume what you want. Like I said, go and talk to Gareth.'

'Mr Lawrence's money was obviously of more concern to you at the weekend than your missing son was.'

Darren's mouth twisted, fighting back the expletives Alex felt certain were struggling to emerge. Whatever explanation he might come up with, nothing could excuse his priorities that week. She could almost sympathise with his wife.

'Wyatt hasn't been around much,' Darren said between clenched teeth. 'You might already know, but his daughter died last year. Anyway, in his absence Gareth Lawrence has been helping himself to whatever extras he can get from the company – as if he needs anything more.'

'And you've been giving him a hand along the way, no doubt. How much did he promise you?'

Darren's hesitation gave Alex her answer. No matter how much he'd been promised, she imagined he hadn't received a penny.

He sighed. 'He said if I drew up the invoices he'd give me a percentage on the lot.'

'But that money hasn't materialised?'

'Obviously not. And it's not as though he can't afford it,' Darren said defensively. 'The pair of them are minted.'

'We know that you had an argument with your son on Wednesday evening last week,' Chloe told him. 'During which he called you a liar.'

Darren looked from one detective to the other, a fresh wave of panic passing across his face. 'How do you know about that?'

'So you're not denying there was an argument?' Chloe asked. 'You seem to keep making involuntary admissions, Mr Robinson. Be quicker for everyone if you just told the truth.'

Darren shot her a glare. 'It's not exactly uncommon, is it, a father and son having a row? It was nothing, all right. I can't even remember now what it was about, that's how important it wasn't.'

'How do you know it was nothing if you can't remember what it was about?' Alex leaned towards him. 'You seem to be making a habit of arguing with people, Mr Robinson. First Kieran, and then last night your wife. It's about time you started telling us the truth. Don't you care what might have happened to your son?'

Just like his wife, Darren refused to speak. It was the kind of 'no comment' attitude that Alex hated more than any other: an arrogant, naïve assumption that silence might protect a guilty person if they were only able to sustain it for long enough.

'Here's what I think happened. I think Kieran found out somehow what you and Mr Lawrence had been up to. The two of you argued, and on Thursday night you went to the Bay knowing exactly where you'd find him. You needed to keep him quiet, didn't you, before he ruined your chances of getting a pay-off from Lawrence.'

'This is rubbish,' Darren said, grimacing and turning his head to the window. 'You don't know what you're talking about.'

'So tell us,' Alex challenged him again. 'Where are we going wrong?'

With a sigh, Darren pushed himself up in the bed, wincing again at the pain the movement prompted. 'I was going to the Bay to confront Lawrence, not Kieran, okay? I changed my mind at the last minute. It was a stupid idea in the first place – as if I could just challenge him with all those subcontractors there to see it. I was angry, I wasn't thinking straight. Kieran didn't know anything about Gareth or the money. That wasn't why we were arguing.'

The two women waited, both eyeballing Darren with impatience. He wasn't going anywhere any time soon, and until he told them the truth, neither were they.

Darren tilted his head back, avoiding their stares. 'Kieran was angry with me because he'd found out he was adopted.'

TWENTY-SIX

Using the list of friends and relatives sent to them by Carol Smith, Dan had spent the afternoon trying to trace someone who might have remembered something of interest about activities that had taken place at 14 Oak Tree Close when Carol had been just a child. He had so far found out little they hadn't already known: Stan Smith had been a local councillor who volunteered as a scout leader; Peggy Smith had worked part time as a sales assistant at a nearby supermarket. By all accounts the family was fairly typical, and none of the people Dan had so far spoken with had shown any reason to suspect the couple of any suspicious activity.

Tracing his finger along the list of names and contact details, he stopped at Eileen Armstrong, the ex-wife of Stan Smith's brother Trevor. Although she would now be in her eighties, there was a telephone number noted that Dan hoped might still be hers.

He called the number and waited just a brief time before the call was answered.

'She doesn't live here any more,' the voice of a young woman told him.

Dan felt disappointment trickle through him, though he wasn't surprised by the woman's absence. Her status as 'ex' meant it might prove unlikely that any of the Smith family had remained in contact with her.

'She's only up the road, mind,' the young woman continued.

'Up the road?'

'Old people's home. They got her a place locally so she didn't have to move too far. Don't know why she was so bothered with sticking around here, mind – I don't think I ever saw her have a visitor in two years. I used to be in one of the flats, see, just across the street.'

'What's the name of this home?' Dan asked, jotting down the name as the woman told him. He put down the pen and moved his free hand to his computer, tapping it into the keypad. A moment later, the contact details of the home appeared on the screen.

Thanking the woman for her help, he ended the call before ringing the care home number. It was answered by a female voice.

'DC Daniel Mason, South Wales Police,' he introduced himself. 'I believe you have a lady called Eileen Armstrong living with you?'

'Eileen? Yes. Can I ask why you'd like to speak with her?'

'We're making some inquiries into a former family member of hers,' Dan explained. 'Someone now deceased. Can I ask ... how is Mrs Armstrong's state of mind?'

'Does she have dementia, you mean? Eileen's sharper than I am. She's physically very frail – kept having falls, that's why she had to leave her own place – but there's nothing wrong with her mind, that's for sure. Anyway,' the woman said, 'I don't mean to be rude, but how do I know you are who you say you are? Sorry, but I can't be sure, can I? You could be anyone. I've got a duty to protect the residents.'

Dan gave her his police ID number, along with DCI Thompson's contact number. He hung up and waited for the woman to get back to him, which seemed to take an age.

'Can't be too careful,' she said once she'd called back. 'Anyway, I'll try to put you through to her room now – she'll probably be there around this time.'

Dan thanked the woman and waited to be transferred. The line fell silent for a while, during which time he began to wonder whether he had been cut off by mistake. When he was finally connected, the call was answered before the first ring had ended.

'Who's this family member?' Eileen asked, having obviously been filled in on the nature of the call.

'Stan Smith,' Dan said, already suspecting from Eileen's tone that social niceties and small talk were something she lacked patience with. 'I believe you were married to his brother, Trevor?'

'Ha,' she said abruptly, the sound bursting down the line. 'So did I, but that turned out to be a joke, didn't it? There were certain parts of him that clearly had other ideas, if you understand what I'm saying.'

Dan raised an eyebrow, the corner of his mouth turning up into a knowing smile. Eileen reminded him of one of his neighbours, a woman in her eighties who had more enthusiasm for gossip than some of the other people living in their street had for their kids. In the small valleys town in which Dan had spent his whole life, it was said that what Mrs Evans at number 42 didn't know wasn't worth knowing. He imagined Eileen Armstrong was built from the same fabric. In just two sentences, she was already proving to be quite a character.

'He was unfaithful during your marriage?' he asked, emboldened to ask the question by the woman's forthright attitude.

Eileen made a noise that sounded like a horse sneezing. 'Unfaithful? He had the clap more times than I've had my roots done, and I went grey at twenty-six. Meeting him, that's what done it. Anyway, you're not calling about him, are you? What do you want to know about Stan?'

Dan told her about the macabre discovery beneath the patio of the Smiths' former family home. A silence followed, but it was short-lived; Dan got the impression that there was little that shocked Eileen Armstrong. He wondered if there was a particular age to be reached when this naturally became the case.

'Good God. It was there all these years? I wish I could help you, but I'm not sure how I can. I hardly ever went to that house – Peggy never liked me very much, truth be told. Mind you, I'm not sure she liked any bugger very much.'

'What makes you say that?'

'Oh, I don't know. Just the impression I got. Sour-faced, that'd be the best way to describe her. Seemed like she had a bit of a chip on her shoulder. Maybe she just preferred to keep herself to herself, I don't know. Anyway, like I said, I hardly ever went there. I had enough to do trying to keep tabs on Trevor. Full-time bloody job that was, I can tell you.'

Dan smiled wryly and looked down at the list of names in front of him. He read them to Eileen in turn, waiting for her to confirm or deny knowledge of each. When he got to the end, he asked her if there was anyone else she might have been familiar with; anyone Carol Smith had been too young to remember who might at some point have had access to the family home.

'There is someone else actually. That boy of Debra's.'

Glancing down at the list in front of him, Dan found Debra's name. Debra Rogers. Stan and Trevor's sister. She had died a number of years earlier, having been widowed in the 1990s when she was still only in her fifties. There had been no mention of the couple having any children.

'Debra had a son?'

'No,' Eileen said, as though correcting herself. 'She couldn't have kids. Caused her no end of heartache, but the grass always looks greener, doesn't it? She went on to have a whole load more grief by the end of it all. Decided to foster, she did. No one could understand it really – she should have adopted, shouldn't she? There's no goodbyes that way. And why she didn't go for a younger kid, none of us could work out, but she wouldn't listen. Said she could do more good with an older child, someone who really needed her help. Always playing the bloody martyr, that one. Can't save the bloody world, can you, but there was no telling her that. She needed to find out the hard way.'

'This boy,' Dan said, keen to get to the details. 'How long did he live with Debra?'

'Oh, I don't know. Not that long, I don't think. He hit sixteen and buggered off, which was always going to happen, wasn't it? That's what she got for trying to play Mother bloody Teresa. He was with her a couple of years at most, I reckon.'

'And this would have been the early eighties?'

'Maybe. I don't know when exactly. Isn't it your job to find all that sort of stuff out?'

With a smirk that was more of a grimace this time, Dan drew the conversation to a close. 'This boy's name, Mrs Armstrong. What was it?'

'Graham something. Sorry … I'm terrible with surnames, always have been.'

Dan thanked her for her time and ended the call, seeking out the contact number for Carol Smith. Had she forgotten about this boy Graham, he wondered, or was there another reason why she had kept his name from her list?

TWENTY-SEVEN

In the car on the way back to the station, Alex and Chloe discussed the revelation of Kieran's adoption. Realising that he wouldn't escape their investigations and that he had been backed into finally telling the truth, Darren had eventually agreed to speak, sharing with them the events that had led up to his argument with Kieran the previous Wednesday.

His admissions might have been controversial, but none were incriminating. He had told the two detectives that he had never wanted to adopt – that he had been happy when Hannah was born but that she was enough. Linda, though, had become obsessed with conceiving a sibling for their daughter, and when she failed to get pregnant for a second time, she had persisted with the idea of adoption until he agreed to make an application. He confessed that he had never been able to feel for Kieran the way he did for his daughter, and that he had been disappointed by the young man he had become. He had tried to help him by giving him labouring work, but the gesture had only been made to keep his wife off his back.

'So Darren agreed to the adoption because Linda wouldn't give up on the subject?' Chloe said, as Alex pulled off the roundabout and on to Manor Way, the main link road between Cardiff and the A470 heading north. 'Seems a hell of a decision to just give in to. Does Hannah know her brother was adopted? She's never mentioned it. Perhaps she was too young to know any different, though there's a few years between them.' She glanced at Alex, whose eyes were fixed to the road ahead. She had fallen silent, lost in her thoughts. 'You okay?'

She had called Alex the previous evening but had received no answer. It wasn't like Alex not to return her calls. Chloe knew there was something going on, but whatever it was, Alex obviously wasn't ready to confide in her with it yet. She just hoped her ex-husband wasn't back in the picture.

'Sorry. I was miles away.'

'I could see that. Anywhere nice?'

'I'm not sure yet. I hope so.'

Chloe studied her with a questioning gaze, but pried no further. Since the incident that had left her scarred months earlier, Alex was often to be found distracted, her thoughts seemingly elsewhere.

'Do you still think Darren's involved in Kieran's disappearance?'

'I don't know,' Alex said, changing gears as she slowed for a set of traffic lights. 'If Kieran's phone hadn't been traced to the water, we'd be assuming now that he'd just gone off somewhere of his own accord, wouldn't we?'

Chloe said nothing. Alex was right: had they known about the argument between Kieran and his father earlier, their assumptions would have been very different. But the phone made the idea that Kieran might have chosen to leave less probable. Even had he wanted to punish his parents for what he might have viewed as a betrayal, it seemed likely that he would have wanted to contact Hannah, if only to let her know that he was safe.

'I wonder how Gareth Lawrence thought he was going to get away with ripping off Michael Wyatt?' Chloe mused. 'They're joint partners – surely he must have known Wyatt would find out sooner or later?'

'He must have thought Darren would get off his back quickly enough as well, judging by the lack of response to his messages. Bit naïve, isn't it?'

'Like Darren said, though, Wyatt's not been at work so much since his daughter's death. Natural that his mind hasn't been on the job, which is probably why they thought they'd get away with it. It looks as though Lawrence decided to exploit Wyatt during his weakest moments. Over two decades of partnership jeopardised for the sake of greed. Nice guy.'

'Lovely,' Alex said with a shake of her head.

Chloe reached for her bottle of water from the door of the car and took a sip before sitting back. 'I just don't get why he'd do something like that when the man's obviously loaded anyway. Those offices they've got, they don't come cheap for a start, and I don't really see why they'd even need them. It seems more of a status thing – you know, look at us with our plush offices and our pointless receptionist. We should get a check on their Companies House records, find out exactly what's been going on.'

Chloe realised she was thinking aloud and might as well have been talking to herself. Alex was only present in part, and wherever her mind was it seemed to be a more engaging place than there in the car, swamped by the noise of Chloe's ramblings. They fell into silence.

*

Alex checked the clock on the dashboard, lost once again to her thoughts. She felt a prickle of anticipation creep through her. She was meeting with a social worker in a couple of hours and whatever the day threw at her, she couldn't miss this appointment.

When they arrived back at the station, she parked the car and the two detectives headed for the building. There was something irredeemably bleak about the station's facade, with its grey walls and darkened windows. It stood at the end of the town centre like a concrete prison, casting a lowering shadow on the traffic that passed it.

'We need to get hold of Gareth Lawrence,' Alex said, pushing open the main doors. 'It seems convenient he's permanently "unavailable".' She was struggling to see how or where the man's extortion of cash from the business fitted into anything else. According to Darren, Kieran hadn't known about Lawrence's activities, but that might not actually be the case. Was there a chance that Kieran had somehow found out, and confronted Lawrence without Darren knowing about it?

DCI Thompson would want something concrete from her soon, but at the moment Alex felt the weightlessness of everything she was able to offer him. She had the impression that he was silently willing her to trip over the mess that the current cases had spewed before her, and the last thing she wanted was to leave the job with failure trailing at her heels.

'DI King.'

As Chloe made her way to the stairs, the desk sergeant left reception and crossed the waiting area to greet Alex. He was holding an envelope, her name handwritten in black biro on the front. He looked at her apologetically.

'What's that?' Alex asked, eyeing it with trepidation. After yesterday's surprise package, further unexpected gifts were the last thing she wanted. Attempts to identify the boy with the bike who had delivered the previous day's envelope had so far failed to locate the youngster.

'Same kid,' the desk sergeant told her. 'Uniform have gone after him this time.'

She hoped they caught up with him, for all their sakes. Morale was already weak: if they couldn't track down a kid on a bike, they might as well all pack up and go home.

She ripped the envelope open as she headed up the stairs to the first floor. Stopping at the top of the staircase, she peered carefully inside to check nothing sinister was waiting there for her.

This time, there was a photograph. Drawing her sleeve over her hand, she pulled it out between her thumb and forefinger, turning it before she focused on its details. She checked back inside the envelope to see if there was anything else: a note to accompany it, or something that might offer a clue as to who had sent it. There was nothing. In the bottom right-hand corner of the photo, a date was printed in faint red letters: 8 March 2018. The previous Thursday.

Alex studied the photo closely, making sure there was no mistake. She felt a surge in her breathing as repetitive drumbeat Her grip tightened ncident room.

TWENTY-EIGHT

DC Jake Sullivan sat at his desk in the incident room reading over the email he had just received. He felt a trickle of excitement ripple beneath his shirt at the realisation that finally they might be getting somewhere, and that if they were, it would be thanks to him. The atmosphere amongst the team had been growing increasingly despondent, with the general feeling that each of the current cases was getting the better of them, but now there was something that looked like a lead, and Jake would have been lying to himself if he'd claimed he wasn't grateful it was his lap it had happened to fall into.

'Jake.'

He turned sharply at the sound of his name. DI King was in the doorway of the incident room, her face set with a look of impatience. He wondered what he'd done this time. It seemed that where Alex King was concerned, he needed to do little to provoke frustration.

'DI King,' he replied, getting from his seat.

'My office,' she snapped.

He pushed back his chair and stood, shrugging as one of the other team members threw him a questioning look. Outside the incident room, Alex was already nearing the other end of the corridor, and Jake hurried his step to catch up with her. He followed her into her office, closing the door behind him.

'There's something I need to tell you,' he began.

'Oh, there certainly is,' Alex said abruptly. 'Something you should have told me last week, perhaps?'

Jake's eyes narrowed in confusion. His superior's attention was distracted from him for a moment, her eyes drawn to something on the desk. He couldn't see its details, but he could see it was a photograph. Last week, he thought. What should he have told her last week?

His face fell at the realisation of what he was about to hear. He didn't know how the DI had found out, but it seemed certain now that she knew. There was nothing else she could have been referring to. His brain raced ahead of him, tripping over the multiple excuses he might offer as some form of defence, but he realised that none of them were going to get him out of this. He had made a huge mistake. It was going to cost him everything.

When her question was met with silence, Alex reached down and picked up the photograph. She thrust it in front of him, her eyes not leaving his face as she waited for his response. 'Explain this.'

Jake looked down at the photo. He tried to hold back a reaction, but it was impossible to stop his face from betraying his shock. Who the hell had taken this?

*

'That's Kieran Robinson, isn't it?' Alex waited, watching as Jake's attempt at composure crumbled in front of her. Gone was the defiance she had detected just moments ago when he had entered her office; now, in its place, there was a look of abject panic.

'When was this taken?'

Jake's lips moved as though he was about to say something, but the excuses he was clearly trying to formulate fell apart in his mouth, meaningless in their lack of substance.

Alex studied him intently, awaiting his explanation. Nothing he could say would excuse what he had done. At no point had he mentioned knowing Kieran Robinson. He had lied to them; he had knowingly withheld information that could have saved them resources and time they couldn't afford to waste. And that, Alex realised, was at best; at worst, she hated to think what else he might be hiding. That he was a member of her own team made the sense of betrayal all the worse.

Realising Alex wasn't going to say anything more until he spoke, Jake cleared his throat nervously. 'I wanted to tell you. I wanted to tell you as soon as I heard he'd been reported missing, but ...' He tilted his head back and drew his hands over his face. 'The longer I left it, the harder it was. There was never a right time. I'm sorry.'

'Sorry?' Alex repeated, observing him with disbelief. 'You didn't even tell us you knew him.'

'I didn't know him. I mean ... not really. I only met him that once.'

Alex narrowed her eyes. 'You'd better start at the beginning, Jake, and unless you've got some serious mitigating circumstances, I suggest you brace yourself. You're already in enough trouble. So come on ... tell me.'

She stared at him, not knowing who she was looking at. She had never felt she knew much about him – she had never felt she wanted to – but now it seemed it would have been better for them all if she had.

'Jake.'

'We met online,' he told her, his voice unsteady as his secret was forced into the room. 'We'd never met up before, we'd only spoken. I knew he was going out that night – he'd mentioned it a couple of days earlier – but on Thursday evening he got in touch to say he wasn't enjoying himself. He knew I lived nearby. He asked if I was busy ...'

He stopped speaking and sank down on to the chair on the other side of Alex's desk. He tried to hide his face from her, but he wasn't able to conceal the flush that had raced up his throat and now mottled his cheeks. Alex couldn't think of anything that would come next that might overshadow or dissipate the frustration she was feeling towards him.

'You were with him on Thursday evening? The missing hours we've been trying all this time to trace … he was with you?'

Kieran's disappearance had prompted a huge search operation involving specialist divers and hundreds of man hours. How the hell was she supposed to explain to DCI Thompson that one of her own team had been hiding information that might have helped the case?

'He went to your house?'

'Flat … yeah. He wasn't there long – two hours at the most. Everything was fine when he left … he told me he was going to get the last train home.'

Alex stood and went to the window of her office. Outside, in the car park, Dan was chatting to a young PC, his hands gesturing wildly as he said something that made the female officer laugh. She felt a knot of regret in the pit of her stomach. Alex knew all about mistakes, but this was something else. Jake hadn't made a mistake: he had knowingly deceived them all.

'What did the two of you do while he was with you, Jake?'

With her back still turned to him, he was spared the awkwardness of having her witness his embarrassment. An uncomfortable silence fell over the room. It was interrupted only by a sharp exhalation from Alex as she realised how naïve the question was.

'Oh,' she said eventually, talking to the window. 'That kind of website.' She realised she'd had no idea that Jake was gay. But why would she? she thought. Chloe might have confided in her about her relationship, but their friendship had developed over the past year into something in which those kinds of details could be deemed appropriate. DC Jake Sullivan was mostly a mystery to her. There had always been something about him – the aloof attitude that suggested he considered himself that little bit better than everyone else – that had kept Alex and the rest of the team firmly at arm's length.

She turned back to him. 'So how had you two communicated up until that night's ...' She didn't know how she should refer to it. Meeting someone online for sex seemed so sordid, so seedy – so dangerous, if nothing else – yet it was apparently something that many people did, without a thought for the potential dangers involved. 'I don't know ... what do you want to call it?'

Though Kieran's mobile hadn't yet been recovered, the police had been able to access his call and text history. If there was anything there that linked back to Jake, it would have been found. 'Internet cafés mostly,' Jake confessed. 'It's less risky.'

'Risky?' It didn't take long for Alex to catch up. Thinking back more carefully now, she remembered that Jake had mentioned his partner on a couple of occasions. Sam, she now recalled. She had always assumed that Sam was a woman. Perhaps she *was* a woman – it wasn't uncommon for men in heterosexual relationships to have affairs with other men – but regardless, his or her existence would explain why Jake had been careful to conceal his online activities by using the privacy of internet cafés.

'This is getting better by the minute,' she said, pushing her hair from her face. 'What about Kieran? He wasn't in a relationship, was he – not one that we're aware of, anyway. Why would he need to keep you a secret?'

'I don't think he'd come out. I mean, we didn't really talk too much about it, but that's the impression I got. His family haven't mentioned anything, have they? I don't think they know.'

Alex pressed her hands on the edge of the desk. 'That's why you were so keen to go there to speak to Darren, wasn't it?' Stepping back, she threw her hands in the air, her exasperation obvious. Jake's interest in the case made sense now; no wonder he had been so keen to take on the task of checking over Kieran's social media profiles. No doubt he was worried there might be something lurking among them that would land him under suspicion. 'You had the audacity to stand in that family's house and say what you did to them, all the time knowing there was a good chance that you were the last person to see Kieran. Why the hell would you do that?'

Jake looked down at the floor. 'I don't know.'

Alex strode past and went to the office door, flinging it wide and standing beside it. 'Get your things. You're suspended from all duties. Consider yourself now officially under investigation.'

'Boss, I—'

'Don't,' Alex snapped. 'Do you know something, I've had reservations about you since the day you joined this team, and now you've proved my doubts justified. You're a liar and a coward. Get out of my sight.'

Jake lingered at the doorway, but said nothing. Alex could guess what he was thinking: it was written all over his face. She had never held much faith in him, and Jake had always known it. He'd done nothing but prove her doubts justified. 'You're going to have to be formally interviewed, you realise that?'

Jake nodded, then turned to leave.

Alex waited to watch him head back to the incident room before she slammed her office door shut. Inside, she took a moment to compose herself before returning to her desk and picking up the photograph of Kieran and Jake. Who had taken it, and why had they sent it to her? She was sure that the handwriting on the two envelopes she had received belonged to the same person. But how? It meant that in some way, somehow, Kieran's disappearance was connected to a mystery that was almost forty years old.

*

Jake returned to his desk. His emails were still open on the computer and he glanced at the attachment he had been studying before DI King had called him to her office. With shaking hands, he touched his fingers to the keyboard. Anger bubbled inside him, making him feel sick. He loved his job. It was the one thing in his life that gave him any sense of stability; the only thing that he could really depend upon to make him feel as though he had some sort of purpose. DI King might not have seen it, but he was good at what he did. All he needed was a chance to prove it.

He moved the mouse, dragging the arrow on the screen to the right-hand side of the attachment and clicking print. Then he waited as the ancient printer in the corner of the incident room spluttered into life. Since going to see Elliot West, he had deliberated whether to share the secret of Kieran's homosexuality with the rest of the team. He had chosen not to, not wanting to draw attention to himself and not seeing how it could be linked in any direct way to Kieran's disappearance.

He closed the attachment on the computer screen, deciding not to save it. Then he glanced over his shoulder before deleting the email.

There was a reason he'd been made part of the team. With all that he knew, maybe it wasn't too late for him to still prove his worth.

TWENTY-NINE

Alex left her office, putting Jake's interview on hold. There was somewhere she had to be and she couldn't afford to be late. They needed to interview him formally as soon as possible to find out all the details about his relationship with Kieran Robinson, but it would have to wait a little longer. On this particular day, her own commitments had to come first. She couldn't mess this up, not now. She had waited long enough for it.

She passed Dan in the corridor as she headed towards the stairs.

'I was just on my way to you,' he said.

'Can it wait? There's somewhere I need to be.'

'I won't keep you. Just to let you know the foster agency got back to me. Debra Rogers, Stan Smith's sister, fostered a fourteen-year-old boy named Graham Driscoll in 1979.'

'Do we know where he is now?'

Dan shook his head. 'No one seems to know where he went after moving from Debra Rogers' house. He was sixteen by that time, and by all accounts it seems the relevant agencies had stopped bothering to check on him.'

Alex wondered how many other teenagers in the care system fell victim to this attitude. No longer children but not quite adults either, they were left to fend for themselves in a world their childhoods had failed to prepare them for.

Dan raised his hands in a gesture of despondence. 'I've tried all the obvious avenues – electoral register, Facebook and so on – but there's no one of that name who knew the Rogers family.'

'Or no one who says they did.'

It seemed to Alex that if Graham Driscoll somehow knew about what had happened at the Smith house, he might not wish to return to the details all these years later. He would be even keener to keep his identity a secret if he was in some way involved.

'Keep going,' she said, making her best attempt at an encouraging smile. With their current progress, even she had to admit it was sometimes a struggle to maintain any kind of motivation.

Pulling on her jacket, she headed down the stairs and into the car park, passing her car and walking out on to the main road that led into the town centre. Kelly had agreed to meet her in a coffee shop just round the corner, meaning Alex wouldn't need to be far from the station. Her job and its commitments was likely to be a central topic of conversation yet again, but she had spent enough sleepless nights envisaging the scenario in all its possible forms that she had had ample opportunity to plan for any question that might come her way.

She entered the coffee shop – a small, generic room housing standard wooden seating painted pale grey and sanded in a trying-too-hard attempt at shabby chic – and saw Kelly sitting in a far corner, a notebook and pen waiting on the table in front of her beside a half-finished bottle of water. Although Alex had met her on numerous occasions already, each of their meetings filled her with the kind of nerves no criminal had ever managed to prompt; not even those she had encountered in recent months.

'Alex,' Kelly said, standing to greet her. She leaned over to take her hand for a brief moment before sitting back down. 'How have you been?'

'Busy' would have been Alex's response to anyone else who might have asked the question, but the reply was inappropriate where Kelly was concerned. Alex needed the woman to know she had sufficient time, even though in her current situation the claim would have been nothing but a lie.

She would rectify the current situation, she thought. Nothing was going to stand in her way any more.

'Good, thanks.' She gestured to the board behind the serving counter, where two young women were bustling about with coffee machines and cocoa shakers that left leaf patterns on the top of steaming mugs of hot chocolate. 'What can I get you?'

Kelly scanned the board. 'I'll just have a tea, I think. Thank you.'

Alex went to the counter to order drinks, using the waiting time to consider any potential questions she hadn't prepared for: mainly, all the ones that she herself might want to ask. She had been so busy fretting over her answers to Kelly's questions that she hadn't given herself time to plan for anything beyond it. But what did she need to know? Her biggest question was *when*.

'You received the letter?' Kelly asked, when Alex returned to the table.

She nodded, unable to keep the smile from her face. For the past year or so, causes for happiness seemed to have been few and far between. She was determined to cling on to the alien feeling for as long as possible, still unsure whether its source might be taken away from her.

'Congratulations. Look,' Kelly said, pushing her notebook to one side and resting her forearms on the table, 'there's still a way to go yet – you know that. But this is great news, obviously. Meeting today is really just a chance for us to go over anything you might want to ask – any last-minute concerns or questions you have.'

'I don't have any concerns.'

Both women sat back as one of the staff brought over their drinks. They stalled their conversation until she had put down the mugs and left.

'In terms of what happens next,' Kelly said, 'it's really difficult to put a time frame on it. We've had placements made within weeks, with others taking a lot longer. Have you finalised your plans about work?'

Alex nodded. 'Everything I told you last time stands. I've just been waiting for that letter.'

Kelly added sugar to her tea before taking a sip. 'You're sure this is what you want? I'm sorry ... I know it's a stupid question, but I have to ask it.' She tapped her notebook and rolled her eyes. 'Form-filling.'

'I'm working on a couple of big cases at the moment,' Alex admitted. 'You're probably aware of them. After that, everything will be in place.'

Kelly's expression changed. She lifted her mug again, peering at Alex over its rim as she took a second sip. 'These cases. You obviously can't have any idea how long you'll be working on them. If this is a bad time for you—'

'It's not,' Alex interjected, a little too abruptly.

'It won't cancel your acceptance – it'll simply put it on hold until you're ready.'

'It's not a bad time. There couldn't be a bad time for this.'

'Okay.' Kelly put her mug back on the table. 'Then the next thing we do is find you a match.'

THIRTY

When Alex returned to the station, she found a uniformed officer waiting in reception with a young boy whose eyes were red with tears. He glanced up as she entered the building and quickly averted his gaze, as though looking at her was likely to result in even more trouble than he'd already managed to get himself into.

'Dominic Price,' the officer told her. 'His mother's on her way.'

Alex ushered them both through to the corridor, finding an empty interview room in which they could sit while they waited for Dominic's mother to arrive. The boy started crying, strangled sobs that he tried and failed to keep concealed from their sight. Alex went to get him a glass of water, finding Chloe on her way back.

'Jake's partner,' she said. 'Do you know her?'

'Sam?' Chloe shook her head. 'He's mentioned her in passing, but no, I've never met her. Why do you ask?'

Alex reached into her pocket and took out the photograph showing Jake and Kieran Robinson together at the door to Jake's flat. Passing it to Chloe, she watched a flurry of unspoken questions pass over her colleague's face.

'When was this taken?'

'Thursday night.'

Chloe's eyes widened. 'He's never said anything about knowing Kieran. I don't understand.'

'He's waiting in one of the interview rooms. I'll be there as soon as I can.'

When she returned to the room where Dominic Price was waiting, the boy's mother had arrived.

'Thank you,' Alex said to the uniformed officer, giving him his cue to leave.

'Why the hell aren't you in school?' Mrs Price shrugged her coat from her shoulders, glowering at her son as she took the chair next to him. 'I can't believe this,' she said, looking up at Alex. 'I took him there myself this morning – I watched him go in. What has he done now?'

Alex took the seat opposite Dominic and his mother. 'Your son delivered a couple of envelopes to the station, Mrs Price – one yesterday and one earlier today.'

'Yesterday?' She glared at the boy, who kept his head lowered, refusing to meet her eye. 'You weren't in school yesterday either?'

She exhaled loudly. 'That bloody school. I didn't have any calls from them yesterday. I'd have gone looking for him myself if I had. What were these envelopes, Dominic? And you'd better tell the truth – I've just about had enough of your stories.'

'I don't know,' the boy said, still looking at his lap.

'You don't know what?'

'I don't know what was in the envelopes.'

His mother rolled her eyes. 'What do you mean, you don't know – you were the one who delivered them.' She sighed and looked to Alex for help, exasperated. 'I'm at the end of my tether with this one, I swear. Never does what he's told, think he's twenty-five rather than eleven.'

'Dominic,' Alex said. 'I believe that you don't know what was in those envelopes, okay?'

He still refused to look up, but he acknowledged Alex's words with a slight nod of his head.

'You're not in any trouble either, but I really need you to tell me who gave you the envelopes.'

The boy hesitated, finally averting his gaze from his lap. He glanced at his mother tentatively, and then looked across the desk at Alex. 'I don't know.'

'Jesus … is that all you're going to bloody say?'

'Mrs Price,' Alex said, raising a hand. 'You mean it's someone you're not familiar with?'

The boy nodded. 'I was in the park,' he said, dropping his head again. 'I was just going round on my bike and this man comes up to me and asks me if I want to earn some money. He said all I needed to do was take something into the police station for him.'

'How much money?' Mrs Price asked. Of all the questions that might have arisen from her son's revelation, this seemed to Alex to be the least important.

The boy tugged at the sleeve of his hoody, hesitating over his answer. 'Fifty quid,' he said eventually. 'He said if I came back at the same time the next day for the other envelope he'd give me fifty quid.'

'What was in those envelopes?' Mrs Price asked, looking at Alex expectantly.

Alex shot her a look that said she'd rather not discuss that in front of Dominic. Panic flashed across his mother's face, her brain clearly rushing ahead of her for a moment, envisaging the worst that her son might have been entrusted with.

'So you went back to the park this morning?'

Dominic nodded. 'He gave me the other envelope and the fifty quid.'

'And you didn't think this was all a bit dodgy? It didn't once occur to you that this bloke could've just gone to the post office like everyone else and spent less than a quid on a stamp? Jesus, Dominic, if you tried staying in that bloody school for longer than half an hour at a time, maybe you wouldn't be so bloody stupid.'

Alex watched the boy, noting how his face twitched and tightened in response to his mother's words. She couldn't help but feel sorry for him.

'Did this man tell you his name, Dominic?'

He shook his head.

'What did he look like?'

'I don't know. Old.'

That wasn't particularly helpful, Alex thought. She could just about remember being eleven. Anyone over the age of twenty-five had looked old.

'What was he wearing?'

Dominic shrugged. 'Jeans. A coat.'

Alex stood and left the room for a moment, returning with a pen and a piece of paper. 'Your mum and I are going to leave you alone for a few minutes, okay? We'll only be out there in the corridor. I want you to write down everything you can think of – any details about this man that you remember, where you were in the park when he approached you, all those kinds of things. Can you do that for me?'

Dominic nodded. He waited for his mother to stand and leave his side before reaching across for the pen and paper.

With the door closed behind them, Alex turned to look back through the glass panel. The boy was already writing.

THIRTY-ONE

Chloe was waiting in the corridor outside the interview room when Alex arrived. They both glanced through the glass in the door, hardly able to believe that they found themselves in this situation, having to interview one of their own. Alex had thought Jake useless, but she had never contemplated that he might be a liar capable of deceiving the team he was supposed to be a part of.

'Who do you think sent this?' Chloe asked, glancing down at the photograph she held in her hand. Alex had left it with her to allow her time to process the latest development.

'No idea. I don't think he knows either. I've just spoken with the boy who brought it in. CCTV from the park will need reviewing.'

'Any fingerprints?'

Alex shook her head.

'Whoever it was, I think it was addressed to you because you're heading current investigations. Anyone could have found that out from the news. I really don't believe there's any more to it than that.'

'Thank you.' Alex realised what Chloe was trying to do. She had been targeted before, and the feeling of vulnerability that had come with it was something she didn't want to ever experience again. 'I suppose only time will tell, won't it?'

She pushed open the door to the interview room and waited for Chloe to go in before her. They both took seats opposite Jake, who was staring forlornly at the box of personal effects on the floor next to him, no doubt contemplating the risk he had taken in concealing something so potentially important.

'Before we do this formally, which we're going to have to,' Alex said, gesturing to the tape recorder sitting on the table, 'I want to hear it from you, between us. You and Kieran were involved sexually?'

Jake nodded. 'It was just the once, though, like I told you.'

'Why didn't you tell us this before, when he was first reported missing?'

Jake sighed and looked at his hands. 'I didn't want Sam to find out.'

With a roll of her eyes, Alex put her fingertips to the bridge of her nose. His deceit had only made things more complicated for him. 'He's going to find out now anyway, I assume. You'll have to explain to him why you've been suspended. I'm right in assuming Sam is a he?'

Jake looked up from his hands and nodded again, then returned his focus to the box. He refused to make eye contact with either of the women.

Alex realised how naïve she had been, and how little she had known about someone she had worked alongside for so long. Had she missed the details, or had Jake purposely kept them concealed?

'Do you have any idea where Kieran might be, Jake?'

Only now did he meet Alex's eyes, his face pinched with alarm. 'No. I swear to God, I don't know what happened to him after he left my flat. And that's another reason I didn't say anything – I really didn't see how it would help. He came over to mine, we spent a couple of hours together, he left. That was it.'

Alex watched him carefully, aware that Chloe would also be looking for signs of further lies. She didn't know what to believe. Jake had proven himself so efficient at hiding the truth that any honesty he now demonstrated would be immediately cast into doubt. He had no one to thank for that but himself.

Reaching for the tape recorder, she started the interview formally and read Jake his rights, though he needed little reminding. For the purposes of the recording, she described the photograph that had been sent to her.

'What do you know about Kieran Robinson?' she asked, once Jake had taken her again through the details of how he had come to meet the man. 'You must have spoken to him quite a bit, all those conversations online.' She would take the details of the website, along with his username and password, at the end of the interview, and would check for herself exactly what had been shared between the two men. For now, she wanted to hear it all from Jake himself.

'Very little. It wasn't that sort of relationship. It wasn't a relationship at all, it was just …'

'Just?'

'Flirting,' Jake said. 'That's all it was.'

'I doubt Sam will see it that way,' Chloe said.

Jake eyed the tape recorder. 'I wish I could tell you something that might help find Kieran. But I don't know anything. We chatted online, it was mostly banter, and when he came to the flat on Thursday, we had sex.' He held Chloe's gaze now, defiant. If he was embarrassed by any of his admissions, he was determined not to show it.

'You and Sam don't live together then?'

Jake shook his head.

'How did Kieran seem to you on Thursday?' Alex asked. 'This was the first time you'd met him in person, you said?'

'Yeah, so I don't really have anything to compare it to. It was just casual. We both knew what he was there for and we were both fine with it.'

'How did he contact you? Did you have each other's numbers?'

'No. He contacted me through the website. I never give my number out.'

Alex raised an eyebrow. So this wasn't the first time he had met someone online for sex, and it was likely that Kieran wasn't the first person he had cheated on his partner with. She couldn't understand how he could be so blasé, or how he could repeat this behaviour without feeling some element of responsibility or remorse. She wondered if life was easier if the only person you really gave a shit about was yourself.

'Did Kieran ever talk to you about his family?'

'Not really. I knew he did some labouring work with his father, but that was about it.'

It seemed to both women that Kieran Robinson's family hadn't known he was gay. When he had been reported missing, the police had asked if there was a girl he might have been with, but his mother had told them he hadn't had a girlfriend in a number of years.

'Do you think Kieran's sexuality is linked to his disappearance, Jake?'

He raised his eyes to the ceiling, his mouth turning down at the corners. 'I don't know. I mean, I would have said no, but now … That photo. Why was someone watching us?'

No one answered the question; no one was able to. Alex could only hope that CCTV from the park might offer some clue as to who had given those envelopes to Dominic Price, and that identifying the mystery man might lead them closer to answers.

'How was Kieran when he left your flat?'

'Fine.'

'Did he say anything to you? Any arrangement to meet again?'

'He said he'd see me later. You know, not in a literal sense, just a general "see you later".'

'As you do,' Chloe said, one eyebrow raised.

Jake turned to her, a smirk flitting across his lips. 'You're not really one to judge, though, are you? At least neither of us was charging for it.'

'Listen to me, you little shit,' Alex said, slamming a fist on the table. 'If anything's happened to Kieran, which it more than likely has by now, you can think yourself partly to blame. Look.'

She put the two envelopes down in front of her and pushed them towards Jake, directing his attention to the handwriting. 'It's the same. Whoever sent this first envelope sent the second as well. So whoever was watching you two on Thursday may very well be the same person who sent me that lovely little gift yesterday. Has it not occurred to you that the finger might belong to Kieran?'

Jake's face paled, but he said nothing.

'Is there anything else you need to tell us, DC Sullivan? I appreciate you're not a fan of the truth, but if there's something that's perhaps slipped your mind then now would be a good time for you to get everything off your chest.'

Jake said nothing.

'Well?'

'No,' he said, with a shake of the head. 'That's everything.'

Alex brought the interview to an end, telling Jake he would be charged with withholding information. She and Chloe went back out into the corridor, leaving him to deal with whatever guilt his seemingly untouchable conscience was able to muster.

'Are you okay?' Chloe asked.

If Alex had had a pound for every time Chloe had asked her that question recently, she'd have been considerably richer. She realised it was uncharacteristic of her to lose her temper as she had, especially at the station.

'And thank you,' Chloe added.

Alex brushed off the thanks with a wave of a hand. Defending Chloe to the likes of Jake was the least she could do after all the support Chloe had given her during her recovery. 'What do you make of this handwriting? It doesn't make sense. How the hell might Kieran Robinson be connected to Oliver Barrett?'

'I've no idea,' Chloe admitted. 'We should speak to Sam, though. Perhaps he knew what Jake was up to. Maybe he took that photograph?'

Alex nodded, but she knew as well as Chloe did that it was unlikely. Sam was far more likely to have just confronted Jake with the evidence rather than sending it to his workplace.

There was something more going on here, she thought: something they were currently missing. Oliver Barrett was linked to all this in some way, and to find the answers she needed, she was going to have to visit the past. 'Thompson's going to love this,' she said flatly.

Chloe offered her a smile that was intended to reassure, yet all it managed to do was confirm that Alex's suspicion was likely to prove correct. 'I don't think it's you,' she said, casting a glance along the corridor to make sure no one was around. 'I don't think he likes any of us.'

Alex glanced back to the door behind which Jake was still sitting. 'Sullivan's made a mockery of us. No wonder the DCI thinks I'm incompetent.'

'He's said that?'

'He hasn't needed to.'

She took a deep breath, clearing her lungs with a fresh intake of air. She wouldn't allow her career to end this way. She owed it to herself to solve this case. More importantly, she owed it to the three young men whose families were waiting for her to find the truth.

THIRTY-TWO

Dear Elise,

Even just writing about it feels strange after all this time. The human brain has an enormous capacity for concealment; we manage to hide things from ourselves – things we don't want to remember, things we don't want to have to think about, things we would rather not admit to. We tell ourselves lies that eventually become our truths. I managed this for years, but I refuse to regret any it, not with you at the end of it all.

Don't be upset by what I have told you. I was so much younger then, and that first love was fuelled by a desire I imagine exists in many first loves; it was fierce and alive, stronger than either of us. Don't think that what I did means that it wasn't real. Don't think for a moment that any of it makes you less loved. I've never told anyone any of this before. You might be wondering why I'd want you to know it, but by the end of it all I need you to understand why I've done what I've done. I want you to know who I am – who I really am. It doesn't matter about the others – they can think what they want of me – but you, my darling, you are the most important thing, more important than any secret I have tried to hold on to.

Please try to be patient with me.

When all this comes to an end, there will only be you ahead of me. You are the only person I need to answer to; the only one whose opinion of me matters. I tried to do my best. I tried to save those boys from lives that would only ever have been half lived, as mine would always have been if it wasn't for you.

In so many ways, it was they who sought me. I saw something in their faces, heard something in their words – all these things that reminded me so much of myself when I was younger. I knew they were silently calling out to me before even they did.

You'll understand, won't you? I promise things will be different from now on, just the two of us.

Benny x

THIRTY-THREE

Alex sat in her office, the cold-case files relating to the disappearance of Oliver Barrett stacked up on her desk. She had looked over and over them, going back and rereading, desperate for some detail missed by detectives at the time. Yet the longer she looked, the less she was able to see. Whatever had escaped the police then, it was continuing to get the better of her now.

Taking a break from the files, she concentrated on the footage running on the computer screen in front of her: CCTV taken from the park across the road from the station. She stared at the screen as the activity on the stretch of path played out: dog walkers, joggers, people pushing prams. Then Dominic appeared, wearing light jogging bottoms, a dark hoody and the swagger usually associated with boys far older than him; an attitude that at some point in his young future would probably cost him in one way or another. He looked so different here to the boy who had sat silently sobbing into his sleeves as he'd waited for his mother to arrive at the station.

He pushed the bike to his left, leaving the screen for a moment, and Alex pushed the recording forward, waiting to play it again when he returned. When he didn't, she wound the tape forward further, willing him to reappear. She paused the recording, went back; paused again. The boy was gone.

'Shit,' she muttered.

Whoever they were dealing with, this man knew exactly what he was doing. He knew where the CCTV cameras at the park were installed, so he knew which areas to avoid in order to approach the child without being detected. Presumably he had watched this boy, picking him out as a target. Was this then the same man who had known where to approach Kieran in Cardiff Bay free from the risk of being captured on camera?

Dominic Price was only eleven years old, and children of that age, no matter how streetwise they might think themselves, could be easily influenced. In Dominic's case, all it had taken was the promise of cash to persuade him to trust this man, forget all the rules of talking to strangers that would presumably have been drummed into him by his teachers and his parents. For Kieran Robinson, circumstances must have been different. Alex presumed he had gone somewhere with someone he had known well enough to trust, but she knew that even that was a presumption she shouldn't make. Hadn't he gone to Jake's flat to have sex with a stranger, someone he couldn't possibly have known, no matter how many online conversations they had shared? Either Kieran was incredibly reckless or there was a vulnerability to his character that had made him an easy target. Either way, there was someone out there who knew him well enough to realise as much.

They were dealing with a clever, calculating individual; someone who knew the areas he moved within inside out and had made preparations for his crimes in advance. It was also likely that they were looking for someone who appeared to others to be an approachable character; the type whose dangers were kept carefully concealed behind a friendly facade. Whoever this man was, he was a clever bastard: a clever bastard who was currently outsmarting them on all fronts.

Alex left the footage paused on the screen of her computer and went to the coffee machine to get herself a drink before walking the length of the corridor, heading for the incident room. The station was silent, and the darkness of the night sky closed in at the windows, enveloping it in an oppressive grip. She pushed open the door and made her way to the evidence board at the back of the room. Mug in hand, she gazed in turn at the array of faces that looked down at her from the wall: the young and the old; those past and those present; the living and the dead. A skeleton missing finger bones; a finger sent to her with no message to accompany it.

And yet somebody was trying to tell her something. She had been chosen, presumably for a reason currently known only to the person who had written her name on those envelopes. Whoever had watched Dominic Price – whoever had singled him out in the park that day – had also watched her in some way, if only for a brief time. Sending the envelopes to her had drawn attention to himself, and it seemed to Alex that that had been done knowingly, intentionally. Someone this calculated didn't make that kind of move without considering the repercussions. It was as though this man wanted to be found, but only on his own terms, when he was ready for it.

She moved her attention from image to image, tracking the faces of each victim in turn, still searching for the links between them. What was it that connected these cases? Had Matthew interrupted something going on in the field? Was there really a chance that the burial ground had been intended for the body of Kieran Robinson? It had occurred to her and Chloe as a possibility; it wasn't to be ruled out as implausible.

If so, the man she believed to be outsmarting them was perhaps not as clever as he thought. Matthew had caught him off guard. Stacey's murder had been clumsy, unpremeditated: if nowhere else, this was the point at which mistakes would have been made, and they should have been able to identify him.

And yet even then they hadn't.

Her thoughts were interrupted by the sound of the door. She turned to see Chloe entering the room, her coat zipped up to her chin in preparation for the cold of the evening.

'I thought you'd gone home.'

'Forgot my phone,' Chloe said, gesturing to her desk. 'What are you still doing here?'

'Nothing,' Alex said, frustrated by how much truth the word held.

Chloe retrieved her mobile from her desk and put it in her coat pocket. 'You're going to have to tell me sooner or later.'

'Tell you what?'

'What's going on.' She raised a hand, cutting short any response Alex might offer. 'And don't even try to pretend it's just work. I know you better than that by now.'

Alex's focus rested on the face of Matthew Lewis. She wasn't ready to talk about the adoption to anyone, not while two young men were still missing. She had made a promise to them and she needed to fulfil it. Besides, she could anticipate Chloe's reaction. Although her friend would be happy for her, she would almost certainly try to persuade her that her career could remain as it was.

'I'm just tired,' she said, knowing the excuse was a poor one.

Chloe studied her for a moment but pushed the subject no further. 'So go home and get some rest. And when you're ready to talk, remember that's what I'm here for.'

She left the room, leaving Alex alone with the faces on the incident board. Days earlier, she had still held on to the hope that they would find Matthew Lewis alive somewhere, wherever he had been taken. She had hoped the same for Kieran Robinson. That hope was disintegrating, so fragile now that she could already feel its cracks widening, separating themselves from her grasp. Each time she had to speak to the boys' parents and tell them that she had nothing more to offer them broke her spirit a little more, making her less and less certain of the profession she worked in.

She had failed people before, more often than she cared to think about. There was always the popular get-out clause that not all crimes could be solved and that some criminals would always remain elusive, but Alex never wanted to be a part of those cases. It wasn't what she had signed up for. She had never anticipated that things might end this way, with yet more faces to add to those she already carried with her: the ghosts of the cases she hadn't been able to resolve; the dead to whom she had broken a promise.

Matthew's eyes looked at her and through her, there but already gone.

'I am so sorry,' she said aloud, her words lost to the empty room.

THIRTY-FOUR

First thing the following morning, Alex assembled the team to give them confirmation that the remains uncovered at number 14 had been identified. An image was projected on to the screen behind her: a head shot of a teenage boy, the picture mottled and slightly out of focus. As she'd anticipated he would, DCI Thompson had shown up for the briefing, no doubt eager to see how Alex would tackle the subject of Jake's suspension. If he was hoping to watch her crumble in front of her team, he was going to be disappointed.

'The body has been identified as that of seventeen-year-old Oliver Barrett, who went missing in 1981. At the time of his disappearance, police believed he had run away from home, although by all accounts his family were quick to dismiss the idea. Barrett was a sixth-form student who was apparently hoping to apply for university. He lived with his sister, Nicola, and their grandmother, having lost both parents to cancer a few years earlier.'

'Christ,' Chloe said. 'Family didn't have much luck.'

'Oliver's disappearance received a lot of publicity, mostly due to the tragedy of the family's background. There was apparently speculation that he might have taken his own life, although his sister and grandmother never accepted that as a possibility either. Oliver was said to be a studious and settled young man with no known enemies.'

'Any leads at the time?' asked Dan.

'According to the files, there was very little to go on. This morning I contacted the retired DCI who was SIO on the case – I'll be visiting him after this briefing.' Alex glanced at the evidence board, and at the photograph of Kieran Robinson that looked down at them. 'Let's get the elephant in the room out of the way, shall we?' she said, shooting Thompson a look. 'You'll all now be aware that DC Sullivan has been charged with withholding information and is currently on suspension. Needless to say, he won't be returning to the team. We're a man down now, so we'll have to compensate for that.

'Priorities this morning: we need to continue to try to get hold of Gareth Lawrence. His absence is well timed, particularly in light of what we found out yesterday. As we all know, Mr Lawrence has been embezzling money from his own business using false invoices supplied by Darren Robinson, who believed he was going to be cut in on the deal. We believed that perhaps Kieran had found out about the blackmail and that this was what Hannah heard them arguing about on Wednesday evening last week, but Darren has now told us that they argued because Kieran found out he was adopted. Other than the possibility that Kieran made the choice to leave, we can't see any link between the news of his adoption and his disappearance.'

Alex sighed. She felt as though she was chasing her tail, and the last thing she wanted was to start showing her uncertainty in front of the team. She turned to the evidence board, indicating the image of the severed finger she had received. 'This,' she said, 'is linked in some way to the photograph of Kieran and DC Sullivan.' She pointed to the second image: a photo many of the team were still struggling to take in. 'Same handwriting on the envelope. That gives us a possible link between Oliver Barrett and Kieran Robinson. These men,' she continued, turning her attention to the photographs of Lawrence and Wyatt pinned to the board, 'need to be a focus of our attention.' She took a marker pen from the table and drew a long line linking Oliver to Kieran. Above the line she wrote the words *linked by handwriting.* She drew another line between Kieran and Matthew Lewis, this time writing *linked by Lawrence and Wyatt.*

'How?' asked Dan.

'Lawrence viewed the farmhouse where we know Matthew Lewis was on Saturday night. Kieran had been working with his father, who was contracted by Lawrence and Wyatt to complete building work on the housing development in Whitchurch. All three cases have these two men as a mutual link.' She stood back and surveyed the complex mass of photographs and notes that covered the board. There was a missing piece, but she felt they were nearer now to finding it than they had been in previous days. With so little hope to be found elsewhere, she had to cling to the belief that they were drawing close to something of significance. 'We need to consider more closely now the possibility that the ground we found disturbed was being prepared for Kieran Robinson.'

Alex appeared to be thinking aloud rather than throwing the statement out to the team, and as such, it was met with silence. The sad fact was that the more time that passed, the greater the likelihood that something sinister had happened to Kieran. She had hoped to deflect such a pessimistic outlook, stop it taking root in the team, but the facts were inescapable.

'We've got no other recent missing person reports,' she said, still apparently talking to herself. 'But we know we've got a link between these three young men.'

'Sorry to throw a spanner in the works,' Dan said, 'but the finger might just be a coincidence. It might not have any connection to Oliver Barrett.'

'Perhaps,' Alex said, still looking at the board. Perhaps not, she thought. It was too much of a coincidence; too improbable. But wasn't the likelihood of these three cases all being connected in some way also improbable? Gauging the reactions of the team, it appeared to Alex that to everyone else her theory seemed unlikely.

'I don't believe in coincidences,' she said, as though concluding her own thoughts. The timing of the discovery of Oliver Barrett's body seemed far too convenient, almost as though someone had wanted him to be found. The builders working at the house had both been questioned, but so far there was nothing linking either of them to any history with the building or its former owners. 'Let's go public with this today. It'll probably garner a decent amount of press coverage – historic cases always tend to create interest. Someone, somewhere, must know the connection between Oliver Barrett and the Smith family – he didn't end up at that property by chance. Let's keep chasing up this Graham Driscoll too, please. He can't have just disappeared. Dan, did you get back to Carol Smith? Any idea why she didn't list Driscoll as one of the contacts she gave us?'

'She claims it was a mistake – she said Driscoll only went to the house on a handful of occasions and she barely came into contact with him. Do we believe her?'

'For now.'

Alex brought the meeting to an end and turned back to the board, assessing the links between the victims that she had proposed. The cynicism of the rest of the team didn't matter to her, not when there was a nagging voice inside her head that wouldn't allow itself to be silenced. Chloe's support for the idea that both missing men might have been targeted by the same person was good enough for her. If there was one thing Alex had learned in almost two decades of policing, it was that nothing was ever impossible.

THIRTY-FIVE

Later that morning, Alex knocked on the front door of retired Detective Chief Inspector Raymond Davies. He was living in sheltered accommodation in Newbridge, a small village twenty miles north of Cardiff. She could hear him shuffling around inside and mumbling to himself. When he finally answered the door, she had to make a conscious effort to hold back her surprise. She had seen DCI Davies's police photograph, taken over thirty years earlier, but even knowing how long had passed since the image was captured hadn't prepared her for the change those decades had wrought.

Now in his early eighties, Raymond Davies was a thin, frail man, his skin an ashen shade. In his younger years he had been a highly decorated officer, with several honours attached to his name and accolades for bravery in service noted on his record. Now, it seemed to take all the energy he could gather to greet Alex and usher her into the small one-bedroom flat he now called home. The ravages of time hit her with all their cruelty, and she felt a pang of sadness for the man and the life that had been left behind.

'Cup of tea?' he asked, leading her into the living room. 'I'd offer you a mocha-chocha doo-dah or whatever it is you youngsters drink these days, but I'm afraid I've got builder's and that's about it.'

Alex smiled. It had been a while since anyone had referred to her as a youngster. 'Builder's is fine with me, thank you.'

'So you want to know about the Oliver Barrett disappearance,' Raymond said, taking two tea bags from a box next to the kettle. 'I'm afraid I can't tell you more than what you'll have seen in the files.' He turned to Alex as he waited for the kettle to boil. 'Played on my mind for a long time afterwards, that one. Every route we took, we kept hitting brick walls. You've found him then?'

Alex nodded.

With a shake of his grey head, Raymond reached up and took down two mugs. The cupboard was almost empty, she noticed: two mugs, two glasses, two plates; two bowls. She wondered how often, if ever, the second set of dishes was put to use.

He still wore a gold wedding band on his ring finger, though there was no sign of a wife now. Alex glanced at the bookcase in the corner of the room, but it housed no photographs. Perhaps they were too painful to have on display, all day every day.

'You must have had your suspicions,' she said.

'Any other case, I'd be telling you yes. There's always someone who surfaces, even when it can't be proven. But not with this one, sadly. Oliver Barrett was one of our few real mysteries. The boy seemed to have just disappeared into thin air. That poor family. I don't think his grandmother ever got over it, especially not after what had happened to her son and his wife. One tragedy after the next. She died a couple of years later, I heard.'

He passed Alex a mug of tea and she went back into the living room. Raymond sat beside her on the sofa. He was studying the side of her face intently, his expression heavy with sympathy. It was a look she had grown accustomed to over the past few months, though it continued to make her uncomfortable. She didn't want to be regarded as a victim.

'That was no accident, was it?'

She shook her head. She preferred it when people mentioned her scars rather than staring and then saying nothing, trying to make it appear that they had somehow managed not to notice.

'Nasty business.' Raymond tutted and took a sip of his tea. 'Take some advice from an old codger who knows … don't give it your life.'

'It?'

'The force. The service … whatever you're supposed to call it these days.' He looked around the room sadly, as though assessing the results of his forty-year career. Whatever thoughts he had about his life and what it had led him to, Alex had a feeling she had already shared the same at some point.

'You won't get any thanks for it.' He rested his tea on his knee while the other hand moved to his hip. 'And another thing,' he said through a wince, slowly stretching out his lower leg. 'Don't get old, love.'

Alex gave him a sad smile. She had seen enough of old age and death during the past year to know that getting older was something she would choose to avoid if the option were available. 'You did a lot of good in your time.'

'I suppose. But the good doesn't stay with you – that's the thing no one tells you. You won't remember the cases you solved, only the ones you failed on. Oliver Barrett was one of the people I failed.'

'There must have been part of you that thought he'd run away from home. Not run away, even – he was seventeen, old enough to leave of his own free will. After everything he'd gone through – losing both parents as he did, and at such a young age – there must have been the thought too that perhaps he'd just had enough.'

'Suicide, you mean? We'd have found a body eventually, though, wouldn't we? The longer he was missing, the more we suspected he'd been murdered. Even in 1981, without all the technology you've got at your fingertips these days, it wasn't that easy for someone to just go missing of their own free will without leaving a trace.'

'But there was no one you suspected might have been involved?'

Raymond took another sip of tea. 'Look, I say no, but … well, there was someone, briefly. It was silly – just my cynical mind going into overdrive, I realised that later. There was no evidence to back it up, and to be honest, I felt guilty afterwards for even contemplating it.'

'Who did you suspect?'

'The grandmother.'

Alex put her untouched tea on the windowsill. 'The grandmother,' she repeated. 'Why?' She had spent hours the previous evening searching through the notes on Oliver Barrett's disappearance. There was nothing in any of the files to suggest that the boy's grandmother had at any point been suspected of any wrongdoing.

'We searched Oliver's bedroom at his grandmother's house after he was reported missing. It's standard practice, as you know. Anyway, beneath the bed we found some pictures. Photographs, you know. Of boys.'

'Boys? Children?'

'No, not children. Teenagers, early twenties. Boys around the same age as Oliver. Young men, sort of ...' He raised a bushy eyebrow, giving Alex an awkward look that wasn't easy to read. 'You know. Tops off ... swimwear ... that sort of thing. He'd cut them out of magazines and books.'

Alex sat forward. 'What are you saying? Oliver was gay?'

'There was no other explanation for the pictures. His grandmother's reaction ... well, you can imagine. She was in her sixties, and this was 1981. She'd have been mortified if anyone had found out about it, so it was kept hushed up. She'd been through enough. It wasn't like it is now. You could use your discretion back then, show a bit of compassion.'

'But you wondered whether she might have already known?'

With a shake of his head, Raymond stood. 'Maybe she did, but logically she can't have been involved in Oliver's disappearance. Do you want another cuppa?' he asked, pointing to the tea Alex had forgotten about on the windowsill. 'That one's probably stone cold by now.'

'No, thank you.'

'If nothing else, she had an alibi,' he said, his back to her as he headed into the kitchen with his empty mug. 'Home all evening with Oliver's sister. Like I said, just my cynical old mind going into overdrive.'

Alex stared at the blank screen of the television set, unseeing. Her mind was back at the station: on the details of Jake's interview; on the secret life Kieran Robinson had been living online. Young men all hiding their sexuality in some way. Jake lying to a lover; Kieran hiding the truth from his family; Oliver seemingly storing his secret beneath his bed. Almost forty years between the cases.

Closing her eyes for moment, she visualised the evidence board back at the station, with all its interconnecting lines and missing pieces. One thought kept returning to her, no matter how many times she tried to work a different route around it: just where did Lawrence and Wyatt fit into all this?

THIRTY-SIX

Once Oliver Barrett's name and photograph reached the public domain, the team expected an increase in calls to the incident room, but the reality of the situation was that the intervening four decades had relegated him to the status of forgotten – or the thought of him pushed to one side, at least – by anyone who might have held any information that would have been of use to the police.

With other members of the team searching for the elusive Graham Driscoll, Dan continued his scrutiny of the Smith family. As he tried to build a picture of who exactly could have had access to 14 Oak Tree Close back in 1981, he sent a page to print and waited for the noisy machine in the corner of the incident room to kick into life. It spluttered and clunked as though not quite sure it was ready to be woken from its temporary slumber. Dan felt he could relate to its general lack of enthusiasm.

He stood from his chair and crossed the room. Someone had left a page in the printer, and he removed it, taking a swift glance before placing it with his own document.

'This yours?' he asked Chloe as she passed him. He held the page out, gesturing to the list of names.

Chloe glanced at the sheet and shook her head. 'Have you seen Alex?'

'Don't think she's back yet.'

'I've just spoken to Matthew Lewis's mother,' she said, crossing the room with Dan as he returned to his desk. 'What am I supposed to say? I'm sorry we haven't found your missing son, but we haven't got a clue what might have happened to him?'

'Well, we do have a clue, don't we? We just don't want to say until there's evidence. No point putting them through that kind of trauma if there's no need for it.'

'What do you make of the theory that these cases might be connected?'

Dan pursed his lips as he considered it. 'I don't know. I mean, Alex is right – there's a link. But it's tenuous, isn't it?'

'Not necessarily. What if Matthew did unwittingly interrupt Kieran's intended burial? Both of them seem to have just dropped off the face of the earth, so if the same person's responsible, he's obviously good at covering his tracks. What if we're looking at a serial killer?'

'But where does Barrett fit in?'

Chloe's eyes rested on the names listed beneath Oliver Barrett's photograph on the evidence board: the remaining members of the Smith family, and other people who at some point had had access to 14 Oak Tree Close. At present, there was no reason to suspect that any of them had had anything to do with Oliver's death.

'Stan and Peggy Smith,' Dan said, following Chloe's eyeline. 'At least one of them was obviously involved. We just need to find out why.'

'With both of them dead, I doubt there's much chance of that, is there?'

Dan shrugged. 'Exactly. So where's the link to Kieran and Matthew now?'

Chloe's stomach rumbled loudly enough for Dan to hear it. 'Sorry,' she said. 'I'm going to pop out and get something – I've not eaten anything today yet. Do you want anything?'

'Watching my waistline, but thanks.'

With a wry smile, Chloe left. Dan returned his focus to the computer screen, but was interrupted moments later by a call that had been transferred to the incident room by reception. The caller had requested to speak to DI King.

'DC Daniel Mason,' Dan introduced himself. 'My colleague tells me you have information regarding Oliver Barrett?'

'Not directly,' the man told him. 'Well, I don't know … it might be. I mean … yeah, I do.'

Dan jabbed the nib of his pen on to the notebook he kept open on his desk. He didn't have the inclination that day for time-wasters, not when there were so many other things that needed his attention. 'Okay. Can I take your name, please?'

'Paul Ellis.'

'Okay, Mr Ellis. Obviously you've seen the news report regarding the discovery of Oliver Barrett's remains.'

'Yes. I knew him.'

Dan rolled his eyes and moved the phone away from his ear for a moment, wondering whether the man was going to have anything more useful for him than an anecdote relating to a child-hood game of football in which Oliver Barrett had played on the opposing team. It wouldn't have been the first time the incident room had received such a call, and it was unlikely to be the last of these unhelpful gems. If everyone who had ever known Oliver Barrett was going to call in, it was likely to prove an even longer and more difficult week.

'How did you know him?'

'We went to the same school. We weren't really friends or anything. I just remember him, that's all.'

Dan exhaled silently. 'Okay, Mr Ellis. What information do you have regarding Oliver Barrett's disappearance?'

'I don't. Like I said, not directly, anyway. But I knew the man who lived at that address where he was found. I know what he was capable of.'

The caller had Dan's attention now, his scepticism cast to one side. 'Which man?' he asked, unwilling to offer any information regarding names that might have been previously unknown.

'Stan Smith,' Paul Ellis said, spitting out the words. 'I thought I'd save you the time. He's been dead for years now, but you'll already be aware of that, I'd imagine.'

Dan had stopped using his pen to jab dents in the notebook and was now instead writing down the caller's name. 'Why do you think Stan Smith was involved in Oliver Barrett's disappearance?'

It was a stupid question, he realised: the boy's remains had been found beneath the man's patio. It was near impossible that anyone would have been able to carry out a burial of such a kind without the involvement of someone living at the address. What was missing from the mystery was why Oliver Barrett had been there at all.

There was silence at the other end of the line; for a moment, Dan thought the call had been disconnected.

'Mr Ellis?'

'I'm still here.' His voice had changed, the anger dissolved. 'Sorry. It's not easy for me to talk about.'

'Take your time.' Dan's brain was already two steps ahead, anticipating the information Paul Ellis was about to offer him. His thoughts had taken a dark turn along a path he hoped for Ellis's sake he wasn't about to take them down.

'I told everyone in 1979 what Stan Smith was. I was fourteen at the time. No one believed me, not even my own mother. He was a married man, well respected in the community. I was just some troublemaker who'd been suspended from school. I had a history of telling lies. No one believed me. Perhaps if they had, Oliver Barrett might still be alive.'

THIRTY-SEVEN

Jake Sullivan parked his car at the roadside and crossed to the electric gates of the imposing property that stood before him. A circular driveway curved around tended grounds, with the first signs of daffodils pushing up through its borders. There was a keypad at the side of the gate where a code could be tapped in; beside that, a button for the intercom that connected to the house.

He pressed the button and stood back, staring at the large, warmly lit building behind a high hedgerow offering privacy from the road. Cyncoed was an affluent area of Cardiff, characterised by sprawling detached properties and populated by the city's high earners. Jake envied them their surroundings, but he knew that money could only keep someone protected for so long. For the owner of this particular property, that time was running short.

There was a long buzz before the gates began to shift slowly open. Jake stayed where he was, having already promised himself that he wouldn't enter the house. He didn't know who else was there, if anyone, and if his suspicions were proved correct, he didn't want to be alone with this man.

He recognised him when he saw him. He appeared at the front door smartly dressed in dark trousers and a white shirt, although his feet were enclosed in a pair of slippers. He raised a hand in acknowledgement of Jake's presence, as though greeting someone he knew. If this was an attempt to play the everyday good guy, Jake wasn't fooled by it.

'DC Jake Sullivan,' the man said.

Jake realised the trouble he would be in if anyone was to find out he had continued to involve himself in an investigation after being formally suspended, but it seemed to him that nothing he did now could possibly make things any worse. There would more than likely be an inquiry into his involvement with Kieran Robinson and he would be taken before a disciplinary panel to explain his reasons for concealing the truth from the rest of the investigating team. There was only one thing he could do now that might get him a second chance at his career, and nailing this bastard was it.

'Do you have ID?' the man asked, eyeing him coolly.

'Not with me, no, but you know who I am.'

'What can I help you with?'

'I think you know that as well.'

The man pulled a face as he studied Jake intently, the creases that lined his mouth deepening. 'I'm sorry. I've no idea what you mean.'

Jake looked past the man and scanned the vehicles on the driveway. A black BMW and a white Audi convertible were parked alongside one another. He wondered whether either car would hold any traces of his victims, but he was surely too clever for that. He wouldn't have used his own vehicle.

'Kieran Robinson,' Jake said, casting his focus back to the man. 'You know him, don't you?'

'We've met, yes.'

'Oliver Barrett. His name familiar too?'

There was a flash of recognition behind the man's eyes that betrayed him. His mouth fixed itself in a set line, his demeanour now changed. The nice-guy act had already been jettisoned, far quicker than Jake had expected.

'Why don't you tell me what happened, Graham?'

The two men stared at one another, both waiting for the other to react. Despite the flicker in the other man's eyes, he remained disconcertingly impassive, defiant in the face of his exposure. Jake felt an uncomfortable heat course through him. He knew he was right about this, he was right about *him*, but now that he was here, the idea seemed naïve and foolish. This man had already been watching him.

'Is everything okay?'

A woman was standing in the doorway of the house. She was immaculately dressed in a navy-blue trouser suit, her hair swept back from her face and pinned in a mass of curls.

'This is DC Sullivan. He hasn't really explained yet why he's here.' The man smiled, though there was nothing pleasant in the expression. Jake caught a glimpse of the wave of darkness that pulsed behind his pupils, hinting at the sinister secrets stored beyond. How could his wife – the person presumably closer to him than any other – not see what lay within the man she had given her life to?

As the woman neared, Jake noticed that she wasn't quite as immaculate as she had at first appeared. There was mascara smudged beneath her eyes, which were red with the aftermath of tears. He wondered whether his arrival might have interrupted an argument between the couple, halting something. Was this woman in danger?

'Is everything okay?' she asked again.

'Everything's fine. Why don't you go back inside, my love?' The man placed a hand on her shoulder. 'I won't be long.'

Jake wondered if she knew about any of it: where her husband had been, who he had been with, what he had done. He wondered if she had any idea of the kind of man he was. He must have told her a multitude of lies over the years they had been together, each more complex and elaborate than the last. Jake was guilty of his own lies – a string of untruths he wished he could breathe back in and make disappear – but even he was not exactly prolific when compared to this man. Maybe the more lies that were told, the easier lying became. Jake had thought so, but the previous twenty-four hours had proven wrong everything he had believed.

The man was glaring at him now, the temper that was flaring behind his eyes concealed carefully from his departing wife with a turn of his head. 'If you don't have anything of relevance for me, I'm going to have to ask you to leave my property.'

'Of course,' Jake said. 'I apologise.' He took his mobile phone from his pocket and swiped the screen to unlock it before holding it out to show the man one of the images that had been saved there: an invoice for materials that didn't exist displayed above a message sent from Darren Robinson's phone number.

'I need to talk to you about this.'

THIRTY-EIGHT

Alex and Chloe stood side by side at the sinks in the women's toilets. It was one of the few places where they got to talk without prying ears picking up on their conversations, and Alex knew there was never going to be a right time to break the news.

'I'm handing in my resignation,' she said, glancing in the mirror and pushing a length of dark hair from her face.

Chloe smiled. 'April Fool's Day is a couple of weeks off yet.' She checked her appearance in the cracked glass, noting the dark shadows beneath her eyes. No amount of make-up was going to conceal the effects of the past week. Scott could be forgiven for thinking he'd been made newly single and that no one, least of all Chloe, had thought to tell him.

She turned to look at Alex, her smile fading at her friend's unchanging reaction. 'You're not serious? But ... I thought everything was okay. You've not mentioned anything before.'

'You'd have only tried to talk me out of it.' Alex raised an eyebrow, challenging Chloe to deny the fact.

'Is this to do what happened with Dan? Because everything's forgotten about now, you know that. I thought things were fine.'

Alex shook her head. 'It's about me.'

Fourteen months earlier, she had been talked out of handing in her resignation by Superintendent Blake. He had presented a convincing argument for her staying in her job, yet it couldn't overrule the other ambition that had been present in her mind for longer than she had known Chloe.

'There are things I want to do,' she explained, 'and if I don't do them now, it'll only be another thing I end up regretting.' She placed her bag on the sink and reached into it, retrieving the letter she had kept there for the past few days, carrying it with her as though leaving it behind might destroy the future it promised. She passed it to Chloe, waiting for her to scan its contents.

During those past couple of days, her fears about becoming a parent had been pushed to the fore by the heartache she had seen endured by so many: Mrs Lewis's grief at her son's disappearance, Nicola Barrett's frustrations at her apparently wayward son; Linda Robinson's violent reaction to the worst kind of not knowing. Dan's daughters were a constant source of worry to him, yet she knew that they were also his life's greatest source of joy.

Yet too many of her choices had been influenced by other people. She had spent so long wanting to prove something: to a mother she had never been close to, a father she missed every day though he had died almost two decades earlier, a husband she had been unable to make happy. Later, she had needed to prove something to herself. The job made her strong at times when she had known she wasn't; it had given her purpose when she had believed that she had nothing to offer. She had done what she'd set out to achieve. Years of trying to prove something had only proved exhausting. There was no one she had to try to please now other than herself.

'This is brilliant,' Chloe said eventually, looking up at Alex with glazed eyes. 'I mean it,' she added when Alex narrowed her eyes as though questioning her enthusiasm. '*You'll* be brilliant.' She handed the letter back. 'You never said anything. I thought the process took years.'

'So did I, but apparently that's not the case any more. I completed what they call a registration of interest form last summer, not long after my mother died. I heard back just after this.' She raised a hand to her face, allowing her fingertips to trace the uneven tracks of the scars that ran down her neck. 'I thought it might ruin my chances, but if anything, it might actually have gone in my favour. I think they see me as some kind of hero or something.'

'You're *my* hero,' Chloe said, adopting a mock-American accent and giving Alex a wink.

'Don't ever do that again,' Alex said with a smile, picking up her bag.

'In all seriousness, though, the selfish part of me is gutted. I'd just assumed that things would always stay the way they have been. I thought we were going to grow old together.'

'Don't think it means you're rid of me for good,' Alex quipped. 'You're not that lucky.'

'What about an income, though? You can't afford to finish work for ever, can you – not unless you've had a lottery win you've been keeping quiet.'

'I can go part-time, hopefully stay within the force somehow. Admin job will suit me fine.'

Chloe raised an eyebrow and was about to question the truth of the statement when there was a knock at the door of the toilets. A moment later, Dan's head appeared around the corner. 'Sorry. Not interrupting anything, am I?'

'Only the obvious,' Chloe said, raising her hands. 'Privacy is dead, apparently.'

They stepped out into the corridor, where Dan told them he had received a call regarding Oliver Barrett. He repeated what Paul Ellis had told him, and also, perhaps most tellingly, what he hadn't been able to put into words.

'I had to say it for him,' Dan explained. 'Stan Smith sexually assaulted him. It happened during a Scouts' trip. Ellis said Smith cornered him in the shower block of the campsite when no one else was around, and when he told one of the other adults, he was accused of making it up. He'd recently been suspended from school and he admitted he had a well-documented history of telling lies. It seems no one believed him when he did finally tell the truth.'

'Could Carol Smith have known about this accusation?' Chloe asked.

'Maybe,' Alex said. 'Though she was just a kid at the time. If everyone else believed Paul Ellis was lying, that's what Carol would have believed too. Perhaps it was kept hidden from her. Even if she did know about it, why would she want to bring it back up now, when all it would do is make her father appear guilty? Either way, we need to speak with her again.'

'So what are we thinking ... Stan Smith assaulted Oliver Barrett before killing him?'

'Seems the most likely scenario, doesn't it?'

Dan looked at Alex. 'There's something else. Before Paul Ellis called in, I found this on the printer in the incident room.' He handed her the sheet of paper. Ellis's name was listed halfway down the page.

'I don't understand. This was on the printer before he called in?'

Chloe stepped towards Alex and scanned the sheet. 'What is that anyway?'

'No idea. I sent something to print, and when I went to collect it, this was just waiting there.'

'Okay,' said Alex, heading towards the incident room, Dan and Chloe following. 'Can you give me Ellis's number? I'll call him back – see if he recognises any of these other names. Dan, is there any way you can find out whose computer this was sent from?'

'Should be able to.'

Alex stopped as Chloe and Dan dispersed to their desks, returning her focus to the list of names in her hand. She couldn't explain why, but a feeling of growing anxiety was beginning to creep through her.

THIRTY-NINE

Jake parked near his block of flats, but he wasn't ready to go home just yet. Sam was busy that evening, working late, and he wasn't looking forward to an evening by himself with only the television and his own thoughts for company.

Instead of going inside, he made the short walk from his flat to the centre of Cardiff Bay, which, despite the encroaching darkness of early evening, was bustling with life: couples with their coats zipped to their throats sipping coffee on the terrace that overlooked the docking area; groups of friends drinking pints behind the floor-to-ceiling windows of the large bar that stood on the corner of the wooden walkway; families heading home for the night, their children dawdling behind them, already resisting their approaching bedtime. Jake loved this part of the city with all its bustle and life, yet sometimes it made him feel lonelier than he had ever thought possible.

He stopped at the railing of the main pedestrian walkway that ran the length of the increasingly popular bar and restaurant area, leaning over to look down into the murky water below. He watched as it sloshed noisily against the dock wall, the repetitive slapping sound strangely hypnotic. Jake had never been much of a drinker. Now, though, he felt he could gladly reach for a bottle in which to drown himself.

Though he'd had no real feelings towards Kieran – no feelings that reached beyond the physical attraction that had spurred that initial conversation – the thought that his life might have ended somewhere near this place filled Jake with an unsettling anxiety. While the majority of his brain told him that it was Kieran who'd been watched that previous Thursday night, there was a part of Jake still clinging to the sickening possibility that he too had been targeted. Someone wanted to hurt him – if only in the sense of ending his career – but he had no idea why. If there was nothing else he could do now, he owed it to Kieran to find out what had happened to him, and he believed that he was now closer than ever.

Pushing his upper body over the railings, he leaned down to scan the underside of the walkway. There was a ledge that ran the length of the water's edge, wide enough for a person to lie on. Surely it wasn't possible that someone could have killed Kieran here, just feet away from the bars and restaurant above, and concealed his body on the ledge to return to later? Unless the divers had somehow managed to miss his corpse in the water, either Kieran had been abducted from somewhere near where Jake now stood, or his body had been removed after death without arousing the suspicions of anyone in the vicinity.

It didn't make sense. It never had. But it seemed clear now: as obvious as it should always have been. If Kieran was dead, he hadn't died in this place at all. He had gone somewhere with someone he knew and trusted. He had gone somewhere with a man he had no reason to fear.

Jake left the waterfront and the busy main roads and took a side street that led him past a quiet pub and an Indian takeaway. At the top of the street was the internet café he preferred to use, a place that was always quiet and where he could find privacy for his online activities. He would never use the internet at his own flat, always fearing that Sam might one day use his laptop when staying over; that he would somehow access the search history and Jake would be forced to explain his deceptions. He didn't want to lose Sam, but there was something in him that needed this other, secret life; an existence that he could keep for himself, that was for him and him alone.

He ordered a large Americano and took it with him to one of the computers in the furthest corner of the café. After using the café's login details to access the internet, he searched for the website on which he had first met Kieran. Curiosity had led him there, but it was an insatiable need to be desired that had kept him coming back. Monogamy wasn't right for Jake, but the safety of his relationship with Sam was something he needed. It had never felt wrong: he lived two separate lives, neither one affecting the other. Nobody was hurt by it. But now he realised how naïve that assumption – that hope, perhaps – had been.

All his conversations with other website users would be stored in his account; it had occurred to him that perhaps Kieran might have mentioned something at some point during one of their online chats – some detail he hadn't noticed at the time – that might now have greater relevance. He had gone through their dialogue once already, but with little else to occupy his time and his thoughts, checking it again seemed as productive as anything else he was now able to do.

He typed in his username and password and waited for the home page to appear on the screen. His profile picture appeared at the side of the page: a heavily filtered selfie that had been taken the previous year; an image that looked barely like he had then and nothing like he looked now. That was the beauty of the internet, he thought, moving away from the photograph and opening his inbox: you could be the best version of yourself, even if it was a version that didn't exist. You could be someone else.

Scrolling back through the message history, Jake felt his nerves begin to regain their strength. That afternoon had made him uneasy, but he felt empowered again now; more confident in his own abilities than he had felt in quite some time. He needed to search that house, but without a warrant, it was going to prove impossible. He had known he wouldn't be able to do it that day, and there was part of him that was relieved. He knew exactly what the man was capable of. There was something that had occurred to him, though. He might not be able to get into the house, but he knew someone already corrupt enough to find a way. Darren Robinson. It had seemed a ludicrous thought at first, but the more he had lingered over it, the more credible it had become. All he needed to do was work out a way in which he might be able to make it happen. Perhaps the threat of a charge relating to his attempted blackmail would be enough to persuade Darren that Jake was his only way of avoiding a potential stretch in prison.

It took Jake another two hours, a second Americano and a cheese toastie to work his way through the conversation thread between Kieran and himself. He had been wrong. There was nothing hidden among the text; no glimmer of a hint that might be later used as evidence. Frustrated at the time he had wasted, he logged out and left the café, turning left to make his way back home. The sky was dark and heavy, threatening rain, and he checked the time on his phone before returning it to his pocket and cutting down a path that led back towards the main road. It was littered with wheelie bins and black bags waiting for the following day's collection. Holding his breath at the stench of rotting waste, he hurried along towards the glow of a street lamp at the other end.

He never made it that far. He was stopped by a figure that stepped from a doorway; by the cold touch of metal that was jabbed to the small of his back, and by a fear that rendered him immobile. He didn't need to see it to know what it was. Bile lurched into his throat, choking any words he might have spoken.

'Keep walking,' a voice told him. 'Get in the van.'

FORTY

Alex used the phone at Dan's desk to call Paul Ellis. Dan was in the corner of the room, still at the printer, working on tracking down whose computer the list of names had been sent from. Alex would have had no idea how to go about even starting the process.

'Mr Ellis?' she said when the call was answered. 'DI King, South Wales Police. You spoke with my colleague DC Mason just a while ago. Thank you for getting in touch with us. I wonder if I could ask you if any of these names mean anything to you.'

'Go on.'

'John Keepings. Emily Llewellyn. Caitlyn Price. Karen Pritchard. June Roberts—'

'I was at school with them,' Paul Ellis said, cutting her recitation short. 'They were all in my year at school.'

Alex scanned the rest of the list, but there was no other name on it that was familiar to her. It only had around sixty names on it – not enough to consist of an entire school year. She couldn't understand what it had been doing on the printer, or where it had come from. Paul Ellis – or the fact of his existence, at least – had been present at the station before his call had come in. But how had that been possible? And why was this list there at all?

'Which school was this?'

'St Joseph's High School.'

'In Cardiff?'

'Yeah, that's the one. Why are you asking about all these people?'

I'm not sure yet, Alex thought. Keeping the doubt to herself, she evaded a direct answer to the question and thanked Paul Ellis for contacting them, telling him she would be in touch again shortly. Once she had hung up, she logged on to the internet on Dan's computer and ran a Google search for the contact number of St Joseph's High School.

Her call was answered on the third ring. There was a parents' evening that night and the staff had stayed working until later into the evening. The secretary Alex spoke to was aware that a request for the list of students had already been made, and Alex asked her to resend it to her own email address.

'Could you tell me who the list was sent to initially, please?'

There was a moment's pause as the secretary checked her sent box. 'It was emailed to DC Sullivan.'

Alex sat up. 'When was that?'

'Uh … yesterday morning.'

She raised a hand, trying to get Dan's attention.

'Right,' the woman said. 'That's just sent.'

Alex thanked her and opened her inbox. As promised, the email was waiting there. She opened it and clicked on the attachment. It was immediately clear that only part of the list had been left at the printer. Someone had taken the first page. Jake.

'Dan. Chloe.'

They joined her at the desk, each peering over a shoulder as Alex directed their attention to a name on the screen.

'So where the hell is he now?' Chloe asked.

Alex's finger traced the name. Graham Driscoll. It had persisted in emerging during their investigations, yet he continued to stay faceless; as absent now as Oliver Barrett had been for all those years. Yet Alex was beginning to suspect that in Driscoll's case, the choice to remain hidden had been made deliberately.

FORTY-ONE

The blow was blunt and sudden, sending Jake flailing into the darkness of the van. His head hit something hard and he groped at the metal walls in an attempt to steady himself, but his ears were ringing and he was too disorientated to keep himself upright. Collapsing into the corner, he raised his arms in front of his face, shielding it from the further assault he felt sure would follow. It never came. The van doors were closed, shutting him inside with his assailant.

'If you make a noise, I'll shoot you. Don't think I won't. I've got nothing left to lose.'

Jake believed every word. He knew all too well what this man was capable of: he had seen the severed finger; the photographs of the remains that had been dug from beneath that patio. If everything he had put together was correct, the man was capable of anything.

He tried to hold his breath against the stench that filled the van: an overpowering rancid, rotting smell. 'I can help you,' he said, choking on the words, his arms still held in front of his face. He didn't believe his own statement – this man was surely beyond any help – but if he didn't hold on to the hope that there might be a way to talk him out of whatever he had planned, Jake realised he had little else to cling on to.

'Tell me what he was like.'

The command was unexpected, and Jake's mind struggled to follow. What was he talking about? What did he want from him?

'I don't understand,' he said carefully, trying to steady his voice; knowing his ignorance might only serve to fuel further anger. 'I'm sorry. I don't know who you mean.'

Glancing into the darkness to his left, Jake narrowed his eyes and struggled to make out the shape that lay beside him. It was a pile of something, something soft and fabric-covered, and the stench was seeping from its corner of the van.

'Kieran. What was he like when you fucked him? That's what you did, isn't it? That's what boys like you do.'

In the darkness, Jake moved his hand to his side, slowly reaching down towards his pocket. His fingers groped quietly in the darkness, searching out his mobile phone, his only means of help. He needed to call someone – it didn't matter who. If he could get someone to hear at least a part of this conversation, then whoever he might connect with would know there was something wrong. They would send for help.

'Come on,' the man said impatiently. 'Tell me.'

Jake shook his head, sickened at the thought of sharing intimate details with this man. Why would he even ask him something like that? 'Nothing happened.'

'Liar!'

The man lunged forward and knocked the phone from Jake's hand, sending it bouncing across the floor of the van. He pressed the gun to Jake's face, making him whimper with a sound he wouldn't have believed was coming from his own body. Everything he had thought about himself was wrong: the bravado, the courage, the carefree persona he delivered to his colleagues on a daily basis was just a mask for everything he tried so desperately to keep hidden. He was alone and he was scared, just as he had been for most of his life, always feeling on the outside of everything; too intimidated by rejection to ever commit fully to anything. He had somehow made it to the rank of detective constable, though even he realised he had done it with luck on his side. He had always had a way of being in the right place at the right time or knowing the right words to say to the right people in order to get him what and where he wanted. DI King had been one of the few people to see through him, and she was probably right, he thought: he hadn't deserved any of it.

'You can tell me, you know. I understand you.'

Jake tried to shut out the sound of the man's voice, but it was so close it was as though he could feel it touching his skin. In the darkness of the van, just a few feet away from where he cowered, was a body. He knew the smell; he had visited the pathologist's lab enough times to recognise the odour emitted by a rotting corpse, and once he had inhaled it for the first time, it was something that had never left him. He could stare death in the face in all its gruesome aesthetics, but the smell of it was something he had never been able to stomach. Retching and swallowing back a mouthful of bile, he tried not to think about what or who was lying in the darkness beside him. He stared at the shape of the gun in front of him, and with a shame that seemed to swallow him, he felt the space between his thighs heat up as his bladder emptied against his trousers.

'Men like you ... little boys playing at being men ... you revolt me. Hiding your dirty little secrets as though no one can see what you really are. Lying to other people, lying to yourself ... taking whatever you can because you think it'll make you feel better about yourself. You deserve to die, all of you.'

Jake watched as the man moved back, the gun still held poised in front of him, and reached down to the floor of the van to pick up the mobile phone with his free hand.

Was he here because he was gay? Jake thought. Was homophobia what all this was really about? He wondered whether Oliver Barrett had died because he had been attracted to other boys. With fear lodged in his throat and a hollow burning in his stomach, he wondered whether he was about to die for the same reason.

FORTY-TWO

The three detectives stood at the evidence board, studying its web of names and dates. It seemed clear to them all now that Graham Driscoll was their missing link; the piece of the jigsaw that until that evening had been eluding them. If the sender of the envelopes had a link with both the past and the present, he needed to be connected in some way to both Oliver Barrett and Kieran Robinson. The link with Barrett was now in place, but to establish a connection to Kieran, they had to start looking at the web in front of them from a different angle.

Though perhaps there was no need, Alex thought, staring at the man's name and the few details that were written below it on the evidence board. Maybe it had always been there, staring right at them.

'Graham Driscoll was fostered by Debra Rogers, Stan Smith's sister. We know that he was put into the care system after his mother committed suicide, and that he left Debra at the age of sixteen. He didn't have the best start, did he? Would you want that hanging over you for the rest of your life?'

Alex had turned to Chloe with the question, immediately regretting her choice of words when she saw the reaction that had spread across her colleague's face. Given Chloe's past, Alex's turn of phrase couldn't have been more poorly chosen. Chloe looked as though Alex had slapped her with the words, dragging everything she had tried so desperately to move away from back into the room with them.

'Christ, Chloe … I'm so sorry.'

'It's fine. You're right … no, I wouldn't want that hanging over me.'

'Shit.' Alex looked from Chloe to Dan, waiting for one of them to catch up with her train of thought. 'Chloe Lane,' she said, throwing emphasis on the surname.

Chloe's eyes widened as she picked up the thread Alex was dangling before them. 'I changed my name to escape my past.'

'Exactly. So what if Graham Driscoll did the same? There's a reason we've not been able to trace him, isn't there? He no longer bloody exists.'

Returning to the phone she had used to call the secretary at St Joseph's, Alex pressed redial and waited for an answer. When the call continued to go unanswered, she glanced at the clock on the far wall: 8.15.

'Shit,' she muttered, fearing that by now everyone had packed up and headed home for the night.

'Hello, St Joseph's High School.'

She breathed a sigh of relief at the sound of the same voice she had spoken with not long earlier. Thank God for overrunning parents' evenings, she thought.

'This is DI King again. I'm going to need a school photograph of the year group you sent me – would that be possible? I can come to you,' she added, glancing again at the clock on the far wall. 'I can be there in twenty minutes at the latest.'

'We're just about to close up,' the secretary said.

'I'm afraid this can't wait until tomorrow. Is a photograph available there, do you know?'

'Yes,' she said, with a sigh she didn't bother attempting to conceal. 'There are copies of all the year photos somewhere in the head's office. But I showed it to one of your officers only yesterday. He took a photo of it on his phone.'

'Which officer?' Alex asked, already knowing what the woman's answer would be.

'Well as far as I know, it was the same one I'd emailed with the student list. DC Sullivan.'

Alex's mind jumped three steps ahead of her. Jake had got there first. All this time spent trying to make the pieces fit together, and he had already solved the mystery, having seen what the rest of them had been unable to. 'Can you get that photograph out again for me, please. I'm on my way.'

Ending the call, she grabbed the list from the desk. 'Dan, I'm sorry, I need you to stay here. Wait for my call. Try to get hold of Jake. I've got a feeling he knows something we don't.'

Fifteen minutes and several broken speed limits later, Alex and Chloe stood in the reception area of St Joseph's High School. The secretary was waiting for them there; a velvet photo album – crimson in colour and embossed with the school logo – sat on the front desk.

'These have been kept for years,' the woman explained. 'Bit of a school tradition.'

Alex opened the album and flicked through its pages, looking for the photograph of the fifth form of 1980–81. When she found it, a couple of hundred faces looked back at her, the image so small that making out any individual detail was difficult.

'Can you see Barrett?' she asked Chloe, who had stepped alongside her to study the photograph.

Chloe shook her head as she scanned the rows of students. 'I can't find him.'

Alex had felt so certain that there would be something here, something that might direct them to their killer; or lead them to someone who knew who the killer was, at least.

As her eyes skipped over the faces, she spotted one that seemed familiar in some way.

'Is that him?' she asked, directing Chloe to a boy at the end of the third row.

'I'm not sure. It could be. It's so hard to make out. A lot of them all look the same.'

Pushing her hair behind her ear, Chloe leaned closer to the image and the two women studied it in silence. The secretary waited beside them, failing despite her best efforts to hide her resentment at being kept at work for even longer than she had previously anticipated.

'Oh no.'

Alex glanced at Chloe. Her gaze had shifted, and she was now fixated on a face that looked back at her from the second row from the top; a face that to Alex looked very much the same as countless other faces in the photograph.

'Is that him?' Chloe asked. 'Is that Driscoll?'

'We don't know, do we?' Alex said, trying not to sound as impatient as she felt. 'We don't know who he is, do we?'

'Or perhaps we do,' Chloe said, moving away from the photo. 'That is him. It's definitely him.' She looked at Alex. 'It's Michael Wyatt.'

FORTY-THREE

Back at the car, Chloe got straight on the phone to Dan and asked him to track any vehicles Wyatt might have access to, the nature of his work making it possible he had the use of more than just his own private car. If he was responsible for Kieran and Matthew's disappearances, he'd have needed a vehicle that made the transportation of his victims easy to conceal. And then there was the other thing that had been preying on Alex's mind: those tyre marks found on the mountain road. Had Wyatt hit Matthew in one of the vans belonging to his company, or had he used it to abduct him from the mountain? Either way, this was it, she thought, her body charged with a pressing sense of urgency; the missing piece they were looking for was now in place, with a link between all the victims: Oliver Barrett, Kieran Robinson, Matthew Lewis, Stacey Cooper.

Dan had tried contacting Jake but had been unable to get hold of him. Chloe tried now, but there was still no answer. Alex's thoughts strayed to DCI Thompson. The next call would be to him, to tell him they finally had a suspect. Just yesterday, she would have been pleased with the result, but now, with Jake potentially in danger, she would take no pleasure in telling the DCI their suspicions.

'Wyatt knew where Kieran Robinson was last Thursday,' Alex said as she left the school gates and headed towards the address Dan had given her. 'He organised and paid for the night out at the comedy club – it would have been easy enough for him to find out whether Kieran was going. Kieran knew him, so the chances are he would have gone with him willingly.'

'Wyatt sent you that photo then?' Chloe asked. 'The one of Kieran and Jake together?'

'Who else could it have been?'

'But why? Why send it to you?'

'That's the part I'm not so sure about. It's almost as though he wants to get found out.' Alex was stalled by her words as they began to take on a greater relevance. The timing of the discovery of Oliver Barrett's body had always seemed coincidental, but perhaps it hadn't been. The builders working on the extension at 14 Oak Tree Close had no connection to Oliver Barrett, but did they have one to Michael Wyatt? She needed to speak to Natalie Bryant again. 'But look,' she said, storing the thought for now. 'He knew that farmhouse up on Caerphilly Mountain was derelict, and he knew that no one would be there. If the ground that was dug was meant for Kieran, and if it was Wyatt up there on Saturday night, what he wasn't expecting was for Matthew Lewis to interrupt proceedings.'

'Why kill Stacey? To keep her quiet as well?'

'She must have seen the van hit him, or been close enough for Wyatt to assume that she had,' Alex said. 'What did he seem like when you met him?'

'Unassuming. Just normal, I suppose.'

'That's the thing, isn't it? Criminals tend to blend in well.' She glanced at Chloe. 'What? What's the matter?'

She slowed for an approaching roundabout and headed straight across. They were only a few minutes from Cyncoed, where Wyatt lived with his wife. On the street to either side of them, the houses had changed in size and style. Inside, lit rooms with drawn-back curtains displayed wealth and comfort; the kind of lives that most people aspired to. Wyatt had it all, Alex thought – he had done everything he could to transform his life from that of his early years – so why had he done any of this? What other secrets was he hiding?

'His secretary told me he was in a meeting,' Chloe recalled, 'but when I went into his office, he didn't look as though he'd just come from anywhere. He didn't really seem to be doing much at all. I don't know … maybe I'm just reading too much into it.'

Alex took a left turn at a set of traffic lights. 'You said his daughter died last year?'

'That's what he told me. Christ … he just seemed so normal. I didn't suspect him at all.' She exhaled loudly. 'Do you know, I even admired him, in a way. How sick does that seem now? It's a great recommendation for my detective skills, isn't it?'

'You wouldn't be the first to be fooled by a psychopath,' Alex told her, wondering if that's what they were dealing with here.

'If Stan Smith killed Oliver Barrett, where does Wyatt fit in?'

'I've no idea,' Alex admitted. 'Wyatt and Barrett would have known each other, or known of each other at the very least. Perhaps Wyatt knew what Stan had done. We need to find Jake. Call Dan back for me – get a trace put out on Jake's phone.'

She found it difficult to accept that Jake had been in possession of that list of names just the day before and hadn't thought to mention it to any of them, yet she realised it should have come as no surprise to her. Looking back on the events of the previous afternoon, it occurred to her that perhaps he had been intending on telling her. He had tried to speak to her when he had first come to her office, but she had interrupted him, cutting him short. If he had been about to tell her what he suspected, she had put an end to it. She remembered the interview that had followed. He'd had a chance then; he had chosen not to take it.

'A labour of love,' Chloe muttered, ending her call to Dan.

'What?'

'Something Wyatt said when I was at his office. We were talking about the farmhouse on the mountain, about Gareth Lawrence's reasons for going to view it. Wyatt said that renovating it would involve a lot of work ... that it would be a labour of love for someone.'

'And?'

'We've been assuming these crimes may have been motivated by homophobia in some way. Maybe we're wrong. Maybe the opposite is true.'

Alex cast Chloe a glance. 'I'm not following.'

'Wyatt and Barrett were in the same school year and we know that there's a good chance Barrett was homosexual, right? We've been assuming Stan Smith was abusing Oliver Barrett, but what if his death was the result of something else? Smith didn't kill Paul Ellis, did he, even though he allegedly assaulted him? So if he'd done the same to Barrett, why kill him?'

'You think Stan Smith found out something was going on between Barrett and Wyatt?'

Chloe shrugged. 'I don't know. It's a theory. What if these crimes are more to do with love than hate?'

'But Wyatt's married. He has a daughter.'

'And? Plenty of gay men hide behind a heterosexual relationship, even more so years ago. Wyatt's in his fifties – things were a lot different when he was younger. He wouldn't have been accepted as a gay man back in 1981 in the same way that he might be now.'

The more Alex thought about Chloe's theory, the more weight it began to hold. Wyatt's motive was unclear, but if Paul Ellis's accusation was founded on the truth, there was another possibility that was making itself increasingly likely.

'Do you think Jake is in danger?' Chloe asked, distracting Alex from her thoughts.

'I hope not.'

The words sounded shallow to her own ears as she spoke them. Wherever Jake was, she hoped for his sake that he wouldn't make any more reckless decisions. As much as he infuriated her at times, the thought of anything happening to him was appalling.

'Jake took that top sheet from the printer,' Chloe said. 'He saw Driscoll's name – he knew that Driscoll was at school with Oliver Barrett and he'd worked out that he had at some point changed his name. Why didn't he tell us all this yesterday? By the looks of it, he sat through that interview knowing he had a possible link and yet he didn't say anything. Instead, he went to the school to confirm his suspicions.'

Alex's lip curled and she put a hand to her head, pressing her fingertips to her temple. 'Stupid, stupid idiot,' she said, pushing her foot flatter to the accelerator.

'What?'

'He didn't tell us because he wanted to go it alone. This is my fault, isn't it? I've been on his case for months and he's known it – you've all known it. What better way to try to get one up on me than to solve this for himself?'

'Surely he wouldn't be that stupid? He's been suspended from duty.'

Alex ran a set of amber traffic lights, a mounting sense of anxiety gripping her. 'This is Jake we're talking about,' she said grimly.

FORTY-FOUR

It was gone 9.30 by the time Alex and Chloe arrived at Michael Wyatt's home. There had been no answer from Jake's phone, though it was little wonder he wasn't picking up. She tried to tell herself that he was fine – that he was keeping a low profile for a few days, taking the sensible option for once – but everything in her suspected that the opposite might be true. If Jake had worked out that Wyatt was Driscoll, and had linked him to each of their victims, there was a chance that he had confronted him in pursuit of some kind of glory. If her suspicions were correct, Jake had put himself in imminent danger.

He had already been targeted by Wyatt with that photograph that had been delivered to the station. Had Wyatt hoped to destroy his career, or was there another reason for sending the photo? Alex was starting to think she had been given a warning sign: one she had failed to recognise though it had been right in front of her.

They pulled up outside the electric gates. 'Impressive,' Chloe said, getting out of the car. She pressed the intercom, waiting for a voice to greet them. 'DC Lane and DI King. Is this Mrs Wyatt?'

'Yes. Come on through.'

The gates opened and Alex and Chloe stepped on to the driveway. Though it was dark, the front of the house was lit with the warm glow of spotlights; sufficient illumination to demonstrate how well kept the property and grounds were. They walked past a BMW and an Audi convertible to get to the front door, where they were greeted by a woman wearing a thin cotton dressing gown tied at the waist. Her wet hair was piled high on her head and held in place with a butterfly clip.

'I'm sorry,' she said, putting a self-conscious hand to her chest. 'I've just got out of the shower.' She stepped aside to allow Alex and Chloe into the house, which was surprisingly traditional when compared to its exterior. An old piano with a sun-bleached lid stood to the left of the wide hallway, whose walls were lined with paintings of stormy seascapes.

'Is this about the fraud?' Mrs Wyatt asked, folding her thin arms across her chest. 'I just can't believe it. I don't know how he could do that to us after everything we've been through.'

Alex glanced at Chloe. 'Fraud?'

'Gareth Lawrence,' Mrs Wyatt said, narrowing her eyes. 'I assume that's why you're here?'

'You've spoken to another officer?' Alex asked. Unless Gareth Lawrence had made a confession, it was the only way she could have known. Darren Robinson was still recovering in hospital, and Alex doubted he would be keen to share the details of his failed attempt at blackmail. Unless Michael Wyatt was already aware of his business partner's activities and was planning on taking matters into his own hands, then Mrs Wyatt had gained the knowledge elsewhere. It wasn't too difficult to work out who she might have spoken to. If Jake had been here before them, it was likely that he had already encountered Wyatt. Where the hell were the two of them now?

'DC Sullivan was here earlier,' Mrs Wyatt confirmed.

Alex felt the knot in her stomach tighten: part frustration with Jake at continuing to make investigations after being suspended; part anxiety at the fact that he had been so close to Wyatt, knowing who he was and just what he was capable of. If it was the only thing she had felt certain of all that week, she believed in her gut that the two men were now together somewhere.

'Is your husband in, Mrs Wyatt?'

'No.'

'Was he here when DC Sullivan came to the house?'

Mrs Wyatt looked from one detective to the other. 'Yes, he was here. I don't understand what all this is about.'

Alex could hear her own voice rising, her panic beginning to show itself. 'Where did your husband say he was going, Mrs Wyatt?'

'To the office. He often works late into the evenings – it's been his way of coping this past year.' She paused before clearing her throat, watching with confusion as Chloe took her mobile from her pocket and made a call. 'Our daughter died. Last year. Michael still can't talk about it. It's as though saying her name aloud might make it all real.'

Alex cast Chloe a glance. Her call to the station had connected; she was requesting that officers be sent to Wyatt's offices on Cathedral Road.

'Why is she doing that?'

Alex turned to Mrs Wyatt, who was wearing panic like a second skin. Had Michael told his wife that he had been at work the previous Thursday evening, when he had followed Kieran Robinson to Jake's flat? Just how much did this woman know about her husband?

'We would really prefer to speak to your husband first.'

Mrs Wyatt looked back to Chloe, whose attention upon finishing the call had been caught by a framed photograph on the hallway table. A young woman with a thick fall of dark hair that swept in waves across her shoulders smiled at the camera, her head turned from the sunlight that pushed through the photo's background.

'That's Elise. My daughter.'

'She's very beautiful.'

'Thank you. She was.'

'My apologies for your loss,' Chloe said, clearly uncomfortable in the presence of the woman's obvious grief.

'She had a rare kidney condition,' the woman explained, reciting the words without emphasis, as though they were scripted and she'd had to repeat them countless times before. 'We'd known about it since she was very young. They warned us it would happen, sooner rather than later, but you never really believe it's going to, not until it does.'

Alex's mind was working faster than she was able to keep up with. Michael Wyatt was a successful businessman, a husband, a father who should have been mourning the loss of his daughter, yet if her suspicions were correct, he was also a killer. She needed a search warrant for the property, but she wouldn't be able to get one until the following morning. It was time they didn't have.

'You said your husband often works late. Is that always in his office?'

Mrs Wyatt turned and headed to the kitchen at the rear of the house. 'More often than not,' she said. 'I think throwing himself into his work is his way of coping with things. He's never liked to bring work home with him. He says he prefers to keep his two lives separate.'

I bet he does, Alex thought. If she had been the gambling type, she would have wagered a substantial sum on this woman having never heard of Graham Driscoll. Throwing all her luck on black, she tossed in the question.

'Graham Driscoll,' she said, watching for a reaction on the other woman's face. 'Do you recognise the name?'

'Graham Driscoll?' Mrs Wyatt repeated with a slight shake of the head. 'No, sorry ... I don't know him. Was he in on this as well? You know, the amount of time Michael spends at work, you'd have thought he'd know what Gareth's been up to.' She paused, assessing the detective's neutral faces; expressions that were obviously being held carefully in place. 'This isn't about Gareth, is it? Would one of you please tell me what on earth is going on?'

'Could you call him for us, Mrs Wyatt? We'd like to know where your husband is.'

Mrs Wyatt eyed them sceptically before disconnecting her phone from the charger by the side of the cooker. She unlocked it, found Michael's number and called him, putting it on loudspeaker so that Alex and Chloe could hear. 'I told you where he is,' she said as they waited for the call to connect. 'He's at his office.'

The call went straight to answerphone.

Alex could feel her impatience rising. She didn't care about the fraud. She didn't care about Gareth Lawrence. All she wanted to know was where Wyatt was. 'Does your husband own an air rifle?'

Mrs Wyatt turned sharply. The question was unexpected, but she also seemed affronted by the mention of the rifle, obviously aware of its existence if nothing else. 'Yes. He used to be a member of some sort of shooting club, but the novelty soon wore off.' Her expression changed, her eyes darkening with the realisation that they suspected her husband of something. 'Why are you asking about the rifle?'

'Do you know where he keeps it?'

The woman looked from Alex to Chloe and back. 'What's this about? You need to tell me now or I'll be calling our solicitor. Should I have somebody here with me?'

'Do you know where your husband keeps his air rifle, Mrs Wyatt?' Alex's tone had changed, the blunt repetition and snipped syllables making it obvious that any politeness was now over.

'I don't know,' she snapped back. 'In the garage, probably. Can someone please tell me what's going on?'

'I need you to take us to the garage, please.'

Mrs Wyatt stepped aside, blocking Alex's path. 'Don't you need a search warrant for that?'

'If the air rifle is in the garage as you say, then we'll have no need to get one, will we?'

The two women locked gazes for a moment, staring each other out defiantly. Mrs Wyatt was the first to weaken. Reluctantly she made her way to the back door, the two detectives following.

The garage was everything the house wasn't: dark and chaotic, tools and rubbish lying in every available space. Scanning the room, Alex's thoughts darkened further. An array of shovels and picks lined the far wall.

'Your husband a keen gardener, Mrs Wyatt?' she asked, gesturing to the tools.

'We employ a gardener,' the woman answered defensively. 'He uses what we have here.'

She went to a cupboard at the back of the garage: a tall metal storage unit with double doors held together by a padlock.

'I don't know the code.'

Alex raised an eyebrow. 'Really?'

'I never come in here,' she said defensively. 'I've got no reason to.'

Alex turned to Chloe. 'Get hold of Dan – tell him we need a trace on Wyatt's phone. What car is he using?' she asked, turning back to Mrs Wyatt. There were two on the driveway, one presumably belonging to the woman and the other to her husband. 'Mrs Wyatt!'

'I don't know,' she snapped, putting a hand to her head and running her fingers through her wet hair. 'He was using one of the works vans, I think. I don't know what you think Michael's done, but you've got it wrong. I haven't seen that rifle in years – he's probably got rid of the thing for all I know.'

Reaching into her pocket for her mobile, Alex checked the screen for missed calls. She hadn't expected Jake to reply, but the longer he failed to get back to her, the more she was beginning to suspect that something was very wrong. He was stubborn, but he had enough intelligence to have made it on to the team. He wouldn't willingly ignore this many calls, of that much she felt certain.

She could hear Chloe outside the garage, talking to Dan. She tried Jake's number again. It rang through to the answerphone.

'What other vehicles does your husband have access to?'

'I don't know. Any of the work vans, I suppose – there are a few that are registered to the company. Will you please tell me what he's supposed to have done?'

Alex left the garage and went outside. Chloe was on the driveway, her phone in her hand. 'He's on to it,' she said.

'We need to find Jake.'

'You think he's in danger?'

'Oliver and Kieran were both young gay men. They were targeted. Wyatt's already aware of Jake – he watched him with Kieran. Now that Jake's been here …' She sighed and shook her head. 'What the bloody hell was he playing at?'

She glanced back at Mrs Wyatt, who was standing at the garage door listening to the conversation. She was looking at them as though uncertain of where she was: as though she had come home that evening in the midst of one life and had now suddenly been transported against her will to another.

'What about Matthew?' Chloe asked.

'He wasn't targeted. He was just in the wrong place at the wrong time. I think—'

She was interrupted by the ringing of her mobile phone in her hand. She looked down at the lit screen. Jake.

FORTY-FIVE

He had no idea where they were or where he was being taken. He had kept track of the van's journey for ten minutes or so, tracing each road in the map of his mind like a web spun by his own brain, more complex with each turn. Having grown up in Cardiff and lived there all his life, he knew the roads as well as anyone, yet fear had made him lose his concentration so that now the only thing he knew was that they had left Cardiff and he had no clue where he was going or why.

He had been so naïve, he realised that now. He should have told DI King what he had found out when he had seen that list of students the previous morning and made the connection between Michael Wyatt and Oliver Barrett. With the original investigation into Barrett's disappearance having already involved interviews with his peers at school, no one had expected to find anything new there so many years later. It was Jake who had seen the photograph; Jake who had realised that Michael Wyatt – known then as Graham Driscoll – had been in the same school year as Barrett. Proving Wyatt's guilt was never going to be enough to get him his job back, not after what he'd done. Now he was here, alone, and no one else had any idea. Jake had never liked asking for help, or admitting that it might be needed. Now he would willingly have begged for it.

He ran his hands along the walls of the van as it jolted over a bump. Falling to one side, he steadied himself as he tried to avoid a collision with the body lying beside him. The smell of decaying flesh made him heave, and he turned to throw up, spilling the contents of his stomach on to the floor of the van. Fighting back sobs, he tried to calm his increasing panic, fumbling around on the floor of the van for anything he might be able to use as a weapon. There was nothing but some fabric in the opposite corner, something that felt like an old blanket, worn and coarse. He thought of the photographs pinned to the evidence board in the incident room: Oliver Barrett's remains wrapped in an old curtain. His stomach lurched and he threw up again.

Hearing his mobile phone ringing from somewhere in the front of the vehicle, Jake turned and pounded his fists on the metal panel that separated him from Wyatt.

'Stop the van!' he shouted.

He'd been about to tell his captor that the police would pick up their location using his mobile signal, but as soon as he alerted him to that possibility, Wyatt would throw the phone out of the window, destroying any hope Jake had of someone finding where he was.

The van came to a sudden stop, throwing him on to his side. The hum of the engine was cut dead and he heard Wyatt get down from the driver's side, slamming the door shut behind him. The sound of his own breaths, short and shallow, filled the darkness of the van and he braced himself for what was to come. If this man was capable of what he suspected, there was no escape for him. His only hope was that someone would find him before it was too late.

When the van doors were pulled open, Jake's eyes took a moment to adjust to what was in front of him. It was dark outside, the black stretch of inky sky only broken by the silhouette of Michael Wyatt. Jake froze as he scanned the man's outline, stopping at the shape of the gun he held in his right hand. He was holding something smaller in the other hand, but Jake couldn't distinguish what it was.

A moment later, he threw the object into the van. It was Jake's mobile phone.

'Call her back,' Wyatt instructed.

Jake fumbled for the phone and unlocked it with clumsy fingers. Six missed calls: Alex. There were several others from Chloe and Dan. At some point he had resented each of these people: their popularity, their positions, their characters. He had envied them in ways he would never have admitted, even to himself. It seemed ironic now that they were the very people he wanted to see more than any other.

With shaking hands, he tried Alex's number and waited for the call to connect. 'You may as well give this up,' he told Wyatt, tightening his fingers around the phone. 'You won't get away with it.'

'I know,' Wyatt said, raising the gun. 'That's as it needs to be.'

Jake held his free hand out in front of him as he heard the sound of ringing. 'Okay, okay,' he said quickly. 'Just wait ... I can help you. We can get you mitigating circumstances, okay? Your daughter's death ... it'll be taken into consideration. There are things we can sort out ... ways I can help you.'

'You can bring her back to life, can you?'

Jake's panic-stricken face pleaded with the man, but he could see that behind his eyes there was nothing. Wyatt had sent that photograph, that finger, knowing that the police would draw closer to him sooner rather than later. He had brought them to him, knowing that he couldn't hide the truth forever. This was a man who no longer had anything to lose, and Jake realised in that moment that there was nothing to be feared more than a person who had lost everything.

'Hello? Jake?'

They were interrupted by the sound of Alex's voice: something once synonymous to Jake with reproach was now his only source of reassurance. Wyatt waved his left hand, instructing Jake to speak to her.

'Alex.' He could hear the shake in his own voice; could hear his fear tripping across the syllables in a stutter.

'Jake. Where are you?'

'I don't know.' Narrowing his eyes and looking past Wyatt, he searched for signs of something familiar that might offer a clue. It was too dark, though, and there was nothing but ringing in his ears and empty blackness ahead of him.

He watched Wyatt step into the van and sit with his back against the wall, the rifle propped on one knee, its barrel still aimed at him. The space between them was small and there wasn't enough room to try to get past him and out of the van. If he tried it, Wyatt had only to shoot him to end his attempt at escape. The version of Jake that had woken up that morning might have tried to wrestle the weapon from him, but he realised now that trying to be a hero meant putting his life at even greater risk. It occurred to him now that had he played by the rules in the first place – had he done things in the sensible way, the way his police training had taught him to – he wouldn't now find himself in this situation. The best thing he could do was try to buy himself time and keep Wyatt talking so that their location could be traced.

But in his heart, he feared it was already too late for that.

'Talk to me, Jake. Is Wyatt with you?'

'Yes.'

'Is anyone else there?'

'No.'

'Do you have any idea where you are?'

'No.' His voice cracked, fear escaping him in a strangled sob. 'Alex, I'm so sorry.'

'Listen to me, Jake, you don't need to apologise now. I want you to try to keep calm, okay? Does Wyatt have a gun with him?'

'Yes.'

There was a brief moment of silence that to Jake felt like an age, and the feeling of wanting to be close to Sam was overpowering; so much so that for the briefest moment it even managed to eclipse the fear he felt. He wanted to apologise to him for everything he had done. He had treated him so badly, always taking what he could with no thought for anything but his own fulfilment. Now he supposed he was paying the price for years of selfishness.

'Help is on its way, okay?'

But the pause had already given Alex away. There was no help coming, Jake knew that: they had no idea where he was. She was good at what she did, but not even Alex was convincing enough to reassure him that he was going to get out of this.

Wyatt waved his free hand towards Jake, gesturing for the phone. He snatched it from Jake's hand, keeping the gun pointed at him. With a tap to the screen, he put the call on loudspeaker.

'Jake? Jake, are you still there?'

'For now,' Michael Wyatt told her.

FORTY-SIX

Alex's hand tightened around her mobile phone. She prayed Dan might be able to track Jake's whereabouts in time, but she knew it had already become time they didn't have.

The sound of Wyatt's voice sent a chill through her. She had the feeling that they didn't yet know the extent of this man's crimes.

'Where are you, Michael?' She tried to keep her voice steady, unwilling to offer him the upper hand by exposing her increasing sense of panic.

'That doesn't matter now,' he told her, his voice flat and emotionless.

'Wherever you are, I want you to let Jake go. He hasn't done anything to you, has he? You don't need to hurt him.'

She was trying desperately to fit the pieces of the mystery together. Why had Wyatt followed Kieran to Jake's flat? Had he known that Kieran was gay? If Kieran's murder had been a hate crime, just where did Oliver Barrett come into the picture? Chloe's theory that this was more to do with love than hate seemed more than a possibility now. If Paul Ellis's accusation was true, then it seemed likely that Stan Smith could have abused Oliver. Was she right in what she suspected, that there had been some kind of relationship between Wyatt and Barrett: a relationship that Stan Smith had found out about and had punished them for? Had Michael Wyatt – Graham Driscoll – been there? Just what had he seen?

'Talk to me, Michael. We can sort this out.'

'He said the same.'

Behind Alex, there was a loud bang – metal against metal – followed by a second, each shattering the silence that had surrounded her. She turned to the noise, but the garage door had swung shut and she couldn't see what was going on. She only knew that Chloe had gone back inside with Wyatt's wife. She still didn't suspect the woman of any involvement in her husband's crimes; it seemed her only crime was ignorance. For now, Alex's priority had to be keeping Michael on the line. The longer she kept him talking, the greater her chance of saving Jake's life.

'He's right. This can end now, Michael – no one else has to get hurt. Let Jake go unharmed and we can talk about it, okay?'

'Talk about what?'

Was this some sort of game, Alex wondered, or was Michael Wyatt a true sociopath? He was speaking as though he had no concept of the severity of his crimes. He had helped lead the police to where he was, and he had done so on his own terms. No, it wasn't a game, she thought. He knew exactly what he was doing.

'Help me understand,' she said. She realised she was still far from comprehending the motives behind the man's crimes. She was yet to know for certain whether the ground that had been dug had been intended as a burial site for Kieran Robinson, or even whether Wyatt had been there at all. Getting him to talk would be the only way to find out, but with each moment that passed, his truths seemed to only be getting further away from her.

'It's too late for that now.'

'It's never too late, Michael. I think I know what happened to you. I think if you talk to me, we can make some sense of all this. No one else has to get hurt.'

She didn't believe that what had happened to Michael as a teenager could ever be made sense of, but if she didn't at least try, Jake's situation only became bleaker. She knew she could only imagine what might have happened to Graham Driscoll to make him the man he had become. She had a feeling she might have worked out part of his story, but she would need him to clarify the details.

'You don't know anything. I don't need to explain myself to you.' Michael's tone was unchanged: he remained distant, remote, as though he was somewhere far removed from what was happening; somewhere far from the things he was responsible for. Was that how he had managed to lead his double life, she wondered: successful businessman and grieving father by day; hunter and murderer by night? Had he kept himself distanced from the truth so that he never had to face up to what he really was?

She supposed that in their own way, that was what everyone was doing.

She tried to travel back in time with him, to the place where this had all started, attempting to piece together what had happened all those years earlier. She had assumed that he had been involved somehow in the murder of Oliver Barrett, but what if she was wrong? What if Stan Smith had abused Michael in the same way he had abused Paul and Oliver?

She couldn't risk raising the subject, not here, not now. If this was where Michael Wyatt's vulnerabilities lay, she couldn't predict what reaction the mere mention of Smith might provoke. If she angered him, she would be gambling with Jake's life.

'Where are you, Michael?'

'Stop asking me that.'

'You obviously want to talk to me. You wouldn't have taken the phone from Jake if you didn't. You've been reaching out to me all week, haven't you? Is that what those deliveries to the station were for? I'm not going anywhere. We've got all the time you need. You can talk to me.'

There was silence for a moment and Alex feared she had lost him. Then she heard him clear his throat.

'Say goodbye, Detective.'

She thought for a second that he was talking to her before realising his instruction was directed at Jake.

'Alex,' she heard Jake say, his voice high-pitched and frightened. Like a child's, she thought, sadness lodging like a tumour in her chest. 'Alex, I'm—'

The sound of a gunshot pierced through the phone, as loudly as if the weapon had been fired right next to her. There was a moment of awful silence in which she could hear the blood pounding in her ears. She waited for something, but nothing followed.

'Jake!'

The line went dead.

'Fuck!' She tried Jake's number again, but the call went unanswered. She called Dan, praying that he had some clue as to where the two men might be. When he didn't answer, she swore again and rushed to the garage. Inside, Chloe was standing at the metal storage unit. Its doors were open and a set of bolt cutters was propped against the wall beside it. Mrs Wyatt was standing at Chloe's side, both hands raised to her mouth.

When Chloe turned, Alex's attention was drawn to the box she was holding in her hands: an oblong metal container with a hinged lid. The lid was flipped back. Inside the box was a collection of small finger bones.

FORTY-SEVEN

Within ten minutes, Jake's phone had been tracked to land near the clifftop at Oxwich Bay, a stretch of beach on the south Wales coastline that during the summer months became a hot spot for families and surfers. For most, the coast was synonymous with the kind of happiness only experienced during those carefree afternoons of summer that seem to stretch to the point of appearing never-ending, but for Chloe, this area brought back nothing but a heart-wrenching sadness that saw her locked into silence any time she was forced to be near it.

'You okay?' Alex asked. Chloe nodded, but her thoughts were gripped by fear for her colleague. No matter what Jake was guilty of, he didn't deserve whatever might be happening to him now. It didn't matter what speed Alex was driving: they both knew they were too late.

Alex turned on to a lane even narrower than the last to reach the spot to which they had been directed, wondering whether this was another piece of land that had been brought to Wyatt's attention via his work.

They had no confirmation of which of the two men had been harmed, but in her gut Alex feared the worst.

'There's the van.'

As they emerged from the darkness of overhanging trees and high, thick hedgerow, Chloe pointed to the near distance. They had entered a wide expanse of field that might have been used as a car park during the day but that now, nearing midnight, was desolate and eerily quiet. The headlights of Alex's car lit up the white van, which had its back doors flung open. Cutting the engine but leaving the beams to light the stretch of ground before them, Alex got out tentatively and scanned the area for any sign of Wyatt.

Chloe climbed out of the passenger side and went to the van. She didn't want to see what was waiting there for her; in her heart, she already knew that Jake was dead. She found him in the back, his body slumped on an old rug and his blood spread out in a dark circle beneath his head. She placed a hand to her mouth, forcing back a surge of sickness. She had seen plenty of bodies before, but she had never seen someone she had known like this.

And then there was the smell. Even with the doors open and the night air flooding the van, the stench was unmistakable. Covering her mouth and nose with the top of her arm, Chloe carefully stepped into the van and crouched beside Jake, placing her fingers gently on his neck as she checked for a pulse. There was nothing. He was gone. She drew back her hand and swallowed down the sadness she felt rising in her throat. Whatever Jake had been guilty of, he hadn't deserved for his life to end so cruelly, so prematurely.

She turned to speak to Alex, but she wasn't there. The headlights of the car illuminated the inside of the van, lighting its chilling contents. There was a pile of blankets in the corner from which the stench was flooding. With tentative fingers, Chloe pulled back a corner, recoiling at the sight that awaited her. Though his features were grey and bloated with the early effects of decay, she recognised the face that had looked down at them from the evidence board that past week: their missing boy, Matthew Lewis. With horror, she realised that he was not alone. Behind him, curved into the corner of the van, lay the body of Kieran Robinson.

*

In the darkness outside, Alex stumbled closer to the cliff edge, losing her footing a couple of times on the uneven ground. The sea stretched out into the distance, vast and blue-black, its sounds swept along with the rush of wind that sped past her. Scanning the drop before her, Alex spotted Michael Wyatt sitting on the grass, his gun on the ground beside him.

Backup was on its way, but she couldn't rely on it to get there soon enough. Wyatt knew it was over and that it had only been a matter of time before his crimes caught up with him. She supposed his acceptance of this was the reason he had sent that photo, that finger, as though he had realised his mistakes and had known that time was against him. If he was here to end his own life, she had to stop him. She wanted to know why he had done what he had. She wanted him to face justice for his crimes.

'Michael.'

He didn't flinch at the sound of her voice. She kept a close eye on his hands, mindful that the gun was within close reach.

'Fourteen,' she said. It was the number of sets of bones collected and stored in the unit in the man's garage. 'Who do they belong to, Michael?'

Still he said nothing. Alex heard Chloe approaching behind her and raised a hand, gesturing for her to stay back. She thought she had an idea of what might get Michael to talk, but what she wasn't so sure of was the reaction she might receive. She was prepared to face it for the sake of gaining the truth, but there was no need for Chloe to put herself in any danger.

'Tell me about Stan Smith.'

There was a visible reaction to the mention of the man's name. Wyatt leaned forward, his hands tightening into fists in front of him.

'We know what he did,' Alex told him. 'Did you see him hurt Oliver? Is that where all this started?'

Wyatt turned sharply to her. His eyes were red with tears, and in that moment Alex saw beyond the cold-blooded killer to the person he had once been, years earlier: just a boy, terrified and alone; a boy who had suffered hardship and was then exposed to more. A picture was beginning to form, but it was still too blurred to see the details, and it was only Wyatt who would be able to shift it into some sort of focus.

'He didn't hurt Oliver. I did.'

A guttural sob escaped him, sudden and loud like gunfire, and he reached for the rifle beside him.

'Alex,' Chloe said softly, the small plea almost lost to the wind.

'It's okay,' Alex said, raising a hand again and keeping her eyes on Wyatt. 'It's okay, Michael.'

The gun was in his hands, pointed upwards to the wide expanse of the night sky above them. Alex could see it moving with the trembling of Wyatt's hand; a tremble that raced the length of his body, shuddering through him. She knew she would never understand, but she needed to know what had happened. It was only he who could tell her what had gone on all those years earlier. Whatever had happened back then, he had kept it with him all those years, burdening himself with a secret that only he now carried.

'What do you mean, you hurt him, Michael? Tell me what happened.'

He tilted his head back and looked up to the sky. 'I didn't want to do it. I panicked. I didn't want to be like him.'

Alex realised he was no longer talking to her. She watched as he ran the palm of his hand across his face, trying to regain some composure. Listening to his words, she attempted to fit them together to try to make some sort of whole. She had assumed that whoever had killed Kieran and sent her the photograph of him and Jake together had been homophobic and the killing had been a hate crime. Now she was surer than ever that Chloe was right.

I didn't want to be like him.

'Who killed Oliver, Michael?'

Michael returned both hands to the gun, his composure regained. 'I did,' he said, his gaze focused on the black expanse that lay in front of them, spread across the horizon in a never-ending pool of darkness.

'But Stan was involved somehow, wasn't he? Did he help you? Did he bury Oliver's body for you?'

'He wasn't helping me. He was making sure I could never tell anyone what he'd done to me.'

And then Alex understood. Stan Smith hadn't abused Oliver Barrett; he had been abusing Graham Driscoll, a boy who should have been able to call him uncle.

'Did you remove Oliver's finger? Or was that Stan?'

At the mention of it, Michael's body tensed and his hands tightened around the rifle. 'He called it a reminder.'

Alex took a tentative step forward, despite the muted protestations of Chloe behind her. 'So why do the same to the others?' she asked, wondering who exactly the other victims were. One of those sets of bones in the garage might prove to have belonged to Oliver Barrett. It occurred to Alex that despite Stan's blackmail, Wyatt had chosen to copy what he had done, repeating the pattern of removing a finger from each of his victims that followed. Had it been an act of ownership, or had he done it to punish himself; as a reminder of what he had done to Oliver and who he was?

I didn't want to be like him.

'Why take a finger, Michael?' she repeated. 'If you didn't want to be like Stan, why do what he did?'

'Because I could,' he said with a shrug, as though there was no reason it shouldn't make perfect sense. 'He didn't have a hold over me then, did he? I chose to do it, not him.'

Alex wondered whether every kill had made Michael feel more empowered: more Michael and less Graham; less the boy who had been blackmailed by his abuser. 'Were you and Oliver at Stan's house?'

'I just wanted to do it there to get back at him,' he said, putting a hand to the ground and pushing himself up. 'It felt right at the time, but as soon as it was over I knew I hadn't proved anything … It was what he'd made me. He'd won.' He stood and stepped closer to the edge of the cliff, the gun still pointed upright.

'Michael,' Alex said, her thoughts racing. 'Come away from the edge.'

In the distance, the first sound of sirens crept into the air. Alex wished them away, knowing that if they came too close too soon, she would never hear the truth.

'You don't want to do this, Michael,' she said. 'You don't have to do it, you know that. Talk to me.'

'So things can all be neatly tied up? It's nice when things work out like that. But life's not so simple. Look at you. You know that.'

'I pity you,' Alex said, though there was little truth in the statement. 'I pity everything you went through as a child, Graham – everything you felt you were unable to confide in anyone about. But what that man did to you doesn't justify any of this. Kieran, Matthew, Stacey … all those lives you've stolen. You say you didn't want to be like Stan, so why do all this?'

She watched Wyatt's jaw tighten in reaction to the implication of her words.

'I'm nothing like him.'

'Why keep those bones?' she challenged, stepping closer to him.

'Alex, please.'

She was too close to the edge, she realised. Chloe had stepped forward behind her too, still pleading with her to move back.

Wyatt turned to her for the first time now, his eyes locking with hers. 'Why should they get to live their lives the way they choose? We couldn't.'

He lifted the gun and aimed it at her. She heard a sharp intake of breath behind her and a rustling of grass as Chloe inched closer, but she kept her eyes fixed on Wyatt's, no longer seeing the vulnerability that might once have existed there; now just seeing him for what he was: a cold-blooded killer whose bitterness and jealousy had led him to rob his victims of a freedom he himself had never been allowed. Graham Driscoll was well and truly dead.

There had been a time not so long ago when a gun directed at her might have seemed of little consequence. Like Michael, Alex had felt she had nothing left to lose. But not now. For the first time in a long time, she had everything to live for. She wasn't going to die out here.

'Kieran wasn't living his life the way he might have chosen, though,' she said, keeping her voice calm and steady; not allowing it to betray the uncertainty that was ringing between her ears at the sight of the gun directed at her. 'None of his family knew he was gay. For whatever reason, he felt forced to keep his sexuality a secret, just as you were. Just as Oliver was all those years ago. You envied a freedom he didn't really have.'

'He was lost,' Wyatt said, his words empty. 'I helped him. I gave him a way out.'

The sound of approaching sirens intensified and his grip on the rifle tightened.

'You took advantage of him, Michael. It might not have been in the same way Stan took advantage of you, but you preyed on his vulnerabilities. You made a choice. You chose to take those lives. You'll have to live with that now.'

'No, I won't,' he said calmly.

He stepped back, lifted the gun upright and rested the muzzle beneath his chin. Then he pulled the trigger.

FORTY-EIGHT

Alex stared at the list in her hand, neatly printed in Wyatt's careful handwriting: handwriting she recognised from the envelopes that had been delivered to the station. There were fourteen names in total, with fourteen dates and the details of fourteen burial sites. Wyatt had remembered each of his victims as though they were missing members of his own family; as though the places at which he had buried their remains were his own back yards. In so many ways, of course, they were.

Each victim – all young men – had been reported missing, but with so many people reported missing every year, each had become just another piece of information that made up the police database statistics. His first victim after Oliver Barrett dated back almost thirty years. In all that time he had managed to keep himself hidden from suspicion, though he had been interviewed by police investigating the disappearance of one young man almost six years earlier. The ways in which he had identified his earlier victims remained unclear, but in more recent years it seemed he had met some of them through dating websites, maintaining his anonymity in the same way that Jake and Kieran had. A couple of the young men whose lives he had taken had worked on properties owned by Lawrence and Wyatt, and when the links were made between them they seemed frustratingly obvious. It seemed that as he grew older, Wyatt had begun to make mistakes; perhaps, Alex thought, why he had introduced the rifle, as a way to overpower victims who were increasingly so much younger and stronger than he was.

She stood in the garden and surveyed the excavation that was taking place. The family who lived in the house had been horrified when they'd been told why they'd have to move temporarily from their home. She wondered whether they would ever return to it. She stared at the ground in front of her, the patio half dug away and the team of officers searching for the remains Wyatt claimed were buried there. It had been almost a week since he had killed himself. During that time, thirteen of his victims had been found, exactly as he had said they would be. Thirteen families had been informed of their loved one's fate. Thirteen heartbreaking mysteries had been finally solved, with thirteen new tsunamis of grief to flood those who had known and loved these missing young men.

The grief that had poured from Matthew Lewis's parents when she had faced them with the news of their son's last moments was something that was going to haunt Alex for a long time to come. The anger that had radiated from them at the filming of the television appeal was lost to a pain that would engulf their lives, and she felt helpless in her inability to offer them any comfort. Matthew's body bore evidence of the impact of the van that had disabled him, but his death had been brought about by Wyatt's rifle.

Kieran Robinson too had been shot. Alex had visited Linda Robinson, who had broken down at the news of her son's death. Kieran's sister Hannah had been there too, transformed by the reality of her brother's final moments from the angry young woman Alex had previously encountered to a sobbing child. Linda was awaiting a court date for a GBH charge for the stabbing of her husband, but with Gareth Lawrence extorting money from his own company and now no business partner to chase it up, both he and Darren had been able to walk away from their crimes. It seemed bitterly unfair to Alex, though her biggest regret was that Michael's death had allowed him to escape justice.

Kieran had been Wyatt's first kill since losing his daughter the previous year, and it was also where his mistakes had begun to show. For years he had got away with his crimes, but Elise's death had made him careless. It occurred to Alex that perhaps he had been intentionally so.

In the glove box of the van, along with the list of names and locations, Wyatt had left a series of letters, each addressed to his daughter. The most recent was dated two days before his suicide.

Dear Elise,

It is almost time now. There is nothing more on this earth that is needed of me and my rightful place now is back by your side, where I was always meant to be. When I see you, I hope I'll have done enough for you to understand what has happened. I hope I'll have done enough for you to find it in your heart to take me back.

I told you in a previous letter that I loved once, a long time ago. He was taken from me, as you now are, and I believe that losing you was my punishment for what happened all those years ago. I was scared of what I was back then and what being with him made me. We could never have been together in the way he wanted us to be, but I am grateful for that. If life had been different for us, there would never have been you.

I took those lives because I saw myself in each of them. They were lost boys, Elise, all of them, all searching for a place in the world that was shaped in their size, made just for them. They could have spent their lives searching, but they would not find it. I know all this because I was just like them. I saw their isolation and their pain and so they gravitated towards me, looking for my help; looking for an escape from their suffering. I helped them. When

I get to you, if I see them, they will thank me for ending their misery.

Save a place at your side for me. I will be with you soon.

Benny x

Alex folded the letter and returned it to her pocket. Benny – the pet name Elise had given her father, borrowed from a character in one of her favourite childhood books; a story that, according to his wife, Michael had read to their daughter every night for a period of three months when she was aged seven. It was all too frightening that a man so seemingly ordinary and good – a man respected by those who had known him – had held such dark secrets and been capable of such evil.

Michael Wyatt had gone to the clifftop knowing he would die there. The list of names had been his confession, though it seemed it was only his daughter he had ever felt answerable to. A search of his laptop had found a history of visits to gay porn sites. With no evidence that he had sexually assaulted any of his victims, it seemed that he had harboured his desires with a shame instilled in him by Stan Smith, as though the sexuality he had kept a secret for an entire lifetime had been enforced upon him by his abuser.

Though Alex's heart cracked for each and every one of his victims, it broke at the thought of Matthew and Stacey. Wyatt had declared a sense of control in his letters to Elise, as though he had planned how and when his crimes would stop, and Alex hadn't at first believed that if he hadn't been interrupted that night by Matthew he would have ended his own life so soon. He had killed Stacey for nothing more than control: it would end on his terms, not hers. He had panicked, made mistakes: been forced to accept that it was all over. But there had been something that contradicted this, one final puzzle piece that suggested Wyatt had planned much further in advance than anyone might have anticipated. A call to Natalie

Bryant revealed that it was Wyatt – after speaking with Natalie's husband about the plans for an extension – who had recommended him. He had sent another man to uncover his crime, knowing what would be revealed beneath the patio.

Wyatt had known his days were coming to an end, but despite this Alex still believed that Matthew Lewis had inadvertently saved the lives of other young men Michael Wyatt might have gone on to kill before he was eventually caught. It was a legacy that would be of little comfort to his parents.

'Boss!'

Alex was shaken from her thoughts by one of the team who stood feet away from her at the excavated patio.

'Found him.'

She crossed the garden and crouched beside the officer. With a gloved hand he drew back a corner of the rotting fabric in which Nathaniel Grant – aged nineteen at the time of his disappearance more than eight years earlier – had been wrapped before being buried. Alex stared at the brown length of dirtied bone, her heart already aching for the Grant family, who would be waiting in trepidation for news.

'Let's get him out of there,' she said, standing.

She headed back towards the house and went inside, stopping in the hallway to exhale the awful air of anticipation she had breathed in while out in the garden. Finally, she thought, it was all over.

FORTY-NINE

The following day, a week after Jake Sullivan's death, Alex was called down to the station's reception area by the desk sergeant. She had been offered some time away from her duties, but with her resignation letter already submitted to the DCI, it wouldn't be long before she was seeing a permanent break from the life that had been the only kind of existence she had really known for the past two decades.

She opened the double doors with her key fob and made her way to the front desk. A man in his late twenties, dark-haired and pencil thin, with a jawline that could have been hand-chiselled, was waiting there, pacing the length of the reception area. The desk sergeant shot Alex an apologetic look, but before she had time to open her mouth, the man had spotted her and hurried over.

'Proud of yourself, are you?'

'Okay,' Alex said calmly, looking again to the desk sergeant. 'Can I ask what this is about?'

'Sir.' Her colleague had left the safety of the desk to come to her aid. 'I'm going to have to ask you to calm down.'

'No, I'll not fucking calm down,' the man said, throwing an arm out to his side to swipe the officer away. 'You're responsible for this!'

There were two other people waiting at reception: an elderly couple who were sitting with their shopping bags at their feet, mouths open at they watched the performance unfolding in front of them. Alex imagined it beat anything that afternoon television might have offered.

'He'd still be here if it wasn't for you.'

Her brain took mere moments to make the connection. 'Sam?' she said, taking a step back. Chloe had broken the news of Jake's death to him, and she had been expecting him to come to the station at some point.

She could have made excuses, but the truth of it was exactly as he had claimed. She felt bile rise in her throat. 'God, Sam, I'm so sorry.' She glanced at the couple still watching, realising this conversation needed to be kept from the view of the public. 'Come through with me,' she said, gesturing to the doors. 'We can talk somewhere a bit more private.'

'Better for you,' he said, jabbing a finger towards her. 'You don't want people knowing what an evil bitch you are, do you?'

'Right,' the desk sergeant said, raising both hands and stepping between Sam and Alex. 'If you don't leave now, I'm going to have you arrested.'

'What for?' Sam spat. 'Telling the fucking truth?' He glared past the officer, redirecting his anger at Alex. 'You had it in for him from day one. The number of times he told me you'd put him down or made him look stupid in front of everyone, like you enjoyed making a fool of him. What was it? Because he was gay?'

'That's not true at all. I didn't even know.'

'Bullshit. People like you, you're all the same.'

'I didn't know,' she repeated, feeling the need to defend herself. There were many things she was guilty of, but she wasn't homophobic. 'The issues I had with Jake were work-related, nothing more. None of us knew about you, Sam.'

The words came out too quickly and all wrong. She watched the reaction spread across Sam's face: he was clearly crushed by the fact that Jake appeared to have kept him hidden.

'I just mean that …' She stopped, realising that any attempt to change the implication of her words was now futile.

'It doesn't matter now, does it?' Sam said bitterly. 'He's dead and it's your fucking fault. I hope you can sleep at night, all the blood that's on your hands.'

Alex watched as the young man's anger dissipated, melting into a grief that seemed to take a grip on his entire body. He shook as he began to sob, lowering himself on to the nearest chair. The elderly couple looked away, embarrassed at the sight of his tears.

Alex sat down beside him. She wanted to offer him something, but she knew there was nothing she could say that would make his pain subside. He hated her. In so many ways, she loathed herself. She would have given anything to undo what had happened, but she knew the futility of wishes and the inevitable disappointment they led to.

'I am so, so sorry, Sam.'

The young man gave a sharp intake of breath and turned to her, his composure regained. 'You couldn't even face me. You're a fucking coward. It should be you that's dead.' He got up and hurried out of the building, angry tears still staining his face.

Countless responses had been on the tip of Alex's tongue, but none had been appropriate. She'd wanted to defend herself, yet she knew that what he had said was true. She had been a coward. She had wanted to go and see him, but the longer she had put it off, the harder it had become. She didn't need anyone to remind her of what she was, and no one could make her feel any worse than she already did.

'Are you okay?' the desk sergeant asked.

'I'm fine.'

Ignoring the looks of the elderly couple, Alex hurried back into the corridor and headed up to her office. She closed the door behind her and went to the window, pressing her hands on the windowsill and taking a series of deep breaths. Sam was right, she thought. Perhaps not about everything, but Jake's death was her fault. If she had made the links to Wyatt sooner, he would never have been able to go after the man by himself.

As she stood looking out on to the car park below, there was a knock at the door. She ignored it, but a moment later Chloe let herself in anyway. She was carrying a mug of coffee, which she put on the desk beside Alex's computer.

'Are you all right?'

She had obviously been told what had happened downstairs.

'I'm fine,' Alex said, keeping her back to the room.

'He's angry and upset. He doesn't mean it.'

'Oh, I think he does.'

She felt Chloe just behind her, but she kept her focus on the world outside the window, wondering whether she might miss this view once she was gone. It was mundane and everyday, yet there was something comforting in its familiarity. She'd lived the majority of her working life here. Saying goodbye to it was going to be a second divorce, messy and final, regrettable, but necessary.

She kept her head tilted to the side, hiding her face from Chloe. Her vulnerability was something she didn't want to broadcast, even now that she was leaving.

'Everything Sam said is right. I did run Jake down. There were times when I just found him so difficult to work with. I didn't think he pulled his weight. But he made a connection to Wyatt before any of us did. So he wasn't so useless after all, was he?'

'He still lied, though. If he hadn't, things might have been very different. I'm not saying he deserved what happened to him, but it doesn't change what he did – you have to remember that. You weren't wrong to suspend him – what other choice did you have? Jake chose to go lone wolf, Alex. What happened to him was tragic, but it wasn't your fault.'

Alex turned to her. 'I should have got there sooner. To the truth, I mean.'

'Well if you're to blame then so am I. So is Dan. None of us worked it out until Jake had already made the decision to go after Wyatt.' She gestured to the coffee on the desk. 'Don't let it go cold.'

Alex gave her a grateful smile and went to her chair.

'So when will you be leaving us?'

'A month's time.'

Chloe nodded, her disappointment obvious. She would be fine, thought Alex; it was only the uncertainty of the unknown that was making her nervous. It was a feeling that Alex was more than able to relate to.

'We'll still see each other,' she said. 'I'm going to need a babysitter, aren't I?'

TWO MONTHS LATER

'All the things I've faced in my years with the police,' Alex said, 'and nothing has ever made me as nervous as today. Stupid, isn't it?'

She glanced through the glass-panelled door at the little girl who was sitting at the table, an array of toys and books spread out in front of her. The four-year-old had thick dark hair that was pulled up into a high ponytail, and on her feet she was wearing a pair of fluffy slippers decorated with colourful unicorn horns protruding from the toes.

'Sounds natural enough to me. It's a big day for you both.' Kelly put a reassuring hand on Alex's arm. 'You'll be fine. You'll have to excuse the slippers, by the way – she won't be parted from them.'

With a smile, Alex looked back at the little girl, who had now picked up a box of crayons and emptied them all on to the table. 'What if she doesn't like me?'

'She'll like you. Stop panicking.'

Kelly pushed the door open and led Alex inside. The girl reacted at the sound of the door – a slight flinch of the shoulders that gave away the realisation that she was no longer alone – though she didn't turn to look at either of the women.

'Hi, Molly. What are you doing there?' Kelly crouched beside the girl and studied the colouring book in front of her. It was opened at a drawing of a ladybird, already half filled in with pillar-box red by another child who had once waited in this same room, in this same seat, with the same uncertainty. 'You're doing a great job. I've brought someone to meet you. Would you like to say hello?'

The girl looked at her nervously, peeping up between the gaps in her heavy fringe. There was an untold sadness in her dark eyes, something cautious and cynical beyond her fragile years. When she finally looked at Alex after what seemed an age, she sucked her lips in as though trying to stop herself from crying. Kelly stood and moved to one side, letting Alex take her place beside Molly, the two of them at eye level now.

Alex waited a moment, letting the child assess her in her own time. She had seen photographs of this girl and had known what to expect, but now she was here in the flesh, it was almost as though she wasn't real, as though the child would evaporate in front of her at any moment, leaving her alone again and taking with her a future that had until now still seemed a mere possibility.

'Hi,' she said, reaching to the carpet and handing Molly one of the books that had fallen from the table. She gave the girl a smile, her heart skipping with anticipation when it was reciprocated after only a moment's hesitation. 'It's lovely to meet you, Molly. My name's Alex.'

A LETTER FROM VICTORIA

Dear Reader,

I want to say a huge thank you for choosing to read *A Promise to the Dead*. If you enjoyed it, and want to keep up to date with all my latest releases, just sign up at the following link. Your email address will never be shared and you can unsubscribe at any time.

www.bookouture.com/victoria-jenkins

Alex and Chloe's story comes to an end here (for the time being, at least), and though I am sad to say goodbye to them, I am excited for what the future holds and where my writing will take me next. And I hope that readers who haven't yet read my other King and Lane novels will look forward to discovering them! The King and Lane series has been more popular than I could ever have hoped for, and I am so grateful to all the readers who have supported the books.

I hope you loved *A Promise to the Dead*; if you did, I would be very grateful if you could write a review. I'd love to hear what you think, and it makes such a difference helping new readers to discover one of my books for the first time.

I love hearing from my readers – you can get in touch on my Facebook page, through Twitter, Goodreads or my website.

Thanks,
Victoria Jenkins

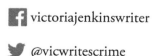

victoriajenkinswriter

@vicwritescrime

ACKNOWLEDGEMENTS

As always, a massive thank you to Jenny, my editor, to Anne, my agent, and to all the brilliant people at Bookouture who have helped put these stories into readers' hands. I feel incredibly lucky that our paths crossed. Thank you to Noelle Holten for all your support and to Kim Nash for being lovely.

Thank you to my family – this has been a horrible year for us, but we have somehow made it through. Thanks to Mia for keeping us smiling and for teaching me – albeit against my will – how to survive without sleep, and to my husband for understanding how much this means to me. Thank you to my in-laws, particularly to Gaynor – I wouldn't have got this one done without you.

And finally, to my dad – I have missed you every minute since you left us, and I will miss you for every minute more until I join you. Until then, I hope I make you proud. This book is for you.

Ingram Content Group UK Ltd.
Milton Keynes UK
UKHW021558290623
424282UK00012B/575

9 781786 816870